W9-CPG-427

The Firing of
Stephen Ledberg

The Firing of Stephen Ledberg

a novel

Allan Lenzner

Copyright © 2012 byAllan Lenzner

Second Printing 2013

Cover design and illustrations by David Suter
Interior design by Jessika Hazelton

Printed in the United States of America
The Troy Book Makers • Troy, New York
www.thetroybookmakers.com

To order additional copies of this title,
contact your favorite local bookstore or visit
tbmbooks.com

ISBN: 978-1-61468-059-8

For Laura, Ben, Sam, and David.

Joe Papp said, You explain too much.
Let them figure it out for themselves.
They have brains. Let them use them.

America

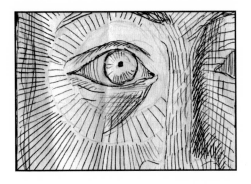

I

"Come in. Come in, my boy. Ledbaum, isn't it?"

"No, sir. Ledberg. Stephen Ledberg."

The newspaper publisher's office was so large and deep that the desk in front of a wall of glass seemed miles away. Stephen Ledberg's impulse was to shade his eyes. He stifled that reflex and walked carefully across the beige carpet. He was aware of three television screens set in the wooded wall to his right, an Eames chair facing them, a black leather couch and chair to his left and above the couch on the mahogany paneled wall the newspaper's name and credo: New Falls Sun Times – New Falls Window on the World.

Christopher Reticent, the publisher and Stephen's boss, was dressed in a blue and white striped shirt, dark blue silk tie, blue suspenders, navy blue trousers, paunch and ass bulging against waistline and seat. He wore no jacket. He had wavy brown hair parted in the middle and luminous blue eyes. Incandescent eyes that caused Stephen's to tear and forced him to glance away. He had not expected this. Some of the more seasoned journalists had warned him about "Ingy" Reticent, "Ingy" being a moniker he cherished because it drew attention to his English heritage, the claim that he was descended from the travelers on the original Mayflower, "Ingy" being short for England. They warned of his belligerence and tenacity to rule the newspaper as he wished. He brooked no disagreement over the slant a story should take. They even suggested he might mispronounce Stephen's name or get it wrong altogether, a device they suggested their boss utilized to give himself an edge. But they had failed to mention the radiance of his eyes.

Reticent, gesturing to the black leather chair in front of his desk, said, "Have a seat, my boy." Then noticing Stephen's tearing added, "The light too much for you? Here, watch this."

He pressed a button under the desktop. Beige curtains moved from inside the wall on either side of the glass, covering it. The late April sunlight filtered softly through the curtains.

"Is that better, my boy?"

"Yes sir."

"Yes, I see your eyes are brown, Ledberg. Mine are blue. Aren't they?"

Stephen looked at Reticent's eyes again. That glow, that blue clearness causing his own to tear up anew.

"Don't worry, Ledberg. It's not the sunlight. It's these eyes. I try to point that out to everyone who comes in here. You're just not used to it."

He reached across the desk and picked up a twin blue leather picture frame. As he did, Stephen had a chance to glance quickly at the desktop – a reporter's prerogative.

Everything was neat and well ordered. A large green blotter, a caddy for pencils, a pipe rack, ceramic jar, large crystal ashtray, desk calendar with the year 1967 imprinted boldly, April 27 in red lettering, a page on which he strained to see, to no avail, if his name had been spelled correctly, and a clock. On the face of the clock the names of various cities – New Delhi, Tokyo, San Francisco, Chicago, New York, Paris, London, Moscow, Nairobi, Capetown…

"Here, Ledberg, look at this." Reticent handed him the leather frame. "See those eyes. I daresay I've given those youngsters more than that. But it's those eyes I'm proudest of."

On either side of the double frame, Reticent's daughters. Light brown hair, pale skin, translucent blue eyes, noses that sloped down and to a point, lush red lips, straight white teeth. The older one wore eyeglasses, her brown hair long, a serious expression on her face. The younger one, ah well, the younger one had shorter hair, bangs, a beaded band around her forehead, a sullenness in her face.

"The oldest is Elizabeth. She lives in Philadelphia. The youngest is Catherine. She's off in Africa right now. Working on the local paper in Nairobi."

He could tell by the way Reticent gazed at Catherine's half of the frame that she was his favorite. Well, so what? What was wrong with that? Fathers were allowed favorites weren't they? If he had had to choose between them based solely on the photographs, he would have chosen Catherine as well.

Reticent replaced the frame, pushed his chair back, and said, "I'll tell you what, Ledberg. Let's go over and sit on the couch. More comfortable there."

As he stood he selected a pipe. Then he lifted the top of the ceramic jar and removed a pinch of tobacco. As he walked toward the couch he pushed the tobacco into the pipe's bowl and said, "Have a seat, Ledberg. Here, or on the couch. And feel free to smoke if you want."

Stephen sat on the couch and felt immediately as if he were in a tanning factory. His clothes steeped in the aroma of leather.

Reticent seated himself across from Stephen, the leather compressing slowly beneath the bulk of his stomach and bottom. He tamped the tobacco in the bowl of his pipe, withdrew a lighter and struck the flint. The lighter gave off a jet of flame which reminded Stephen of war movies in which Marines used flame throwers against the Japanese in the South Pacific, and he wondered if Reticent's lighter were a commercial spin-off of that earlier and larger model.

Reticent puffed a few times, pale blue smoke curling in the room, an aroma of expensive tobacco, a redolence sweet and rich and mysterious.

"What you smell, Ledberg, is latakia. I've always felt that even the best cigarettes or cigars cannot compare to a finely blended pipe tobacco. This special formula has been handed down in my family from one generation to the next. Neither of my daughters smokes of course but… it's the latakia that gives it its distinct fragrance. Remember that if you ever take up the pipe. Make certain your tobacco has a goodly portion of latakia in it."

And then, "I'm told your story about the new highway shows sentiment running against it. That true?"

"Yes, sir."

"I'm told you're one of our bright young journalists."

Stephen blushed. "Well, I don't know, sir. But thank you."

"Ledberg, let me tell you something about journalism. You're the eyes and ears and smells for the reading public. They're not just your own eyes and ears and nose but everyone's who reads the paper. Now I believe there must be people out in that neighborhood who think this highway is a good thing."

"There are, sir, but…"

"But, Ledberg? But what? It's a simple story. We're not building six lane highways out there. They're just going to widen the road a little bit on each side."

Stephen wanted to say that front yards would disappear, in some cases houses altogether, but Reticent, contrary to his name, gave him no opportunity.

"Look at me, Ledberg. I like a man who can look me in the eye."

He looked at Reticent, tears welling up.

"You know, Ledberg, I have found in my short time on this planet that many communities do not know immediately what is or is not good for them. People have a difficult time envisioning the future. They make the wrong decision only to regret it later. Do you see what I'm getting at?

"Ledberg, I want that highway now. This paper wants that highway now. I don't give a crap about the people out there. Shit, they'll be long gone and dead when this paper is still running its presses. We need that highway. Do you know what it will mean for this paper to be able to run its trucks right to our front door with all that raw newsprint? Christ, it could mean savings of thousands of dollars."

Ingy Reticent was puffing furiously on his pipe. The room filled with the smells of latakia and leather.

"Let me ask you something, Ledberg. I don't want you to take this in the wrong way. I was just wondering. But Ledberg, that's not Jewish, is it?"

Stephen had been confronted by this question only once before and that had been in college. Then the question had confused him for he had never been aware until that moment that his name was anything but what it was – Swedish. He, of course, could have been, or could not have been, or was, or was not … but what was in a name? A name was only a name. That which we call a rose… would smell as sweet – as a Rosen? Or a Rosenberg? Or even, a Rose?

The query in college had upset him, not only because of the possible mistake in identity but also because of the implications. Why had the question been asked? He had been eating lunch with other students and they had been talking about girls. Jewish girls. Hebrew girls who were, if you listened to one particular boy, more sexually active than others. Why should that be? How had that boy come by that lode of information? And why had the boy sitting beside the worldly one nudged him? Nudged him and nodded in Stephen's direction. That was the first time he had heard the question.

Had he been honest with himself, to say nothing of with those boys, he would have admitted that the first girl who ever excited him erotically, even though he had never touched her, nor had he ever heard the word eros, was Jewish. She was the younger sister of a star athlete at his high school. She caused him to feel a sweetness and excitement in his groin and stomach which he had experienced only once before as he slid softly down a thickly fibered climbing rope in gym class. With the sensation of the rope rubbing against his male- ness an ecstasy had groped him, the pressure of the fibers massaging his organ. He had touched the gym floor, too embarrassed to look at anyone, wondering if they had felt the same or could see what he had just experienced. The delicious sensation bewildered, frightened, and pleasured him. He wanted to go right back up that rope and do it over and over again and he thought that was mad and irrational. The sister of that senior caused the same sensations, causing him to hang around within eyeshot of her house, thrilled with anticipation as she stood on the lawn stretching her legs, toes up, toes down, calves and thighs beckoning, imagining where they led, some deep dark mystery which caused him to swoon, not comprehending in the least what was happening inside him, but only aware that it gave him great plea- sure, more pleasure even than that climbing rope. Maybe those boys were onto something. Maybe Jewish girls were more erotic. Maybe Jewish girls were more like that climbing rope. Or come to think of it, maybe a Jew had made the climbing rope. Or, at the least, the fibers had been grown in Israel.

"No, sir. Ledberg is a Swedish name."

"Swedish, eh? I guess that could be. Now don't get me wrong, Ledberg, we're an equal opportunity employer here. We've never turned anyone down because of race, color, or creed. Punch Sulz- berger's one of my best friends. I just wondered, that's all."

Stephen had no idea who Punch Sulzberger was, but he thought, from Ingy Reticent's insinuation, the man must be a Jew.

Reticent paused and sucked on his pipe. Then he said, "We're a team on this newspaper, Ledberg. It doesn't do anyone any good if one of us goes off in one direction while the rest of us are moving in another. I don't suppose you ever rowed crew?"

Stephen shook his head.

"I didn't think so. Well, if you had you would have known that the person who did not pull in exactly the same rhythm as everyone else caught what we call a crab. He was usually thrown from the boat. If you get what I mean.

"Tell you what. Let's take you off the highway. There's an interesting story out at the golf club. No harm there. I've wanted to do it for a long time. There's a man out there who's been caddying for almost thirty years. A good human-interest story. Why don't you go out and cover that. Yeah. Go out there today. See the caddy master. He'll fill you in. There may even be another story out there. I'll call the caddy master and tell him you're coming. You report directly to me. Okay? Yeah, let's see how you handle this."

II

THE CADDY MASTER, HOLDING A COCA COLA in one hand and a golf club in the other, said, "So, Mr. Reticent wants you to tail Lefty for a week or so. You play golf?"

"No."

"Well, you'll get the hang of it. Did Mr. Reticent tell you there's another story he wants you to cover?"

"He did."

"Yeah, well, this one's a bit more difficult. See, there's one hole out here, it's the sixth, the shortest on the course, a hundred and thirty yards. Well, you can hit the green easily with an iron, might even make a hole-in-one. Might. But you wouldn't make as many as the women members been making. Nope, and the men are damned pissed off about it.

"See, the thing about that hole is that as short as it is you can't see the green from the tee. No, you can't cause there's two large mounds, tits we call 'em here at the club, right in front of the green. Because of them tits we call that hole Mae West.

"See, because you can't see the green from the tee, the caddies always walk down there behind Mae's tits before the golfers tee off. That way they can see where the balls go after they're hit. Well, the women been making too many holes-in-one out there and the men want to find out what's going on. I have no idea how you're going to deal with that, but if Mr. Reticent says you're good, I'll just let you figure it out. You got any questions? No? Good. Let's go and meet Lefty then."

As Stephen followed the caddie master outside he felt Ingy Reticent was trying to humiliate him. Why was this man talking about a hole on a golf course as if it was a woman? Who cared whether or not women were scoring more holes-in-one than men? Was Ingy Reticent hoping he would just quit the paper? Well, he thought, if Ingy was attempting to bend him, he would find out so much about Lefty and that golf hole, information that Ingy Reticent never dreamed existed, that it would knock his boss right out of his leather chair.

"Oh, there's one other thing I forgot to mention, Mr. Ledberg."

"What's that?"

"The other caddies, they're all niggers."

There was a sweet smell of fertilizer in the air, as Stephen followed the caddy master down a grass slope toward an open lean-to shaded by trees, his brain flooded by images and thoughts. Of the portrait of Abraham Lincoln hanging in the kitchen at his parents' house. Of him in front of that portrait telling his parents of a riddle he had heard in school. "What did Abraham Lincoln say after he picked his nose?" Recalling a quizzical frown on his dad's face, as Stephen said, "I freed the boogies." His father exploded with anger, "I never want to hear that filth in this house again." What, Stephen wondered, was Ingy Reticent trying to prove?

"Boys, this is Mr. Ledberg. He's a reporter. He's going to write a story about Lefty and maybe about you boys, too."

The caddy master embarrassed him, doing more harm than good, the story becoming more intricate than he had imagined as the caddies reminded him suddenly of George Morris, who had been for a while his best friend freshman year at college. George who always called himself one crazy nigger. George who had killed himself. He had not thought about George in some time. He did not want to think about him now.

"Where's Lefty?"

"In the clinker."

"Well, go and get him. Tell him I want to see him."

When Lefty appeared he surprised Stephen, not because he was white and so much older than the other caddies, nor because of the day's bristle covering his weather-beaten face, a face that had seen too much sun, too much wind, too much rain; nor because of the toothpick sticking from the corner of his mouth, a mouth chewing on tobacco, a spurt of saliva spit to the ground. No, it was not any of those things. What surprised Stephen was that Lefty was missing a left hand, left wrist, left forearm. His left arm severed slightly below the elbow, half an arm hanging from the sleeve of a soiled tee shirt. Stephen tried not to look, but he could not help himself.

He spent the next day accompanying Lefty on the course, not only as a journalist but as a caddy as well. It was clear very quickly that there was an art to caddying. That it did not just require the toting of bags, but also a knowledge of golf – "caddie, what club should I use from here?" And not only a knowledge of golf but exquisite eyesight, or at least some reliable method of following the small white ball, a ball Stephen was forever losing sight of. So often in fact that the golfers for whom he caddied threatened to have him fired. So often that the men for whom he caddied yelled at Lefty, "Can't you teach him anything? For chrissake, kid, what did you say your name was? For chrissake, Ledberg, just watch what Lefty does. Just copy him."

And that was most of the problem. Stephen was so involved in studying Lefty that he was useless, except as a beast of burden, himself.

The most difficult motion for Lefty was removing a club from the bag on his right shoulder. Had he had a left hand, he would have used that. But without that natural maneuverability he had to use the fingers of his right hand to inch the club from the bag. What usually happened was that the golfer whose bag it was, would grab the correct club as soon as Lefty touched it.

And that was another thing about Lefty. He knew that course backward and forward. He knew his golfers backward and forward. And not just because he had caddied for them for so many years, but because he could tell the moment they teed off what sort of golfer they were and what club they would need for each particular lie of the ball. No matter whom he caddied for he always earned a large tip. He no longer needed, as the other caddies evidently did, the hole-in-one on the sixth green.

What Lefty told him, what Lefty explained as they lay with their backs against the grassy hillock facing the green, was that everyone got a hole-in-one out there. Both the men and the women. And everyone knew why. The men knew why. The women knew why. "Why shit, boy, ah done it once or twice mahself when ah was younger. You go down there and put one a them balls in that cup and you get a big tip outta it. Nobody can see you doin' it cause Mae's tits block the view. It's a tradition here at the club. Everyone expects it. Ah don't know this newspaper fella but ah'm sure it happened to him. Ah don't do it any more 'cause ah'm getting too old and ah don't really need it. But them niggers, they do it all the time. Why you can do it too if you want. Just go down there and find the Maxfli 'cause that guy pays the biggest and there ain't no sense in wastin' your time with anyone else. So ah don't see why there's any mystery there. Ah don't see what you got for a story there."

Stephen lay with his back against the hillock, the hillock and a copse of spruce trees about ten yards beyond the green protecting it, large billowy clouds scudding across the sky, covering the sun, chilling the air.

"Well, that's a story. The caddies doing that and everyone know-ing. You think I could get anyone else to admit it?"

Lefty shrugged. "Don't know. Not the caddies. Probably not anyone, but it's the story."

Lefty stared at the distance beyond the green, gazing at the small wood of trees. His tan windbreaker was pinned double at the left shoulder, his brown eyes squinting from the glare, crow's feet at the corners of those eyes. Beneath the bristle, the creases, the wind-burn, Stephen thought Lefty's face kind and gentle and truthful. A face he could trust even if Lefty had used the word nigger.

Lefty treated him to dinner that evening. He took him to his fa-vorite bistro, a place called Stan's. Lefty ordered a schooner of beer, the waitress and bartender greeting him as if they had known him all his life. The waitress brought a meal of antipasto and spaghetti and veal parmigiana and salad without their even ordering it.

Lefty maneuvered his one hand in and around that food as if there were no tomorrow. He scooped up a piece of bread and with his thumb a slice of salami, and in the same sweeping mo-tion brought them to his mouth. He reached for the schooner of beer, his face covered now by the glass, half the beer gone, the glass placed back on the table, the back of that hand wiping the foam around his mouth.

As Lefty popped an olive into his mouth he noticed Stephen look-ing at his stump. He said, "You wonderin' about mah arm? That's okay. Everybody does that at first. Might as well begin there. Prob-ably wouldn't even be here if it wasn't for that. Ah lost that, the good part a that arm when ah was ten.

"Yup, ten. Lost more than that, ah'll tell you. Lost mah whole goddamn family. Down in Florida. Mah father was drivin' along lickety split at a hell of a pace. That son of a bitch loved to drive fast. We'd just finished lunch. He'd a had three or four beers and goin' out into that afternoon heat and everythin', well, his reflexes was none too good. We hit a intersection and there was this other car comin' across runnin' a stop sign. Mah father hit the brakes as hard as a man is gonna hit the brakes. The car just took off into the air. Turned over. Smashed on its head like a accordion. The only way they could get me out was to cut me from mah left arm. Pain. Son of a bitch ah'll never feel pain like that again. Ever."

He picked up his beer and drained it. He consumed that beer as if it were the last glass of beer he would ever drink.

"Blood all over the fuckin' place. There was nothin' they could do for mah parents. Ah remember through this blood and haze a priest goin' on with last rites. Mah father, he was never a very religious man neither."

Stephen winced and said, "Jesus Christ, I'm sorry."

"Shit, it happened years ago. And here ah am not too much the worse for wear. The doctor who took care a me, he told me to start caddyin'. Mainly to build up mah shoulders. And ah been doin' it ever since. Up here in the summer, back south in the winter. Not a bad life. Make enough money to survive on. More than most. Ah ain't got no family to worry about. Only mahself. Yup, ah guess if ah had to do it all over again ah wouldn't do nothin' different. Ah had mah share a good times and bad."

As they ate dinner, Stephen asked Lefty questions. "Is Lefty the only name you go by?" Lefty answering, "It's as good as any."

"How many years have you been caddying?"

"Forty. Twenty-six years at the club. Ah seen a lot a changes. Ah thought those electric carts was gonna do me in, but those carts can't tell you what club to use. Yup, ah guess ah'm the last a a breed. Those niggers don't study the game. All they want is their twenty bucks a day. Some a 'em even want more. There was one who wanted to get rid a me. Wanted only his own kind. Threatened to strike. Didn't want them sendin' me out with all the best tippers. Well, shit, if ah'm the best caddy why in hell shouldn't ah get the cream a the crop? Well, the only one who got fired was that wise guy. Never had any trouble since from any a 'em. For me it's a life. Keeps me outside. No one tells me what to do. The money's important but it ain't everythin'. Ah got some saved up and maybe when ah retire ah'll buy mahself a farm somewhere where it's warm and sunny. Yup, that's what ah'd like to do, just sit on the porch a mah farm and relax, mah feet up and …"

Lefty paused, his fork in mid-air, "A course it'd be nice to share that farm with a woman but no woman's gonna want to put up with me. There was a time though. There was a time."

He had a faraway look in his eyes, those brown eyes staring above and off to the left of Stephen's head. He looked at Stephen and said, "I'll tell you what, Ledberg. A lot a people feel sorry for me 'cause a this." He moved his stump in the air. "But not me. Why it gets mah blood up right now just thinkin' about some a them women who go crazy with this stump a mine. Biggest fuckin' cock they ever saw."

Stephen's arm froze, his slice of veal falling into his lap, leaving a grease mark slightly to the right of his fly. Who the hell was this man sitting across from him, with one good arm and talking about what was left of the other as if it were a penis?

"Ah'll tell you what, Ledberg, let's you and me make the rounds a the bars in this little town. Okay? By the time you an' me gets through you'll know all there is to know about this town. Right, kid?"

They did hit every bar in town, or so it seemed. Stephen could not believe there were so many bars in New Falls. Or so many ethnic groups. He realized later that the only area they missed was the black one. Niggertown, was what Lefty called it. They didn't go anywhere near there. Where they did go was to dimly lit Irish bars, dart games, pitchers of beer, beer settling in tiny puddles on the wooden tables, slopped over from the pitchers, the carbonation still bubbling in the tiny pools, the jukebox playing When Irish Eyes Are Smiling, Take Me Home Again, Kathleen. They went to fluorescently lit Polish bars with polkas blaring from the jukebox, hardboiled eggs in little dishes at the bar. And to Italian bars with their posters of small fishing villages, Chianti bottles wrapped in straw, plastic grapes hanging over the mirror, Caruso singing Vesti la Guibba, Sinatra crooning, That old black magic has me in its spell… Bars with plate glass windows, neon signs, reds and whites and blues, the windows covered, now that the days and evenings had become warmer, with all kinds of insects, insects banging away trying to get in for a drink.

Stephen became more and more inebriated, relaxing, trusting, enjoying Lefty's companionship, revealing at one point that he was adopted, how he hoped one day to find his real parents. Lefty responded by raising his glass, touching Stephen's, exclaiming, "Well, here's hoping you do, kid," draining what was left.

III

STEPHEN SHOWED HIS STORY TO INGY RETICENT who said only, "It's got to be more than that, Ledberg. I like what you've written about Lefty, but it's got to be more than just tipping out there. If it were just tipping there'd be more men getting holes-in-one. Dig, Ledberg, dig. Go on back and find out what you can. I don't care how you do it, just do it."

At dinner the next evening Stephen said to Lefty, "My boss isn't satisfied with what you've told me. He thinks there's more to it than just the tipping out there. Lefty, I need to uncover anything you can help me with. I need to show him I can come up with whatever it is he imagines is happening out there. Is there anything else you can help me with? You've been here longer than anyone else."

Lefty fiddled with the label of his beer.

He said, "Well, ah know at one time, years ago, there was stories a things goin' on on that green."

"Stories? What kind of stories?"

Lefty glanced out of the corner of his eye, a gesture Stephen took to mean, "Can I trust you?" Or even, "I wonder how you're going to handle this?"

"It's all right, Lefty. You can trust me."

"Well, there was stories, this was years ago mind you, there was stories a hanky-panky goin' on out there."

"Hanky-panky?"

"Course that was when we was all white. Now them niggers wouldn't dare do anythin' like that. Besides it was only a story. Just a bunch a caddies braggin'.

"Ah wouldn't worry so much about that green if ah was you. Ah always find the more you worry about somethin' like that, you find out it's never as big a deal as you thought. But if that newspaper fella is so hell bent on the story why not try to hide yourself out there?"

"Hide? Where?"

"You could do it in the woods behind the green. Or..." and a huge smile came over Lefty's face, revealing tobacco stained teeth, "or you could hide in one a Mae's tits."

"You're pulling my leg. You're..."

"Nope, ah don't see how else you gonna find out what's goin' on out there. What you got to lose? Ah'll even help you. It shouldn't take more'n a night to dig out one a them mounds." Lefty raised his glass of beer and said, "Here's to Mae's tits."

When Stephen made the suggestion to Ingy Reticent he expected to be laughed right out of his office. But he wasn't. Ingy said, puffing on his pipe, looking him square in the eye, causing Stephen to well up, "A good idea, my boy. I agree with you. I think you might be seen in the woods. And if you think it'll only take a night... Tell you what. You go to the photography department and tell them I said you could have one of their best cameras. Okay? That way we'll have it on film as well. I'll arrange with people out at the club to leave you alone. Do what you have to do."

Two nights later he and Lefty were pushing wheelbarrows across the deserted course. In the wheelbarrows were picks and shovels and blades and flashlights, timber and chicken wire. The early May evening was chilly, the earth already having given up whatever warmth it might have absorbed from the source responsible for the pale light reflecting from the moon.

He looked across at Lefty pushing his wheelbarrow, his stump propped under the handle, the left side of his body lower than the right.

Lefty nodded toward the sky. "You think there are any other a us out there?"

"Do you mean do I think are there any other people crazy enough to be pushing wheelbarrows in the middle of the night? I hope not. I hope there's no one else that's as stupid as us."

"Hey, this ain't gonna be so bad. Fact is we just might have some fun."

Fun? Stephen did not think they would have any fun. When he thought about what he had agreed to he thought they were crazy. Fun? He thought it would take a lot longer to dig out a hole in one of the mounds than Lefty or Ingy thought, if they were able to do it at all. In fact, it took until almost dawn to do it. But do it they did.

They worked in silence. For hours they worked. The earth crumbling away, getting into their shoes and socks. Sweat soaked their clothes, pouring down their faces, their bodies covered in sweat and grime. Whiskey drunk. Lefty swinging his pick with enormous energy, clods tumbling to his feet. A distinct indentation forming in the hillock, a suitable cavity formed. They crawled in, stood, brushed the loose dirt from their clothes. It was cool and damp and smelled of the freshly dug earth, sweet, intoxicating, an aroma Stephen loved.

When they had finished and taken the chicken wire and tied to it each piece of sod that had been cut away so that it camouflaged the entrance, the two men embraced.

"God, we've done it," Stephen exclaimed. "I didn't think we would but we did. Does it look all right to you? Do you think they'll notice what we've done?"

"Them? The golfers? Nah. The only thing they're interested in is whether that little white ball goes into that little ol' cup. Nah, they ain't gonna notice nothin'. Now let's get these things outta here and go into town for breakfast."

Stephen spent over a week in that dank cave before he discovered what was going on. He thought he might be bored waiting day after day. But he had not realized quite how active his brain could become, if he allowed it.

It was too dark inside the space to see right away. But the smells were primal. Of decay and his own aromas. Of walks in the woods in the fall around his home in Kansas. Of rotting leaves and his own mucus on a hot summer day. And, like Anna's.

He bit his knuckle as he remembered how she threw herself at him that New Year's Eve of his freshman year in college. She ripped the shirt from his back. She unbuckled his belt, undid his zipper, massaged his organ. He had been startled by her sudden violent movements.

They had been necking, french kissing, he stroking her breasts, her ass, his hand inside her pants feeling the mucus, a light, dry oil, smelling the sweetness, should he move his hand further? What would she do? Suddenly she stopped him, held his hand and said, "Do you really want to go all the way, Stephen?" That had shocked him. Did you go all the way with someone you loved? What would that mean? Would he have to marry her? "Do you really want to go all the way, Stephen?" What will she think if I say no? "Of course, Anna, I love you." I love you? I do, don't I? "Are you sure, Stephen?" "Of course, I'm sure." She had gazed into his eyes. What did she expect to find there? He never found out. She had shocked him by her ferocity. By her animal passion. Anna. Like that?

Only later did he understand that the hate he began to feel toward her was also directed at himself. For making believe he loved her when he knew from the beginning he did not. And he thinking she was pretending to be someone she was not. It bothered him that everyone thought she was such a nice girl. What was it about that feeling? Something he did not trust. That she seemed so innocent and sweet when they were with other people and so passionate and voracious with him. There was something about that difference. When she was in bed with him, and in a gathering of their friends. Something she was trying to hide about herself. Something that he had not trusted.

Everyone was so happy that they were in love. Love? Whatever that feeling was, he knew it was not what he felt for Anna. Nor she for him, despite what they said to each other in bed and in public. There were times he had wanted to say, when his friends smiled and proclaimed what a great person she was and how lucky he was, that she was not what they thought. But he did not; he just nodded in agreement. He hated himself for that. And Anna. She seemed to know so much more than he. They never discussed it – he did not want to know – but he felt she must have had many affairs. He had had none. All he had had was that slim blue volume in his father's closet, the Jewish girl in high school, and that climbing rope. He resented her for all that experience and all those other lovers. Was it because she wasn't pure? For him. A nice girl. Was that what he really wanted? I thought you never liked the nice girls mom and dad always wanted you to meet? But this was different. This was Anna passing herself off as a nice girl, fooling him, until that New Year's Eve.

Why had he continued with the affair when he knew it would lead nowhere? Was it because it was the first, would it be the last, the only one, until death do us part? He knew it was not. He thought everyone must pretend that first time. Else how did you get over that first hump, so to speak? It certainly was not the first one for Anna.

So why had he been so jealous of George Morris when he and Anna became lovers? Was it because George was supposed to be a friend? Friends do not take away your girl, lover, mistress, the woman you were going to marry so many thought, even if you did not love her. Or was it because George was black? It drove him mad thinking of Anna, whom he did not love, in bed with someone else. In bed with George Morris. His best friend.

Was George better than he was? Was it true what he had heard about Negroes? Did Anna scream louder and scratch deeper with George? Jesus. He never loved her but he was crazy thinking about her and George. Thinking about another man, his friend, his black friend, hearing, watching, tasting, touching, and smelling Anna.

Then one day George came to his room. He was wild-eyed, crazy. "She's pregnant, Stephen. Help me. She hates me. I want to marry her. It's my child, too. But she hates me. Talk to her for me." Pregnant? Anna was pregnant? And he wanted me to talk to her? It made him sick to his stomach. Why should I help him? George looked as if he had not slept for days. "She'll always hate crazy niggers now," he said.

Stephen had had a premonition about George that day. Wild-eyed. Crazy. Like he was going to kill himself. He had this feeling that George was going to take Anna's car and crash it. Drive it off the road or into another car. He had listened. George had said, "Help me. Talk to her for me. She'll listen to you." Stephen said, "I don't know. I don't see her much anymore." Why should I? Why should I do that for him? And then George had left, got into Anna's car and killed himself. Guilt. Could he have helped him? And Anna, whom he heard had had an abortion, who did not go to George's funeral, and whom he never saw again. Anna. That seemed like eons ago.

Now he studied the earth around him. Occasionally he noticed a slight movement in the soil. A worm struggled from the earth, dropping back to the ground. Sometimes he saw grayish maggot-like creatures pushing grains of soil, then they too dropped to the earthen floor. These he crushed with the sole of his shoe. These frightened him. They sent shivers up his back, then to his groin. His groin feeling impotent. Dead. Dismembered. Why did that happen? Why did that always happen when he saw disgusting things like maggots or imagined killing something?

There would be many such worms and maggots and remembrances before he finally discovered what was going on on that green.

IV

Wʜᴇɴ ʜᴇ ᴅɪᴅ ғɪɴᴅ ᴏᴜᴛ ʜᴇ ꜱᴜꜱᴘᴇᴄᴛᴇᴅ ᴛʜᴀᴛ Lᴇꜰᴛʏ, who just happened to be there that day, had known the truth all along.

Lefty with his eye to his peephole as the caddies dropped a ball in the cup. Stephen with his thirty-five millimeter camera clicking away as one of the women found the ball, held it up, and then began removing her skirt. "My god." Lefty shouting as the caddies unzipped their trousers. Stephen whispering, "Shhhh. They'll hear you." Lefty answering, "Hear me? Shit. They ain't gonna hear no one."

And Lefty was probably right. The green was a jumble of rolling bodies, moving pelvises, brown organs. Stephen felt disgusted, and dropped the camera as he heard the women crying, "Ohhhh, sweet tootsie rolls, let me have more of that tootsie roll."

"Tootsie Rolls? They're not talking about Tootsie Rolls."

"Damn right they're not. Them women are talkin' about them caddies' peckers."

Stephen gave the story and film to Ingy Reticent. His boss thanked him, shook his hand, walked him to the door, sucking on his pipe, calm and cool. What could his boss possibly do with this story? He certainly wasn't going to print it, was he?

That evening he met Lefty again. Lefty arrived at Stan's bistro shaved, scrubbed, wearing a clean set of clothes, making excuses, "Sorry ah'm late, ah had to get mahself a woman." Stephen wondered why he himself did not have a similar need. Was something wrong with him?

"Why did those women do that?"

"Why? Who knows? A little adventure. It don't harm no one. Unless you get caught."

"But you knew what was going on out there, Lefty, you knew. Everyone must have known. You couldn't keep a thing like that a secret."

"Ah swear to you, kid, ah didn't know. Ah didn't know nothin'."

Stephen studied his friend's face, not entirely believing him. Maybe Lefty had participated in such a scene years before and did not wish to admit it now. But so what if he did not want to talk about it, that was his prerogative, wasn't it? Anyway, maybe he'd just forgotten. Forgotten? Was that possible?

It was the following morning that Ingy Reticent sent for him. Stephen expected to be lauded for his work. He thought he had accomplished exactly what his boss wanted. He did not believe the story could have been covered as well by anyone else. He did not think the story would be published but he knew it was the story. He even added a fillip by telling Reticent, "I don't mean to get the caddy master in trouble, but I thought you ought to know that he uses a crude word to describe the caddies out at the club."

"Well, he is a little old-fashioned. He doesn't mean anything by it. But don't you worry. We'll talk to him about it." And then, "I'm afraid this is your last day here."

What? What the hell was Ingy Reticent talking about? "What are you talking about? Why that was one of the best pieces of investigative journalism I have ever done. You're firing me? Why would you do that? What did I do wrong?"

"You're a good reporter, son. Don't worry. You'll find another job. You might even thank me for this some years down the line. I just don't think you fit in here with the direction we're going. You'll find a check in this envelope."

A check? What good was a check? He had just been fired from the only job he ever wanted as an investigative journalist and Ingy Reticent was handing him a check? He was frightened. He felt his bowels loosen. He felt alone and lost. He did not understand. His parents had told him not to go east. There are dozens of newspapers out here, they had said. Had they known something about the newspaper and its owner and kept it from him?

When he told Lefty what had happened he said, "Shit, son, it ain't your fault. That guy wanted to find out what happened out there. Well, he did. But ah'll tell you this, there's sure somethin' about this ol' life a ours ah don't understand. Ah don't want to make you feel any worse but believe it or not them caddies was never fired. Ah don't understand it. You got fired but not them caddies. Now, there's a rumor out there that they're only gonna level them mounds. Yup, they're gonna change that ol' hole out there and get rid a Mae's tits. That seems to be their way a solvin' that particular problem.

"But listen, you an' me, we're buddies, right? Well, if you need any money to tide you over why ah can lend you some. Ain't no problem there."

"Thanks, Lefty. But right now I've got to contact other newspapers about any job openings. Some of the other journalists on the paper are helping. I just hope I can get another job soon."

"Shit, son, if ah was you ah wouldn't worry. You're young. Somethin'll turn up."

V

AND SOMETHING DID. A few days later, after mailing out resumes to newspapers suggested by some of the other journalists, he received a telephone call from an Esther Maroon. She had heard he was out of a job.

"How did you hear that?"

"New Falls is a small town," she answered, "I hear things. Would you be interested in coming out and listening to what I have to say?"

"Sure, why not?"

"Fine, Mr. Ledberg. I run the Bridle Street School. Here's the address."

The Bridle Street School straddled the boundary where the black section of town began – or ended – depending from which side of the fence you viewed it, an area Lefty had avoided the evening they went drinking. The school occupied an old red brick building, the only brick building on the block. The others were made of wood, with laundry flapping on clotheslines in backyards, the breeze and sun drying the sheets and trousers and blouses and underwear. The school was the only building with flagpoles, flying from one the American flag, from the other a flag of cerulean blue onto which had been sewn in cloth the color of chrome yellow two figures: an adult and child studying a book and under them, the spring breeze unfurling the flag so it could be read, the school's motto: Every Student A Teacher, Every Teacher A Student.

The moment Stephen opened the fire door to the stairwell the scent of a familiar cleansing agent assaulted him. Did every school use the same detergent? On the walls of the stairwell were finger paintings, collages, and murals. On the stairs a compressed piece of pink bubble gum.

Two children pushed open the door to the second floor, bolted past him, jumping the three steps from one landing to the next. He caught the door before it closed.

Esther Maroon's reception area, where her secretary sat, was well ordered. A bookcase stood opposite an oatmeal-colored couch, the bookcase containing hardbacks with the word child or teacher or school or parent or cognitive or education on their spines. On the walls were more children's paintings, these with little notes scrawled on them. For Esther. Love Miranda. Or Peter. That was her reception area. Her own office was a shambles.

Books and papers were scattered everywhere. The room was in need of a paint job, and it smelled of stale cigarette smoke. Esther Maroon, on the other hand, wore a dark green wool skirt and a short-sleeved, pastel green cashmere sweater and on her feet brown pumps. Why, he wondered, was she dressed so immaculately while her office was in disarray?

"So nice to meet you, Mr. Ledberg. Please excuse the mess. Here. Sit here." Her face exploded with a smile, a smile that puzzled Stephen.

Esther Maroon picked up a pack of Kents, withdrew one, lit it, exhaled and said, "So I hear that son of a bitch fired you."

Stephen felt his face flush, not so much from embarrassment as surprise. "Are you talking about Ingy Reticent?"

"I certainly am. He's my ex-husband. But that's the past, Mr. Ledberg. That happened too many years ago. It's water over the dam. I don't suppose you have any idea why I've asked you here?"

"Well, my parents are teachers but…"

"Are they? Where do they teach?"

"They teach in a high school in Wichita, Kansas."

"Wichita, Kansas? I've never been there. What do they teach?"

"My mother teaches English. My father is a music teacher." Stephen felt an impulse to add, they're not my real parents, but he stifled that thought, never knowing when such information would be appropriate.

"Well, I haven't asked you here because of the school, although I will show you around later. We're very proud of what we do here. You've seen our flag as you came in? Yes, well spend some time with us. You'll see that in fact every student is a teacher and every teacher is a student. We learn from each other every day. But no, it's not because of the school I've asked you here. I have friends on the paper who still talk to me. They tell me you've done good work there."

"Mr. Reticent didn't seem to think so. I…"

She picked up her cigarette, ground it out, and said, "Forget him. He's a strange, warped man. Trust me. You're better off not working for him. So… here's my proposition. I'm on the board of a foundation that needs some work done in Houston. It's not exactly newspaper reporting, but it might be even more interesting. You might find it's a needed break right now from journalism."

"Houston, Texas?"

"Precisely. Have you ever been there?"

"No. What sort of investigative work?"

"I'd rather not go into the details. The man who runs the foundation can fill you in."

"Who's that?"

"His name is Pete Codding. He's an old friend. We've known each other for years."

"I appreciate you thinking of me, but I'm not sure I want to give up journalism right now."

" All I ask is that you think about it. It will require a good deal of your journalistic skills. Who knows, after you've finished you might even be able to write a piece about it. I have friends at various magazines. Even other newspapers. Who knows where this might lead. Here's Pete Codding's business card. He's in New York. Give him a call. Hear him out. Keep an open mind. Okay? Now let me show you around my school."

She led him down the staircase, Esther Maroon taking three steps at a time, just as the children had done, past the finger paintings and collages and murals, back to the first floor, where she announced, "If you're going to see one classroom it might as well be Betty's. She's my old pro."

Betty's room shocked him. Scattered across the floor were pools of water, piles of mud, scraps of paper, crayons, a discarded peanut butter and jelly sandwich, saltines, paper cups, and adding an additional air of terror, a half-caste child with tight curly brown hair and thick-lens eyeglasses, light blue grayish eyes magnified through the lenses, the child clutching tightly a closed black umbrella, swinging it wildly about the room, bringing it down hard on one of the tables, thwack.

Stephen recalled a cold, drizzly night when he and George Morris saw a black man – "He's one crazy nigger," George had said – beating his wife or his girlfriend or his sister with a closed umbrella. George had rushed over to stop him, receiving a blow across the face for his efforts. But the most damaging injury was the woman screaming at George, "Leave us alone. It's none of your business." George had returned with a welt across his face, his eyes tearing, not only from the blow but also from the cruelty, while Stephen had slunk in the shadows ashamed.

"How old is the child with the umbrella?'

"How old? Adam is almost five." Esther Maroon astonished and horrified, just as he was, he thought, gazing at Betty, "her old pro", until she could bear it no longer and shouted, "Adam, what are you doing? Adam, come here. Stop that nonsense right now."

Adam stood before him, gazing, eyes intent, staring as if there was a connection. Unexpectedly, a great smile erupted across the boy's face as their eyes met, a smile that forced Stephen to return one in kind.

"Stop that now, Adam. Sit down. Leave Mr. Ledberg alone," Esther Maroon admonished.

"No. No. It's all right. He's not bothering me. In fact, I'd like to hang out here for a while."

And before Esther Maroon had an opportunity to respond, Betty, her old pro, said, "Of course. Spend as much time as you want."

VI

BETTY SAID, AFTER THE CHILDREN HAD LEFT FOR THE DAY, "Why don't you come and have a drink with me?"

"Where to?"

"Just follow me."

He said, as they sat at a table with their drinks, "I've been here before."

She did not answer. She had ordered a double martini, finished it in one motion, motioned for another, lit a cigarette, half-smoked it, and lit another. Her behavior puzzled him. His parents drank a glass of wine at dinner, but no one he knew, not even any of his college compatriots, drank as Betty was doing. She did not even acknowledge his presence. He wondered why she had invited him. She sat agitated, her right leg a piston moving frantically up and down. She made him so uncomfortable that he felt compelled to say something. But before he could she exclaimed, "He took a liking to you."

"He?"

"Adam. I saw him smile at you."

Stephen flushed.

"What are you embarrassed for? Instead of being embarrassed you should feel good. You didn't see him smile at that son of a bitch, did you?"

"Esther Maroon. You mean Esther…?"

"Exactly. You didn't see him smile at her, did you?"

"No."

"Exactly. She comes into my classroom spewing hate and fear."

"Whoa. Hate and fear?"

"You and she," Betty spat out the "she", "come into my room. You saw what you saw. You thought things were falling apart. You thought my classroom was in chaos, didn't you? Well, didn't you?"

Stephen hesitated. He did not wish to hurt her feelings.

She sneered. "Oh, come on, of course you did. You don't even have the courage to admit that. Did either of you have any idea what happened a moment before you entered? No. Did she even make an attempt to talk to me about it before she shot her mouth off? No. If she had I would have told her Adam was fine. Leave him alone. He had asked Emily to play with him and she didn't want to just then. Did any of the children look upset when you came in?"

"Come to think of it, no," he answered.

"Exactly. Of course not. They are used to Adam. He has never harmed anyone. They know he would not now. But she scared the hell out of them."

"She did?"

"You didn't notice their expressions when she began berating Adam?"

"No."

"No, of course you didn't. You didn't notice the fear on their faces. Suddenly they thought, Miss Maroon is scared so we must be as well. God."

She finished her drink, noticed a waitress, raised her hand, waved the glass, and said, "You know who Adam is, don't you?"

"No. Is he someone special? Is he…"

"He's her kid. Adam is her kid."

"What? Adam is Esther Maroon's child? I don't…"

"I don't mean her kid. Her adopted kid. She adopted him. She gave him her name. No one knows who his real parents are. She's been absolutely closed mouthed about that."

Had Stephen wanted to he could have reeled off an encyclopedia of knowledge about adoption that would have dazzled and informed her as to why Esther Maroon – and Adam – did not know, could not know, would not ever know his real parents.

"Course I have my own idea who the parents are," Betty said.

"You do?"

"Yeah. See, I think it's her daughter's kid."

"Her daughter's?"

"Yeah. See I think it's Catherine's kid."

"You do? How…"

"Yeah. Catherine. The youngest. She's always been the wild one. I have no proof mind you, just my intuition which is usually right on. My gut tells me it's Catherine."

"Catherine? The youngest? Why…"

"You know her?"

"No, no. I've only seen a photograph."

"A photograph? Well, a photograph is as close as you would want to get to her."

"Why?"

"Why? You haven't fallen for her, have you? Look at your face. You're blushing. Jesus Christ, you've fallen for Catherine Reticent."

"No, no. I mean, I thought she was attractive. But it was only a photo…"

Dragging deeply on her cigarette, the ash aglow, Betty said, "Anyone who's a product of those two, my advice is to give them the widest berth you can. Yeah, I think Adam might be Esther's grandson. But no one's saying and I've known her for years. An adopted child my foot."

"But what makes you think that?"

"What makes me think that? Well, for one thing, Catherine disappeared from the face of the earth about a year before Esther announced she was adopting a child. She was so proud of herself. A biracial child. Yeah, I think they hid Catherine away somewhere until Adam was born. The question of course," she smiled, "is if Adam is Catherine Reticent's child, who knocked her up?" She relaxed in her chair and gulped the remains of the martini.

Stephen felt nauseated. The memory of George and Anna seized him, his past rushing into his gut.

"It runs in the family."

"What? What runs in the family?"

"Getting knocked up."

Stephen's mind was reeling. Who was this woman smoking cigarette after cigarette and consuming gallons of gin? Was she really a teacher? Or just a madwoman?

"I bet she didn't tell you about her third child, did she?"

"She had a third child? Esther Maroon had another child?"

"Yup. A son. You know what happened to that kid? You know who her former husband is, don't you? He owns the goddamn newspaper in this town. Well, she had a third child only he was born with brown eyes. Well, that son of a bitch took that child and left him on someone's doorstep. 'Can't be my child,' he said. 'No child of mine, even if it is a son, is going to have brown eyes.'

"Yeah, yeah, you don't believe me, I can see it on your face. You think ol' Betty's a drunk and a crackpot. Go ask her. Course she'll tell you what she tells everyone else."

"What's that?"

"She'll tell you that kid died. Died my ass. There'd be a record of that. We would have heard about that. Death you can't hide. No, that husband of hers just took that kid and left. God knows where he deposited him."

"I don't believe it. You can't just go around dropping off babies. I don't care who you are you can't just up and drop off a baby somewhere."

"Really? You don't believe it? It happens all the time. You know what a foundling home is, don't you?"

"Yes."

"There you are then. The real question is who was the father? Yeah, that's the real question. I mean if her husband, her ex-husband, thinks he only produces blue-eyed children, then who the hell knocked up Esther Maroon?"

She winked, moved back in her seat. "Get what I mean?"

Stephen did not believe her. It was too wild a story. Ingy Reticent left a child, even if it were not his, on someone's doorstep? How could anyone get away with something like that even if they did own a newspaper?

"I still do not believe it. This town is too small for someone not to know."

"Not to know what? Not to know what happened to that kid? Listen, whoever that kid is, he's lucky he has nothing to do with those two. She's got those two daughters. You think Catherine Reticent is attractive? Well, let me tell you something. If you ever run into her, be warned. Keep on running."

She remembered the cigarette in the ashtray, picked it up and inhaled.

"Listen, Esther Maroon and I go back a long way. Why she and I started the school. She had the money from the divorce. I had the brains. But does she give me any of the credit? She calls me her old pro. As if that should make me feel good. Well I ain't her old anything."

Betty sat with one leg crossed over the other. She seemed comfortable, as if a burden had been released. Sipping her martini, she glanced at the door each time it opened, as if expecting someone she might know.

It was not someone she knew who finally entered, but Lefty. Stephen sat with his back to the door but knew instantly whom Betty was following with her bloodshot eyes by the way the bartender and waitress greeted him.

Stephen turned and beckoned him. Lefty was dirty and sweaty from the golf course, but the dirt and sweat and missing arm seemed to make no difference to Betty. Lefty hit it off with her, and she with him. They ordered dinner and while Betty and Lefty discussed golf, Betty commenting on the importance of eye-hand coordination, how necessary it was to develop that in a child, how Lefty's coordination must be so much sharper than the average person's what with his handicap and all. A handicap, she added, which didn't look much of one to her, Betty winking lasciviously at Lefty, eyeing his stump and then his face. Lefty and Betty huddled over the table, Stephen feeling left out, finally excusing himself, leaving his two friends deep in conversation, himself going home.

VII

HOME FOR STEPHEN WAS A ONE-ROOM BASEMENT APARTMENT with an electric hotplate and a tiny refrigerator. It was dark and shadowy and had bars on the only window, a window that looked out on a yard he did not have the use of. It was an apartment he had furnished sparingly. Furnished as he imagined his hero, Ralph Nader, whose photograph was pinned to the wall, the only such adornment on those grimy bare walls, arranged his living quarters. He had read somewhere that Ralph Nader lived frugally, ascetically, a monk's existence, not even bowing to the most elementary of American comforts, the telephone. That Nader used the pay phone down the hall for both incoming and outgoing messages. Stephen did not go quite that far. He did have a telephone and a black-and-white television set and a clock radio, a night table and a lamp and a small desk and chair, some pots and pans, and on the floor a mattress on which he slept exactly like, he imagined, his hero. His hero's theory was that you only used your apartment to sleep in, devoting your full waking energies to your vocation.

Now Stephen lay on the mattress thinking over the events of the past few weeks, wondering where he had gone wrong, how he could have been fired from the only profession that interested him. He did not feel he was a born journalist. Not in the sense that he heard people say, "he was a born musician", or "she was a born actress". He knew that. He thought he could trace his career to the day of his thirteenth birthday. But he knew it began long before then. He often wondered why he was so unlike his parents, why nothing matched. Not the color of his hair, his black, theirs light brown; nor the color of eyes, his brown, theirs light blue gray; nor his complexion, he swarthy, they pale; nor height, his dad over six feet, his mother at least five ten. Even now he thought himself as short for his age; nor for that matter the size and shape of penis, his tiny, bullet-like, his dad's hanging, hooded, looking for all the world like the head of a turtle.

He thought it was that mystery that had compelled him to sneak into his parents' bedroom when he was eight or nine or ten. He could not recall exactly how old he had been. What was he seeking? Was it the pad of gauze that he later realized was a tampon, protruding from a partially opened box high on a shelf in his mom's closet? Or the blue covered book with no title hidden under a pile of clothes in his father's closet, my god, inside that book? What did his dad do with that? Page after page of naked men and women, what were they doing? What was his peewee up to? The men with their peewees inside a woman's place, upside down, sideways up, eyes shut tight eyes wide open.

And in one of his mom's drawers, a picnic hamper, a topless tattered picnic hamper lined with yellowing, flaking newsprint. He wondered why the hamper was there, shrugged, closed the drawer, and left.

He remembered that summer day of his thirteenth birthday. His father called him into the kitchen. He knew immediately there was trouble. "Come in here, young man. There's something mother and I want to discuss with you."

Almost as if he had done something wrong. "We're in the kitchen, Stephen. Come into the kitchen," his mom beckoning him in a voice he had never before heard. The kitchen, where all the crucial decisions in the Ledberg family were made. In other families he knew it was the living room or the dining room or the bedroom or sometimes even the bathroom.

He wanted to say "you're scaring me," but he stood transfixed, glancing at the wall, eyeing the two portraits staring at him. "Why are they there?" he had asked once. "Because they are the two greatest presidents this nation has ever had," his father had answered. George Washington and Abraham Lincoln, side by side. The Gilbert Stuart reproduction and the Mathew Brady facsimile, the one man with powdery hair, white ruffles, pink skin, glowing aura; the other with black hair, black beard, black clothes, brooding, closed countenance. I cut down the cherry tree, father. All men are created equal.

He wanted to stop whatever it was they were about to say. "Where is the Red Schoendienst glove you promised? The Stan Musial bat?" But even now he remembered how cottony his mouth had been, how he desperately needed to relieve himself, trying to hold in his gas.

"We're not your parents, son. We adopted you at a very young age. We knew you should have been told sooner. I wish we had." His mother was sobbing, shoulders heaving, rivulets running down her cheeks. His father stalwart, tall, ramrod, brushing the forelock of hair from above his eyebrow. Those two men on the wall pensive, patient. He wondered what their thirteenth birthdays had been like. His was a disaster.

He ran into his room, slammed the door, threw himself on his bed, crying, scared, different, his fears confirmed. The children in the park across the street, their shouts and excitement, caused him to feel even lonelier. His dad had knocked on the door, "Please come out now, Stephen. We want to take a photograph. You know we always take a photograph on your birthday."

No, no, no. His thirteenth birthday was a complete failure. No, a tragedy, because as it turned out they had bought him a Jackie Robinson glove and bat. How could they? What were they thinking? No one growing up in Wichita, Kansas followed the Brooklyn Dodgers. Everyone was a Cardinal fan. (Although he had to admit that the bat was perfection, the thick handle an extension of himself, carved for his grasp, comfortable, reassuring, cradled in his palm and fingers as if that bat had known him his whole life; handle and barrel perfectly balanced, any part of that bat able to strike the ball fully, unlike the Musial, the head of which felt leaden and unbalanced, the handle a toothpick. Each time, which was not many, he used the Jackie Robinson he got a hit, each hit a line drive. The bat stunned him with its magic. But he had used the bat sparingly ever since the day his coach humiliated him, "Do you use the Robinson bat because you and he are pigeon-toed or because you are a nigger lover?")

He began to consume books. Books about boys with lost parents, boys with hidden pasts, men seeking answers: Oliver Twist and Captains Courageous and Huck Finn and The Prince and the Pauper and Tom Jones and Catcher in the Rye and Great Expectations, poring over them, discarding one for another, devouring those books, feverish, holding the thermometer near the reading lamp, watching the mercury rise to a hundred, staying home, ill, to read his books.

Later he was influenced by Rachel Carson's The Silent Spring, an expose of the damage caused by pesticides, a book that infuriated the pesticide industry which convinced him even more of the book's authenticity, otherwise why would they spend so much effort to discredit her? And Richard Rovere, who authored a caustic biography of Joseph McCarthy, the scandalous senator from Wisconsin who, himself, was not unlike a pesticide gone mad attacking everyone whom he thought a communist, a pinko, a fag.

One day in the college library he noticed a newsletter lying on a tabletop. He picked it up and began to read. He sat down to read more, even though it gnawed at him that he had reams of homework to finish. He read the newspaper, I. F. Stone's Weekly, from front to back. I. F. Stone, whoever he or she was, seemed to be writing for him, explaining in great detail, supported by documentary proof, the intricacies of legislation wending its way through the Congress. Stone pinpointed where money was being spent and wasted. I. F. Stone was a journalist practicing a form of journalism Stephen had never before seen. Each week he sought out the next issue. He researched Stone, tucked away the information in the back of his mind, thinking this was exactly the kind of journalist he would like to become. He even imagined that one day he might work for "Izzy" Stone.

Still, no one could hold a candle to his real hero, Ralph Nader. None of the others, not even Rachel Carson, had stopped an entire industry in its tracks. Unsafe At Any Speed had changed his life. He would have given anything to meet Nader, to work for him. But for now the photograph would have to do. Ralph Nader hanging hangdog on Stephen's wall. Nader appearing, Stephen thought, particularly around the mouth and eyes, a little like the deceased senator from Wisconsin, the subject of Mr. Rovere's book. But that did not deter Nader from being his hero.

He attributed the influence of all those writers to his success his senior year in writing a series of articles for the school newspaper on adoption agencies, adopted children, and their search for their real parents. A series of articles that won the newspaper an award and actually influenced the state legislature to consider whether they wanted to change the laws governing the secrecy surrounding the adoption process. But the articles were written by a college kid, an adopted college kid at that, and who would want to adopt a child if that child might at some future date wish to make contact with his or her biological parents? Who knew what might follow that? The very idea, he understood, was a threat to the adoption process, and more particularly to the adoptive parents. And the latter had the child outnumbered two to one.

While the success of the articles was gratifying, his parents' responses to the questions about himself were not. For the first time they told him his biological mother had been a young woman with an unwanted pregnancy "just passing through town", then disappearing into the vastness of America, the woman shedding no illumination on the name of his father. "We have no idea where she is, son", his mom and dad swore as he questioned them, saying they had sworn to the young woman they would never reveal her name. An oath he accepted even though there was something about the telling which perturbed and upset him.

None of his research diminished his fantasizing that one day he would find a clue. He would hear something, notice an expression, and then circle, sniff, pounce, and follow the lead. Now he pondered Betty's story about Esther Maroon's third child, "She'll tell you he died," Betty said, "but that's a lie," wondering if it were possible, could it be? Ridiculous, a long shot, yet his parents had discouraged him from going east. "Why that paper, son, when there are so many out here?" Stephen wondered if something had not just gone kerplunk with the drunken jabber of an angry frustrated teacher. What he did not wonder about was whether or not he would pursue the opportunity Esther Maroon presented to him. He knew he would go to New York City as soon as he could to meet Pete Codding.

VIII

NEW YORK CITY, STEPHEN THOUGHT, from the approach to the Holland Tunnel, seemed seductive, those towering buildings clad only in a transparent film of summer haze, not male symbols, but tall, lanky, restless women, women of the night, or even of the day, beckoning, attracting. He drove into and through the tunnel, the noise, the trucks, the traffic all converging, oblique lines meeting, that seductive feeling evaporating, the excitement and energy yet there.

The offices of the African-American Friendship Committee where Pete Codding worked were located across the street from the United Nations building. Stephen drove east on Canal Street, north on Bowery and then wished he had not, wondering if there was a better route.

The traffic was backed up. A sweet sickly stench hovered in the air, his nostrils invaded by that offensive yet oddly attracting aroma, that scent day old dirt and grime and sweat and urine which rose from the sidewalks and the bodies of the derelict men sprawled in doorways flat out on the baking concrete. He dared not look at them, but as with Lefty's stump, he had no choice.

He parked the car as close to Pete Codding's building as he could, stepped out and locked it. The back of his shirt was soaked with perspiration. The heat and the traffic made him lethargic. He shook his head in an attempt to clear it, but the heaviness remained. He walked to the building and sidled in through the revolving door. The air conditioning caught him unawares. It cooled him so swiftly that the back of his shirt felt cold and clammy. He shivered, but the frigid air cleared his head.

He walked to a bank of elevators and took one to the twenty-third floor. The elevator was sleek, silent, swift, doors gliding open, shut, floor lights flashing, air conditioning cooling, the doors whooshing open at his stop.

He stepped out onto a burnt orange carpet. A receptionist sat in a chrome chair, the back and seat covered in a royal purple cloth. On her desk were a telephone and paperback book that she held open with her left hand. Behind her on a dove-gray-colored wall in gold lettering was the name of the organization and beneath it a logo etched on a metal plate: two hands clasping, one shaded black, the other not. Dangling from each wrist were severed chain links. Beneath the logo the words "Liberty and Justice For All".

Magazines with names like Drum, Transition, and Spearhead were neatly arranged on a glass-topped table. In the corner of the room was a bookcase with magazines and books that reminded him of George's bookcase. He felt ill. He thought he might vomit. He recalled the moment he realized Anna was attracted to George. She had been browsing through his books, ticking off the names of the authors. "Oh, Ralph Ellison, I love him, and Richard Wright and Langston Hughes, oh, he's so great and Marcus Garvey and John Williams, I don't know him, who's he? I don't see any James Baldwin here. I love James Baldwin. Why isn't there any…" George exploded, his face contorted, veins popping, screaming, "Baldwin, that fag. Baldwin doesn't speak for me. No fag speaks for me."

Anna had been dazzled by George's anger and energy, her face a sea of lust and sensuality, while George eyed her knowingly. Stephen froze, invisible, dismembered, lost. He tried to drive those thoughts from his mind. That was his past.

"Mr. Ledberg?"

"Yes."

"I'm Mr. Codding's secretary. Please follow me."

He followed her down a long hallway and entered Pete Codding's office. Codding stood, extended his hand and as he did, Stephen caught sight of cufflinks holding together the cuffs of Codding's shirt. He had never before been in the presence of a precious metal, but he knew instinctively by its luster that those cufflinks shaped like the continent of Africa were golden. Codding squeezed Stephen's hand forcefully, a handshake Stephen thought his dad would have appreciated, and said, "Pete Codding, Mr. Ledberg. Nice to meet you. They're beautiful, aren't they?" He moved his arm so Stephen could have a closer look.

"Yes. Yes, they are. Are they…"

"Gold? Yes. They are pure gold. Twenty-four carats. Here. Come over here." Codding led him to a wall covered with photographs, all of them of men.

"Do you know this man?"

"No."

"Kwame Nkrumah. He gave me these. He was the first president of Ghana, which was once upon a time called the Gold Coast. So these are very special." Codding moved his arm again, exposing the cufflinks. "But now I am afraid Kwame must live his life in exile. It's a great tragedy. But life goes on. And that's why you are here."

"Because of Kwame Nkrumah?"

"No. Forgive me. I was simply ruminating. What has Esther Maroon told you?"

"Nothing really. Only that I might have to go to Houston, Texas. She said you would fill me in on everything."

"Precisely. Sit anywhere you like while I retrieve the file."

Stephen sat on a charcoal gray couch and glanced about the room. Windows overlooked the East River and the dappled marble of the United Nations building. African artifacts were placed here and there. In one corner stood a tall wooden carving of deformed people. Hunchbacks, drooping breasts, sagging jaws, skewed eyes, grotesque facial expressions. On the wall behind Codding's desk was an oil painting, primitive in form, of a sepia-skinned Christ slumped on a cross. A full moon illuminated the scene. Africans gathered at the foot of the cross gazing up at the dying man, a name, "Ntiro", daubed in the right hand corner. Ntiro? What sort of name was that?

Codding returned with a file, which he handed to Stephen, saying, "This is the file for Marcus Aurelius Brown." Stephen opened it, to find a number of photographs of a young, handsome, sinewy black man whose aviator-style sunglasses covered his eyes, sunglasses that reminded Stephen of photographs of Douglas MacArthur, corncob pipe clenched between teeth, wading ashore in the Philippine islands. Marcus Aurelius Brown, his shirt- sleeves rolled up, his right arm upraised, a fist clenched, led other young men and women, their arms punching the air, their fists clenched as well. The final photograph showed a manacled Brown walking into a courthouse, the label said, with the sheriff of Harris County, Texas.

Stephen looked up. "Marcus Aurelius Brown? Does that mean he was named after Marcus Garvey?"

Codding shrugged. "I don't know. Could have been the Roman emperor. Have you finished?"

"No."

"We'll talk after you finish."

Under the photographs were a number of clippings from Houston newspapers describing how Brown was arrested trying to buy drugs. And under those articles was a clipping from another newspaper, one in which Stephen had more than a passing interest. The New Falls Sun Times described Brown's arrest and noted that he was a former New Falls resident.

"You didn't say Brown lived in New Falls."

"I'm glad you noticed that. Yes, I think Esther was correct about you. You do your homework. Now let me tell you why we want you to go down to Houston. You see, we think he's been framed. It's not the drug charge that has brought him to the attention of the police, but his organizing skills. That used to happen constantly in Africa. The British or the French or the Portuguese would find one excuse or another. Well, Brown was supposed to be out on bail by now, but he's not. We're not sure why. That's your job, to go down there and find out why. We'll pay all your expenses, your flight, food, plus a hundred dollars a day. You'll stay at the YMCA. We have a relationship with them. If you want time to think about it, that's fine."

Stephen sat on the couch and wondered what he was getting himself into. He imagined the black Christ in the painting on the wall staring at him, wagging his finger. "You did not help George Morris. All you had to do was talk to Anna. That's all he asked. Now I've come for you. Tit for tat." But he realized that that melanochrous Christ was not interested in him at all. That dying man too busy with his own misery and agony and betrayal to worry about anyone else, much less Stephen Ledberg.

"Does Esther Maroon know Brown?"

"Why do you ask?"

"Well he lived in New Falls. Is that why she is interested in him?"

"No. No. No. I don't think it makes any difference to Esther where he's from. She just wants to see justice served. I think this is just a matter of chance. But if I were you, why not ask her the next time you see her."

"I will."

He thanked Codding, shook his hand, and left the office.

As he drove back to New Falls he could not escape the feeling that Codding had been evasive, that he never answered directly his question about Brown and Esther Maroon. She just wants to see justice served? He did not think so.

IX

Lefty said, "You know, ah'm not sure but ah think that nigger, that Marcus Aurelius Brown was a caddy at the club once. The same one who wanted me fired. Ah figure whatever that nigger got down there in Texas he deserved. Ah wouldn't go if ah was you."

"What I don't understand is why she is a part of this." Betty was drinking and smoking and throwing out thoughts offhand.

"None a it sounds right to me. Why, they're gonna pay you more than ah make on mah best days."

"I wonder," Betty interjected, "if this has something to do with the boy."

"The boy?" Stephen inquired.

The three of them were eating dinner again at Stan's. Stephen had asked to meet with Lefty who brought Betty along. Stephen had not felt that would be helpful but now changed his mind.

"Adam. You remember Adam. The smile. The umbrella."

"Adam? You think Brown might have something to do with Adam?"

"Something? I think he's Adam's father. He's the guy who knocked up Catherine Reticent. That's what I think. Course it's only a guess. There's no proof and Esther is certainly not going to admit it. But I don't know any other reason for her involvement."

She stared at Stephen waiting, he thought, for a response. When he was silent she said, "Of course the question I keep asking myself is how you fit in all this?"

"Me? What do you mean?"

"Lefty tells me you are adopted."

"That's right."

"Well, how did you get here?"

"What do you mean?"

"Did you ever ask yourself why her ex-husband hired you and then fired you? Lefty tells me you hope to find your biological parents one day."

"That's true."

"Well, then, there you are. It wouldn't surprise me knowing that son of a bitch…"

She gazed at him intently, making him feel uncomfortable.

"I don't know. I don't see any physical resemblance in you to either of them. I'm probably way off base. But you do have brown eyes."

Stephen felt light-headed. Betty thought Ingy Reticent and Esther Maroon were his real parents? She was mad and a drunk. She had no idea what she was talking about. Yet his parents had not wanted him to work for the New Falls Sun Times. Why go east, they had said. But they had told him earlier that his mother was a young woman just passing through Wichita. Betty had no idea what she was talking about. Did she?

"You think he should go down there?" Lefty interrupted his thoughts.

"Why not? Anyway, you never know what you might find. But if you meet this Brown fellow, ask him about Adam. Ask him about Esther. Ask him about her former husband. And definitely ask him about Catherine Reticent. I can't wait to hear his answers."

X

THE FLIGHT TO HOUSTON WAS UNEVENTFUL except for the thoughts cascading through his brain. Why did Betty bother him so? She was just a sad drunk, wasn't she? But if she was, why did Lefty spend so much time with her? They weren't in love, were they? Ask Marcus Aurelius Brown about Esther Maroon and Ingy Reticent and Adam and Catherine Reticent, Betty had said, when he had absolutely no idea what to expect in Houston.

The first thing he discovered in Houston was that the lobby of the Y was not air-conditioned. How was that possible? Houston, even at night in the middle of June, was more humid and debilitating than New York. He took the elevator to the ninth floor. The elevator was ancient, creeping slowly toward each floor, lit only by a thirty-watt bulb.

The door opened slowly at the ninth floor. At the end of the corridor a window was open and a large rotating fan stirred the heavy air. Unlike Codding's office, not one of the public areas in the building was air-conditioned. But Stephen's room was.

He thought the room felt like a meat locker, an air conditioner the size of a small refrigerator vibrating in the window. He lowered the dial and returned to the lobby. He walked to the telephone booth, picked up a directory and returned to his room. He always did this when he was in a new city. He thumbed through the L's having no idea why. Even if he found a Ledberg it would be meaningless.

As usual he found nothing and tossed the book onto the floor. He undressed, pulled back the covers, crawled into bed, but the sheets were cold and damp and uncomfortable. He slept that first night, when he slept at all, restlessly.

The following morning he gave the cab driver the address of Moses Short, Marcus Aurelius Brown's lawyer. Outside, the day was scorching and humid, the city of Houston resembling a kiln. A bright yellow sun hovered in the deep blue Texas sky, that sun cooking, baking, firing everybody and everything. Inside the taxicab, Stephen sat shivering in the air-conditioning wondering why the cab did not move.

The driver said, "You sure you want to go out there, mister?"

Stephen glanced at the address again. "Yes, that's where I want to go. That's the address Codding gave me."

The driver shrugged. "Okay, mister. I just wanted to make sure." He glanced at Stephen in the rearview mirror, shook his head and eased the cab into traffic.

Stephen should have known what the question and the shaking of the head meant. He should have known Moses Short's office was in niggertown.

The taxi passed through an area of ranch homes, manicured lawns, white children playing on the pavement in front of those homes. It was just like in Wichita. Just like where he lived. He could have been going home.

And then the scenery began to change rapidly as the cab moved past a shopping mall filled with fast food stores. The cab turned off the main road into back streets. They passed old wooden houses standing next to dilapidated wooden shacks. The driver glanced in the rearview mirror again. "You're going to have a tough time getting a cab to come out here to pick you up. And I sure ain't gonna wait for you."

Stephen answered, "Well, don't you worry. I'll get another one."

"Me? I ain't worried, mister. I'm gonna get outta here as soon as I drop you off. You may get another cab, but it ain't gonna be no good cabbie."

The car stopped in the middle of the street. A series of wooden horses stood in the gutter blocking the sidewalk. The sidewalk had disintegrated, large potholes gaping where the sidewalk should have been, tufts of wild grass growing in the uncovered earth. Maybe the taxicab driver was correct. Maybe he should not have taken on this project. He paid the driver and climbed from the cab, the torrid air heavy, causing him to feel as if he could not breathe.

Beyond the crumbling sidewalk was a two-story house, itself in a state of disrepair. Its coat of dark gray paint was peeling, blotches of weathered wood showing through. The lawn was overgrown with weeds and in need of mowing. Implanted on the far side, its back to Stephen, was a large sign.

He moved one of the wooden horses to the side and made a slight jump over the decaying sidewalk. He walked through the wild grass and weeds, seeds from the weeds catching and clinging to his trousers, sensing that someone was watching from the second story window. He glanced up, but saw no one. Perhaps, he thought, it was the taxicab driver's suggestion and the condition of the neighborhood that caused him to picture imaginary figures. He reached the sign. Painted in bold black letters on a white background was not a "For Sale" notice as he thought but SHORT FOR CITY COUNCIL and under it REMEMBER MARCUS AURELIUS.

He studied the house again. A series of steep wooden steps led to the front door. He had felt a few moments ago as if someone was observing him from the second floor, but now it seemed as if the house was empty. He walked through the wild grass to the steps and climbed them. To the right of the door was a bell, under it was a small black laminated plastic sign with white lettering: Moses Short, Barrister. He pushed the button and heard, "Yes, may I help you?" "Stephen Ledberg," he replied, and heard a buzzing sound. He twisted the doorknob and pushed against the door. It opened more easily than he had expected and he stumbled inside. What he saw startled him.

The room was covered with zebra skins. Floors, walls, chairs, stairs leading to the second floor, all covered in zebra skins. Only the ceiling, which was painted white, and the ebony-colored banister of the staircase were not. The room smelled of animal hides. It was as if he walked into the lair of a trapper, and it caused him to be anxious.

He heard a woman's voice call from the second floor. "Yes? Can I help you?"

He walked across the skins, his shoes leaving imprints on the black or dark brown sections. He reached the first step and looked up. Standing on the landing looking down at him was a black woman. Not black or brown like the zebra skins, but caramel. She wore a white dress scooped low in the front. The swelling of her breasts above the scoop neck excited him. For a moment he felt his legs weaken. A pinging sensation coursed through his body. She stood looking down at him, her legs slightly apart, a quizzical expression on her face.

She asked again, "Can I help you?"

He told her who he was and continued up the staircase.

She said, staring into his eyes, "Oh yes, Mr. Ledberg, we've been expecting you." She extended her hand and announced, "I'm Stephanie." As if that was enough to tell him everything there was to know. Stephanie who? Was she Short's assistant? His wife? His lover?

He grasped her hand. Was it his imagination? Had she pressed with slightly more pressure than she need have? And why is she star-

ing at me like that, he wondered? He averted his eyes onto the up-
per part of her body. Breasts and nipples pressed against the dress,
breasts overflowing above the neck of that dress, breasts whose skin
was so smooth it reminded him of the texture and color of butter-
scotch pudding. She smiled at him and ran her tongue over her bottom lip. Had she done that on purpose? Was she flirting with him?

Stephanie said, "Won't you sign our guest book, Mr. Ledberg?" She moved toward a desk at the right of the stairs. As
she turned he caught a glimpse of her buttocks outlined against
the dress. She wasn't wearing any underwear, was she? He felt
his legs go weak again. She turned her head and smiled as if she
knew that her turning and the slight clinging of her dress would
affect him as it did.

He signed his name in the guest book. She said, "Isn't that
interesting, Mr. Ledberg, your first name is Stephen and mine's
Stephanie. What's your sign?"

"My sign?"

"When were you born?"

"In June. In another ten days actually."

"Really? Well, we'll have to help you celebrate, won't we?" She
smiled. "Well, I'll let Mr. Short know you're here." She walked to
the closed door, while Stephen followed her with his eyes, watching
her buttocks brush against the back of her dress.

"Mr. Short will see you now."

As he entered Moses Short's office he did not see him right
away. What he did notice was a desk piled with papers, books, files,
an ashtray filled with dead cigarette butts. The walls were grimy and
in need of fresh paint. Except for the flash of color Stephen caught
from the corner of his eye, colorful birds flitting in a wire cage,
everything in that office was black and white and grim.

He heard a chair move. Moses Short stood, a cigarette between
his left forefinger and thumb. He said, "You'd like to get into her
pantsh wouldn't you, Mishter Ledberg? I shaw you, sho don't make

believe you don't. You're in good company. Shshshshshshsh." Moses Short was blowing a laugh from the right side of his mouth.

Moses Short upset Stephen. He thought Moses Short an oddity, a short black man less than five feet tall, deformed, his torso twisted to the left to such a degree that his right breast bone pushed against his soiled shirt. And his mouth never seemed to change shape, his lips forming an opening at the corner, which meant Stephen realized, that when he used a word with an "s" in it, the "s" was followed by an "h".

"Don't get all hot and bothered, Mishter Ledberg. She'sh been shpoken for." He nodded at the photographs behind the desk. "Marcush Aureliush, she'sh hish girl. Come around here, I'll show you.

"He'sh a great man, Mishter Ledberg. Shome day he'll be ash great as theshe two."

He moved down the wall to a photograph Stephen had seen before, of Martin Luther King Jr. making his famous Dream Speech in front of the Lincoln monument. It was a speech he had watched on television alone, a speech he knew Anna and George had attended together. Even now the remembrances jolted his bowels, millions glorying in King's words, while he had been sickened, not by the speech but at the thought of Anna and George together, ecstatic, touching, embracing, loving. He did not want to think of that now.

"You shee, Mishter Ledberg. Dr. King hash written a note."

And indeed he had. "To my good friend Moses. May his dreams come true. Martin."

"And thish is the old man." The photograph Short pointed to was of an African at a political rally. This, too, had an inscription. "To Moses. May the zebra skins remind you of Africa."

"Thish ish a man who has shurvived everything. May he live forever."

All the time Short had been talking, his cigarette had burned dangerously near the fingers that held it. He noticed and snuffed it out.

"Well, Marcush Aureliush will shurvive, too, Mishter Ledberg. They think they've got him on thish frame-up but they don't. He'll be out shoon and then they'd better watch out."

"Well, you know that's why I'm down here," Stephen said. "Mr. Codding wants me to find out why Mr. Brown is not out on bail yet."

"Yesh, yesh, I know. But Pete Codding knowsh thingsh are much shlower here than in the North. Nothing ish eashy here. He should know that. Here. Have a sheat."

Stephen sat down. Short sat as well. He picked up a square red box with gold lettering, opened it and withdrew a cigarette. He lit the cigarette and blew the smoke through the right side of his mouth. "Are you familiar at all, Mishter Ledberg, with the cashe?"

"I only know the little Mr. Codding told me about it, which is not much actually."

Short rummaged through the flotsam on his desk and pulled out a thick file. He handed it to Stephen who glanced through it, recognizing most of the same material Pete Codding had shown him.

"I've seen all this. As I understand it, Pete Codding has had bail money sent and I'm supposed to find out why Mr. Brown is still in jail."

Short said, "Why, Mishter Ledberg? Are you queshtioning me? Marcush Aureliush will be out shoon. I can guarantee that. Do you think thish community would shupport me if they did not trusht me? Do you know theshe people have contributed nickelsh and dimesh to my campaign. That may not mean much to you, but they can barely afford to do that. Do you know they bring food here for Marcush Aurelish becaushe they know I shee him every week? Did you know that, Mishter Ledberg? That I'm the only one who sheesh him. Trusht, Mishter Ledberg, you should trusht me. M.A. doesh."

Trust? Stephen had to admit that he did not trust Short. What was it that he did not trust? The fact that, the community believing in him or not, Marcus Aurelius, or M.A. as he had just been called, had been sent bail money and he was still in jail. Short kept evading that. If Short could not give him a more definitive answer as to why Brown was still in jail, or even when he would be released, someone else might be able to help.

"Well, if you don't mind I may try to see if anyone in the sheriff's office might help. It might be that an outsider might actually…"

"I wouldn't do that if I wash you, Mishter Ledberg. We don't like northernersh coming down here shticking their noshesh in our bushinessh. Particulary Jewish northernersh."

Short paused and glared. A pause and glare that gave Stephen the opportunity to say Ledberg was not a Jewish name, nor that he was not from the north having grown up in Wichita, Kansas. But so startled was he by Short's invective that he said nothing.

"M.A. will be out after the election. I promish you that. Now ish that all? I'm a very bushy man."

"Yes. I'm finished," Stephen replied.

"Good. Then do you have a car or shall I have Shtephanie call a cab?"

"I don't have a car, yes do please ask her to call a cab."

As he waited with Stephanie, she said, "Why don't we talk downstairs and wait for the taxi outside?"

They stood in the hot sun on the stairs leading to the wild lawn. She said, "Whatever he said, don't trust it. He's a shit. Here, take this." She handed him a piece of paper with a telephone number written on it. "You don't have to contact me if you don't want to. But I think I can help. Just don't call me here."

"I won't."

A taxi stopped in the street beside the wooden horses and gave a brief honk. She extended her hand. He took it – there was that pressure again – as she said, "I hope I'll see you again." She paused, her mouth open slightly as if she were debating what to say next, finishing with, "Stephen."

He walked down the steps and across the lawn. The heat did not bother him now. Now he could feel its warmth tanning his face. Now he enjoyed the feeling of sweat pouring from his body. Now he felt energized. What had changed? The position of the sun? The consistency of the air? Or was it just the sound of his name on Stephanie's lips?

Had he been more aware of what he was doing and less affected by Stephanie, he would have wondered about the black-and-white checkered cab. Had he been in less of a dreamlike state he would have taken in the name of the company printed on its side. Had he been more himself he would have wondered what the words – Uhuru Ltd. – meant.

XI

THE FOLLOWING MORNING HE TOOK A TAXI to the courthouse. The early morning golden light was mirrored by the glass sides of the skyscrapers, bathing the ochre and sandstone of other buildings in a lutescent glow, casting long shadows over the streets. The skyscrapers were like pieces of sculpture, commissioned by the wealth of Houston. Built by the rich, for themselves and to themselves, if not necessarily by themselves. Downtown Houston reflected the Southwest back at him – ochre, sienna, sand, gold – and always that deep blue sky.

The taxi stopped in front of the courthouse. Stephen followed the stream of people through the vault-like doors. So many hurrying in, he thought. So few leaving. The contrast between the brightness of the morning and the shadowy interior momentarily obfuscated his vision. Men passed each other in the dim marble lobby, the lobby cool, refreshed not by a machine, but by the thickness of the walls and the high vaulting rotunda. The men greeted one another, acknowledging each

other's presence by a "Hiya, Bob" or "How's the wife, Dick?"
or "You want to have lunch later, Will?" Men who must have
known each other for how many years, who must have swapped
how many stories over how many lunches? Their familiarity and
bonhomie made him feel wistful, wishing he, too, could partake
of that camaraderie.

The sheriff's office was not what he expected. It was tiny,
cramped, with gray metal filing cabinets occupying most of the
room. A large, fat bellied man sat in a swivel chair behind a cluttered
desk. He eyed Stephen suspiciously and said, "Whaddya want?"

"I'd like some information on a prisoner."

"Which one?"

'Marcus Aurelius Brown."

The man stared at Stephen as if he were mulling something over
in his mind. Then he said, "Never heard of him. You sure he's
here? With us?"

"Yes. He was arrested on a drug charge. It's a well-publicized
case. He should be out on bail now, but for some reason he's not."

The man stretched what little neck he had, looking around Stephen to the hallway. He yelled, "Hey, Frank, come on in here."

A tall, handsome, suntanned man wearing a gray uniform with
a holster and weapon hanging from it entered the room. The fat
bellied man said, staring intently into Frank's eyes, "This guy, what's
your name anyway, buddy?" – Stephen told him – "this guy wants
to know if we got a prisoner called Marcus Aurelius Brown. You
ever heard of him?"

Frank said, "You a relative of his?"

"No. But…"

"You his lawyer?"

"No."

"Sorry then. Can't give you any information on any prisoner unless you're one of those people."

The fat-bellied one said, "And you ain't either of them." The
room exploded with his laugh.

The laugh embarrassed Stephen. Frank's black leather holster and the two men in gray uniforms intimidated him. He left the room and walked through the marble lobby, through the heavy doors, out into the bright sunshine, the heat and humidity shocking his body. He remembered how yesterday other words and another attitude had given the sun and heat a different character.

He thought of approaching the problem as if it were a story and he still a journalist. He wrote out a list of all the individuals connected to the case. But when he called them, none of them would tell him a thing. Not the district attorney, not the judge, not the lawyer who had handled the case originally, not even the journalists who had covered the story.

"That? That's old news. I don't know who's covering that now. Probably no one."

"But don't you think there's a story there if he's supposed to be out on bail now and isn't?"

"Could be. But I'm on another story now. Have you talked to the D.A. or the…"

He hung up, disgusted. He was angry with the members of his chosen profession. If it had been him, he thought, he would have been more helpful.

So he called Stephanie. "You gave me your number."

"I know. I didn't expect you would call. I'm glad you did."

He was elated by her friendliness. "You said you might be willing to help."

"Yes, I did."

"Well, I wondered if we could meet."

She did not respond immediately. Then she said, "I'll tell you what. There's a party tonight. Are you interested in going?"

He hesitated for a moment, and said, "All right."

"Great. I'll pick you up around eight. The Y, right?"

"Right."

Stephanie arrived in a white Ford Mustang.

"Wow, is this your car?"

"Of course it's mine. What do you think? A nigger can't own a 1966 white Ford Mustang coupe?"

"I didn't mean it that way."

"Oh yeah. What way did you mean it?"

He realized the more he tried to explain himself the more entangled he became.

"I'm sorry."

"That's better."

Whatever he imagined the evening would bring, he felt he had just put an end to it.

Stephanie drove the way he had gone the other day. Past ranch houses, manicured lawns, sprinkler systems now watering those lawns, past the fast food stores, the neon signs turning slowly in the dusky sky. She turned left into the ghetto area, the houses and shacks looking more rundown and unwelcoming than during the day.

Stephanie drove confidently. She was proud and in control of that automobile. She asked, "So what's going on?"

"I'm stumped. I went to the sheriff's office."

"Uhuh. That's a no-no. You shouldn't have done that."

"I had to start somewhere. What else could I have done?"

"You should have contacted me."

"Well, now I have. What I don't understand is why Short doesn't want Brown out on bail. The money's been sent."

"He doesn't want M.A. out because he's scared of him."

"Scared of him?"

"He thinks if he gets out he'll run in the city council election. He's scared the people will want M.A. to run. He's scared he'll take his place."

"Would he?"

"M.A.? He wouldn't do anything to harm Short. Short's like a father to him. At least that's the way M.A. sees it."

"But you don't?"

"You know what I think about Short. You're wasting your time here. I don't even know why you bothered to come. Houston's nothing but a shithole anyway. If I could, I'd get out tomorrow."

"Why don't you?"

She glanced at him and then back to the road. "Why? 'Cause you need money to get out of here and Short pays nigger wages. That's why."

Her words confused him. For one, how had she come by the Mustang if her salary was meager? But more, how was it she used an expression, nigger, just like George Morris, his college friend? He understood why Lefty used the word, but he did not understand why Stephanie and George did.

Stephanie parked the car across the street from a house from which he could hear music. He followed her up the walk and into the house, which was jammed with bodies, all with two things in common, perspiration and music. Music blared from speakers in each corner of the room. Drums. Electric guitars. Pianos. Bongos. Vibes. Organs. Strings. Horns. Music so loud, drumbeats so piercing that Stephen could feel them vibrate deep within his belly. Drumbeats, bass notes, rhythm, and sweat wrapped around everyone, like a cocoon, enclosing himself and Stephanie and all the people she greeted, "Hi, Steph, how're you doing?" "This is my friend Stephen." "Nice to meet you."

Stephen felt odd, as if he did not belong, and not only because he did not know anybody. He felt exposed, a thought flashing through his mind; did anyone here know George Morris?

Stephanie led him toward the center of the room, her body moving to the beat of the music, her eyes closed, her teeth pressed gently on her lower lip, her breasts undulating, pressing against the black knit top. They danced and danced. On and on the rhythm pulsated through the room, so penetrating that it blocked out everything else. Stephen might have gone into that house with certain thoughts and impressions, but within half an hour only the music mattered. Everything else, even Marcus Aurelius Brown, no longer existed. The music never ceasing, never letting up, blasting from speakers in each corner of the room. So overpowering was its influence that even he became caught up in its rhythm, his body moving now, awkwardly at first, then closing his eyes, his body swaying, himself transported. They danced until the music broke, covered in sweat; their clothes drenched, Stephanie grasping his hand, palms perspiring.

She said, "Let's get out of here for a while. Let's go somewhere and talk. We can always come back."

Holding his hand she wended her way through knots of people. She led him outside, the night so still; nothing was moving, the sky so dark, nothing stirring save for the beads of perspiration cascading down his body and the pounding of his heart and the fullness of his penis.

XII

STEPHANIE DROVE THEM TO SHORT'S OFFICE. Had Stephen not been there before, had he not actually walked across that lawn and into that house he would have thought she was taking him to a derelict building. The house and lawn and crumbling sidewalk were now illuminated only by a solitary street lamp.

Stephanie took his hand as if to reassure him. She led him around the wooden horses, across the disintegrating pavement and through the grass. She unlocked the door, the streetlight throwing eerie shadows onto the floor and walls and ceiling. He could smell the zebra skins as she led him toward the stairs, squeezing his hand warmly, brushing her hip against his, not a word exchanged. Stephen was excited and not only by the closeness of the house.

As they reached the first step, she turned and still grasping his hand, placed it on her breasts. He did not have time to think, he was aware only of the feeling of her breasts, soft, firm, the nipples suddenly erect; his own organ mimicking hers; Stephanie breathing heavily; Stephen in a frenzy.

He threw his body against her, their chests brushing wildly, Stephanie gasping as if she were drowning. They fell to the floor. His hand moved uncontrollably up her skirt, up those legs. Knowing all along what he would find. Lubricants. Sopping. Stephanie as wet as the air itself. She let forth a groan, sucking in what oxygen she could in that heavy sultry atmosphere.

She grabbed his hand. "Woooeeee. Old passionate Pete. If we want to do this properly let's get undressed. We'll just ruin our clothes this way."

He did not have time to say no. He did not have time to say I don't think this is a good idea. No time to say I thought we came here to discuss Marcus Aurelius Brown. Stephanie unhooked her skirt and dropped it to the floor. The knit top was not a top but a body suit. She peeled the black body suit from her torso like a snake shedding its skin.

Stephanie stepped out of the dark puddle at her feet. She stood naked, her breasts dusky melons, black curly forest, heavy thighs, and strong lithe legs. Stephanie standing, the light from the street lamp reflected on her body, only white hoop earrings remaining. She removed even them.

"Now it's your turn. It isn't fair if I'm the only one who does this."

As he undressed he wondered what he was getting himself into. Certainly she caused his legs to weaken, other parts to stiffen. But had the earth opened up? He barely knew her and here he was almost naked.

"Moses Short says you're Marcus Aurelius' girl."

"Is that what that shit said? I'm no one's girl. M.A. doesn't even know I exist. He doesn't have time for anything but his cause. But I do."

She took a step toward him, touching his chest, stroking his body, the excitement overcoming him, his mind a whirl, images spinning. Stephanie was drawing him down to the zebra skins. He felt the roughness of the skins beneath his naked body, Stephanie rolled him over on his back – how had she managed that? – and was atop him, lying flat out on those black-and-white skins, her breasts inches from his face.

He touched her nipple with his nose, Stephanie emitting slight gasps and moans. He could feel her hand searching for his wand, finding it, guiding it, feeling it slide into her juicy tunnel, loving warmth, wishing his whole body might disappear into that luscious lair.

Stephanie gasped, moving her body, slowly, accelerating, rocking, undulating, friction, warmth, lubricants, muscles expanding, vessels flushed. Suddenly she screamed, her back arched, her face toward the ceiling, "Come on, whitey, give it to me. Ohhh, yeah. Tootsie Rolls ain't for me. Bazooka bubble gum's what sets me free."

Stephanie was moving wildly, as she grabbed his hand screaming, "Feel my prick, lily of the valley," Stephanie gurgling breathless yeses and ohs, until Stephen fell out of control, senseless, blank, unaware that he had dug his fingers into her shoulders.

They lay on the skins that felt cool against his body.

"Bazooka bubble gum, Stephanie? I…"

"Bazooka bubble gum and Tootsie Rolls, Stephen, don't you get it?"

"The tootsie rolls I get."

"You do? If you know that how come you don't get Bazooka bubble gum?"

"I don't."

"I'm not talking about the individual pieces, silly. I'm talking about the package shaped like a Tootsie Roll. You know the package they sell that has the pieces segmented just like a Tootsie Roll. You have to break them off to chew them, just like the large packets of Tootsie Rolls. Tootsie Rolls and Bazooka bubble gum used to be big hits in women's prisons. But they banned them when they discovered why they were so popular. Get it?"

He felt shy and embarrassed. How did she know that? Why was she so much more worldly than he was?

"Shhhh. What's that?"

"What's what?"

"That rustling sound upstairs."

"Oh, that. That's just his birds. His birds from Africa. Didn't you see them when you were in his office?"

"Yes. Yes, I did."

"It's part of his business in Africa."

"Short has a business in Africa?"

"Are you kidding me? He's got all sorts of businesses out there. These," she ran her hand over the zebra skins, "were given to him by Kyangu, the old man's nephew. They are partners. They're like that." She crossed her fingers forming an X.

"They own a restaurant and cab company here. The taxi you took was theirs. They've been friends for years."

He became pensive. He felt in a bind. The reason he had met with Stephanie was to ask for help, but the evening had evolved in a way he had not foreseen – or had he? – and he felt it would be crass and opportunistic to pursue the question of why Marcus Aurelius Brown was not out on bail if funds had been sent by Pete Codding. He was thinking of different ways to ask the question without offending Stephanie, when she did it for him.

"So what is it you want to know? I'll help you if I can but no one can know I told you."

He did not think on it at that moment, but later he would come to understand how silence suddenly can be breached with, if not the absolute truth, then at least with movement toward it. That most people were so uncomfortable with silence they would break it of their own accord and in the breaking reveal immense knowledge, if not about a subject he was pursuing, then certainly about themselves. He wondered if that was where the expression "silence is golden" derived from, the gold mined from the person who broke the silence.

He said, "Well, I guess the most important is the bail money. What's happened to that?"

"Has there been bail money?"

"That's what I'm down here for. To find out what has happened to that."

"Really. Well, then I would say that's easy. Short uses it. All the money he receives, campaign money, money for M.A., it all goes for his companies."

"But isn't Marcus Aurelius aware of any of this? Doesn't he know he should be out on bail by now?"

"Why should he? His only source of information is Short. When Short's ready, M.A. will be out."

She began stroking the back of his head as if she felt the question and answer period was over. As if they should return to a more intimate and familiar subject, one that had engaged them body and mind only minutes before. She was caressing his hair, relaxing him, while he was trying not to let her seduce him. He wanted to engage her a while longer on one more subject.

"Brown lived in New Falls, Pennsylvania," he said. "Did you know that?"

"He did? M.A. lived in Pennsylvania? I didn't know that." She paused. "Maybe that's why we get that envelope every month from there."

"An envelope? From New Falls, Pennsylvania? From whom?"

"Don't know. I don't open the mail. I just pass it on to Short."

"Then how do you know where it's from?"

"The postmark. The odd thing about that envelope is it only contains a check."

"How would you know that if you don't open it?"

"That's what I think anyways. What else could it be, folded in half and the only thing in the envelope? Short gets a lot of those, but this is the only one that comes regularly."

"Is there any way you can find out who's sending him the envelopes from New Falls?"

She studied him as if she were searching for something. She looked into his eyes as if she wanted to tell him something. And then she said, "Maybe. Maybe I'll do that for you. But I just gave you an early birthday present and now I have to know what's in it for me. Yeah, I'll have to know that. What's in it for me?"

XIII

He telephoned Pete Codding the next day and told him that Marcus Aurelius Brown was not out on bail yet, that, according to Stephanie, Short's assistant, the bail money was used for Short's businesses, and that he, Stephen was at a dead-end. And all Codding said was, " Well, we can't just take his assistant's word for it. I'll call Short from here and emphasize that you're going to stay down there until Brown is out. The foundation is committed to this. You're doing a good job. You let me know anything else you hear. Call me in a couple of days. I just wish we had another source in addition to Stephanie."

Stephen did not think they even had her as a source any longer. Not a word had passed between them as she drove him back to the Y. Then Stephanie turned off the engine, looked at him, and with a hint of desperation said, "Take me with you, Stephen. We're good together. Take me with you when you leave. We'd make a good team. Get me out of this shithole."

He said nothing, not because he had nothing to say but because he thought it was not what she wanted to hear. Take her with him? How could he do that? He wasn't in love with her, was he? What was love? An orgasm? What did he feel for Stephanie? What had he felt for Anna? The Jewish girl? The climbing rope?

"What's the matter? I'm not good enough for you? I was plenty good back there. You want to find out who's sending those checks? You know what you have to do."

He had not responded to her ultimatum, not because he did not wish to, but because he had no idea what to say.

The day after he spoke to Codding, the elevator at the Y broke down, lodged between the sixth and seventh floors. And while afterwards, a good three hours afterwards, everyone said it was an accident, that the elevator was old and had to be replaced, Stephen, who happened to be the only person in the elevator, did not see it that way. Whether or not it was his imagination, he thought the event was planned, that someone was trying to give him a message, a message scratched on the elevator door. A graffito he had not noticed before: the onle gud niger is a ded won And under it the word simeon. Was that the tag of the person who wrote the graffito, he wondered, or had he misspelled the word simian or even his own name, simon?

He called Codding again, told him what had happened and said he was leaving. "I don't think there is any more to be gained by remaining here. I'm going to stop off in Wichita to see my parents before returning to New Falls."

Codding responded, "I'm glad you called, Mr. Ledberg. I was just about to call you. Just stay another day or two. Short has promised me Brown will be out within the week. I'd like you to see him if he is. Make sure he is all right. See if there is anything we can do for him."

Stephen spent most of the next two days in his room, venturing out only for something to eat, descending or ascending the elevator only if there was at least one other person in it. Trying to avoid the graffito each time, but drawn to it as he had been to Lefty's stump, as he had been to those derelict men sprawled out on the streets of the Bowery. Maybe there was nothing, he thought, one could do about those men or Lefty's arm, but the elevator could be painted, couldn't it?

On the third day he received a call from Short. "You better get over here right away, Mishter Ledberg."

"Why? Is Marcus Aurelius there?"

"Can't tell you that. Jusht hop in a cab and get over here."

Stephanie surprised him by opening the door. She stood in the doorway and said nothing, then wheeled around and walked toward the stairs. She walked briskly across the zebra skins, across the area on which they had loved, and up the stairs. As they reached the top she said coldly, "He's here."

Short stood outside his office. He said, in a voice loud enough for anyone in his office to hear, "Sho, Mishter Ledberg, you didn't trusht me. I told you he'd be out of the shlammer, didn't I? I told you Marcush Aureliush'd be here."

Short's office was the same, except for the man silhouetted against the window at the far end. A tall, well-built man wearing a white tee shirt, jeans, work boots, sunglasses. Short said, "M.A., thish ish the man I wash telling you about. Mishter Ledberg, thish ish Marcush Aureliush Brown."

Short shuffled through papers on his desk, found his cigarettes, put them in his pocket and said, "I'll be back later, M.A."

The room was silent except for the movement of the birds. Marcus Aurelius stood at one end smoking a cigarette. Stephen stood awkwardly near the door. He walked to the other end, moving to his left so as to see Brown more clearly.

Brown was no longer silhouetted against the light from the window. Without that distraction he appeared even stronger, more muscular. To Stephen it seemed as if all that strength and power resided in his neck. The man's neck was pulsating, the veins popping against his tan skin; his neck was strong and graceful, like that of a deer or an antelope.

Stephen said, "I'm glad you're out of jail."

Brown did not respond. He stood, Stephen thought, staring at him. He could not be sure because he could not see his eyes through the lenses of the sunglasses. Stephen glanced out the window.

Marcus Aurelius said, "How come you didn't trust Moses?"

He spoke in a deep, soft voice. A voice that had the strength and power and suppleness of the speaker's neck, as if the voice and neck and throat were one, in harmony, not separate and distinct entities, but one flowing from and into the other.

What could he say? Why didn't he trust Short? He couldn't say anything about the bail money, could he? Would Brown believe him if he told him that? Or Short's partnership with Kyangu? Or the cab company? To say nothing of the birds. He glanced at them. They were flitting wildly about the cage as if all they wanted to do was escape both the cage and that room, which was exactly how Stephen felt.

"It wasn't that I didn't trust Mr. Short. I don't know if you know, but bail money had been sent down some time ago. I came here to find out why you were still in jail. I know Mr. Short...'

"Moses Short is the only man I trust."

"Yes, I know. Stephanie told me. Stephanie told me he's been like a father to you."

As soon as he said it he knew he should not have.

"Stephanie told you that? Well, he isn't. I don't have any father. And no mother either."

Marcus Aurelius ground out his cigarette, pulled a pack of Kools from his jacket pocket, tapped one out, pounded the filter end on his watch crystal, and lit it. He dragged deeply and exhaled. His eyes, or at least the lenses of the sunglasses, were riveted on Stephen.

"I never knew my mother. She died when I was born. And I don't know who my father was. He just took off as soon as he heard she was pregnant. I don't hold any grudge against him, I understand. It doesn't make any difference. What's important is the struggle. What's important is for me to help my people. If my father's still alive somewhere he'll know that. That's all that matters.

"All those people out there," he moved his head in a quick sideways gesture towards the street "are my brothers and sisters. They're my family. Do you know what it's like to grow up in a wooden shack? A shack that stinks, that's infested by rats, that could go up in flames at any time. Do you?"

He dragged on his cigarette, exhaled the smoke, dust particles floating in the sunlight, blown willy nilly by the extended smoke.

"Do you know how many of my brothers and sisters have been burned to death out there? In this city, with all its money? Do you think they give a shit what's happening in this part of town? As long as everything's calm out here they don't care. But let one person begin to question, shit, they'll find a way to throw that person in the slammer. But I'm out now and I'm going to help Moses win the election. That's the beginning."

Marcus Aurelius took off his sunglasses in order to rub his eyes, eyes which shocked Stephen because they were not brown as he had assumed, but were the clearest, most perfect pale translucent gray, the color of chalcedony. So clear a color that the sunlight poured right through them, forcing Marcus Aurelius to shut his eyelids. Sensitive eyes that Stephen observed were tearing, causing his own to sympathize in kind. Was that why Brown wore those sunglasses? Because his eyes were photosensitive? Or because he was ashamed they were not brown?

He replaced the sunglasses. "I've got to get back on the street now. I've got to thank all those people out there for remembering me."

"Is there anything else we can do for you? Anything you need?"

"I have my freedom. That's all I need."

Stephen thought to ask him about his years in New Falls. He could have asked if he knew about the monthly check Short received from there, but he had only Stephanie's word to go on and he did not wish to involve her any more than he already had. After all, he was leaving Houston. She would have to remain. He could have asked M.A. if he knew Catherine Reticent, or even if Adam Maroon, the half-caste child in Betty's room, was their child. That was what Betty wanted him to do but, he did not. He did not because it was a direction he was terrified of traveling.

As he shook Brown's hand he said, "I hope the trial exonerates you."

Brown said, "They don't have anything on me. It's one lousy cop's word against mine. After Moses wins this election they'll be too scared to bring me to trial. This community is getting itself together."

Stephanie sat at her desk and stared at him, as if she were waiting for him to say something. He wondered if she thought he was going to change his mind and ask her to leave with him.

She said, "I suppose you want me to call a cab?"

He smiled inwardly at that. A joke on his own expectations.

After she replaced the phone she said, "You're leaving. Looks like I'm going to be stuck in this shithole."

"You'll get out, Stephanie. You don't need me to get you out. Here."

He picked up a pen from her desk and wrote his address and telephone number on a piece of paper.

"If you get east, call me. And if you ever find out who's sending those checks and you feel like telling me, that's where you can reach me."

He heard a honking from the street.

"That's your cab." She held out her hand. He took it, this time feeling no pressure, this time sensing another message entirely.

He turned and walked down the stairs, across the spot where they had loved, across the zebra skins and out into the bright, hot sunshine.

And this time he noticed the black-and-white checkered cab. This time he saw the name of the company on the door. And this time he asked the driver what the words meant.

"Uhuru Ltd.? Don't know. Don't think it means anything. It's just the name of the company."

XIV

HIS MOM MET HIM AT THE AIRPORT IN WICHITA. She seemed older than he remembered. Her hair was grayer, her body neither as strong nor as upright, as if she had shrunk or he had grown. But he knew from past visits that that initial impression would fade, that his mother – and father – would quickly return to their former selves, to the image he knew all his life.

He kissed her cheek lightly.

"Dad's out at the house waiting for you. He's been puttering around in the garden cleaning the barbecue.

"We called you on your birthday, but you weren't home. Then when you called from Houston we realized the paper must have sent you there. What sort of an assignment was it?"

They had left the comfort of the air-conditioned terminal, the Wichita heat stunning him, the glare from the sun forcing him to shut his eyes momentarily.

"I'm not working for the paper anymore, mom. I have another job."

He shook his head to clear it of the heat's effect, squinting, studying his mom's face, wondering what her response would be.

She said nothing. He thought actually that her face relaxed slightly, facial muscles easing, tension evaporating, his mom magically younger than when they had embraced. He did not tell her why he had left the paper. And she did not ask.

He followed her to the old navy blue Dodge station wagon. Heat waves shimmered from the metal. She unlocked the rear door and he threw in his bags. She unlocked the passenger side and he climbed in.

His mom inserted the key in the ignition, put the car in gear and accelerated gently. How many times, he thought, has she done that? His mom in control. An expert driver. Nothing bad ever happening on all those trips of the past. The automobile was traveling serenely down the highway, and he was relaxing, wishing as always that the trip would not end, that it would go on and on. But as with all those trips of the past, this one finished where it always began.

The small two story wooden frame house was exactly the same. The trim tiny lawn sloped down to the sidewalk, a hose snaking across the grass, the hose connected to a faucet at the front of the house.

Across the street was the playground. He noticed a few young children on the swings, and farther in the distance teenagers playing basketball. He never went near the park now. Not to play tennis, nor to play basketball. He had not gone there since the day he returned from college after George died - died? - after George killed himself. It was after that that he returned home and walked through the park to see the boulder where he used to play king of the mountain. He remembered struggling up the side of the boulder, other children trying to pull him off, grabbing his shoulders, occasionally ripping a sweater. Scratching hands, and bloodied knees, grass and dirt-stained trousers. He recalled the feeling of invincibility after battling the other children and standing proudly astride the rock slab, fists clenched, legs planted firmly, daring any of them to come up to challenge him, the king of the mountain. It was not that he was bigger or stronger than the others. But he was tougher, craftier, instinctively always one step ahead.

He remembered sneaking glances at his mom sitting on the bench conversing with other mothers. Was she watching him? He wanted to shout, "Mom, mom, look at me". Instead he yelled loudly at the other boys, loud enough he hoped for his mom to hear, "You can't come up. I'm the king of the mountain." He did not dare look over at her for fear she still sat and chatted with the other mothers. But in his mind he pretended she was watching him as he defended his position atop the rock. And, imagining that her eyes were focused on him, he felt swell and strong and proud.

The only times he knew for certain she saw him was when she yelled, "Stephen, come down from there. Let Tommy on top now. You've been there long enough." Let Tommy on top now? But, mom, that's not the way the game goes. And that day back from college he had walked to the boulder and had not believed it was the same one. It could not have been this boulder they had struggled over, it was too small. But it was. The same one. That day he felt something inside him had been lost. A secret revealed. His mom and dad had changed back to their old selves, but not that boulder.

That was the day he realized that one of the most dangerous things a person could do was to go back into the past. At least with the unknown you entered with your eyes wide open. With the past, scales covered your eyes. You expected one thing, and you found another. What had changed? You. It was impossible to gauge how much, until you had confronted the past. You could never be prepared enough for what you find there. And now he was home again.

They did not enter the house through the front door. He followed his mom through the gate leading to the garden and picnic area in the rear, and through the kitchen door. It had not changed at all, in any way.

XV

WHILE HIS DAD ROASTED SIRLOIN STEAK over hickory briquettes his mom prepared a salad and waited for the exact moment to drop the sweet corn into the boiling water, his dad shouting, "Let it go, mother," his mom gently lowering the corn into the steaming kettle.

As his dad placed a slice of steak on Stephen's plate he said, "Mother tells me you're not working on the paper anymore."

He glanced at his dad's face. Was he angry, or relieved?

"I'm glad you're not working for that paper anymore. We never thought it was much of a paper. What were you doing in Houston then?"

Stephen picked up a steaming ear of corn and placed it on his plate. He wondered if that was all his dad was going to say. He was quite prepared, if need be, to tell them what had happened. I was fired, dad. And to tell you the truth I don't know why.

He rolled a slice of butter over the steaming cob and shook salt and pepper on it. Succulent aromas rose from his plate. The steak was burned charcoal, blood seeping from it, butter melting, running over the yellow kernels down onto the plate, mixing with the blood and fat of the meat.

"Stephen, did you hear your father's question?"

"Yes, mom, I did. I was on a job there."

And he went on to tell them almost everything that had happened since he left the New Falls Sun Times. What he did not tell them about was Stephanie. That he omitted. He had never mentioned any information about girlfriends since the episode many years ago when Katie Williams invited him to the seventh grade dance. After he accepted and returned to the table his dad asked who that was on the phone. He told him, not dreaming what would follow. His dad had broken unexpectedly into song. "Stephen's got a girlfriend, Stephen's got a girlfriend." That had embarrassed and humiliated him. His mom just sat at the kitchen table smiling at her husband's teasing. His mom, and those two men whose reproductions hung on the wall, failed to come to his support. The very next day he telephoned Katie Williams to tell her he could not go.

"Why not, Stephen?"

"I forgot I have a baseball game."

Not only a lie but he felt something for Katie Williams he had never before experienced. What was it? He did not know nor understand, but he was aware that the lie had caused him to feel vacant and sad. A loss he could never retrieve.

Somehow, he did not know how, Katie Williams had touched him. She had, he felt, understood him. Somehow – he did not know how – she loved him. And he had betrayed her. And more, although he did not understand, he had betrayed himself. Katie Williams was before the Jewish girl, before Anna, before Stephanie. That year in school whenever their paths crossed, which was frequently, she would smile and, expressionless, he would pass her by, his heart thumping madly, but the rest of him paralyzed. Katie Williams and her family left Wichita the following year. He never saw her again but when on occasion he experienced something wonderful, something that brought a smile to his lips, he thought of her and it caused him to feel vacant, lonely, and sad.

There was one other girl who affected him as Katie Williams had. Once when he was visiting his cousins in Binghamton, New York, a group of their friends were playing a version of spin the bottle. In this variation the boys formed a line opposite the girls. Whoever was at the front of the line kissed the other. There was a girl in the group who stunned him with her beauty, the only kind of beauty he knew, what he saw in her face. He did not understand what it was he saw there. All he knew was that she looked at him with openness and honesty, as if there were a secret they shared, a mystery, and no one but they were aware of it. He counted how many girls were in front of her, then counted the boys in front of him, realized he would be one too early, turned to the boy behind him and exchanged places. His heart was knocking as he reached the front of the line, and with eyes shut, they kissed. It was as if no one else existed. All the other boys and girls, the world itself, vanished. The following day he asked his cousin, "Who was that girl last night?" His cousin smirked. "You like her, you really like her." "No, no. No, I don't. I just wondered who she was, that's all." He never found out, nor did he ever see her again, but he never forgot her.

His dad was sitting across from him now, an ear of corn poised between his large hands, scarred hands, the hands of a concert pianist which he had been until Stephen's mother had accidentally spilled a pot of steaming coffee on them years before Stephen was born. His father said, "Well, I admire you for trying to help the Negroes. If old Abe were alive today he'd be pretty proud of you, too. But we wonder, son, if you can make a steady living out of that kind of work? We wonder if that's possible."

"I wonder about that myself, dad. But I'm still using my investigative skills. That's interesting. And they are paying me."

"It doesn't seem all that secure to us, son. Do you think it can lead you back to journalism?"

"I certainly hope so."

"Well, when the time comes, mother and I would love to see you closer to home."

"I know, dad." But he did not think he would be home now if he had not been in Houston earlier.

Two days later he received a telephone call from Pete Codding.

"Have you heard Marcus Aurelius jumped bail?"

"He did?"

"Yes. We'd like you to come to New York as soon as you can."

"Why?"

"We think we know where he is and since you have already made contact with him you would be the natural person for this."

"Where do you think he is?"

"I'd rather not discuss it over the telephone."

Stephen wondered about that statement, but said, "Why not? Okay. I'll get there as soon as I can."

Pete Codding said, "That's just great, Stephen. I look forward to seeing you again."

It startled him that Pete Codding had unexpectedly used his first name as if they were intimate friends. Why, he thought, did he do that? It made him uncomfortable. But he could not possibly respond, I prefer to be called Mr. Ledberg, could he?

When he told his parents, his mother said, "Why do you have to leave? You barely arrived. We thought you would be around for the fourth of July. We planned to go out to the park for the fireworks and barbecue. You used to love that when you were younger."

"I'm sorry, mom. They want me to come to New York now."

"Is it something we've done, Stephen?"

"No, mom, it's nothing you have done." He wished it had been.

XVI

"JOURNALISM, MR. LEDBERG? You're worried that if you take on this project you'll stray too far from journalism? Well, of course, I respect your ambitions and perhaps I'm prejudiced, but let me tell you something about your chosen profession." Esther Maroon inhaled deeply on her cigarette, blew the smoke out into the room, and continued.

"Journalists are children. I know, I've lived and worked with both. Have you ever observed a child at play, Mr. Ledberg? He'll play for a while with whomever or whatever he's interested in. Then the moment he becomes bored he looks around for something else to engage him. Journalists are like that. If they're not the center of attention they'll go off in the corner and pout until they find someone to listen to them. That's the nature of their profession. They can't help themselves. No sooner are they writing one story than they're looking around for another. Anything to prevent them from focusing on their own lives. I know of no other profession like it.

"You might say the rhythm of a reporter's life is set by the head-line and byline. In what other profession, Mr. Ledberg, does one have the instant gratification of seeing one's name in print every day? Not even actors and actresses are allowed that. I've often won-dered what would happen to the journalist's ego if he wasn't per-mitted a by-line. What if no one knew who wrote which stories? What would happen then?

"No, Mr. Ledberg, I think if you scratch the surface of most reporters you'll find a child who never outgrew tantrums. And I don't think that's you. I don't think you're interested in a life that's limited to the by-line and headline. Do you?"

Before he had an opportunity to answer she added, "And let me tell you one other thing, Mr. Ledberg. Never marry into the news-paper profession. You'll regret it."

Earlier that day, he had gone straight from the airport to Codding's office, the air-conditioned elevator whooshing open at his stop. The reception area was exactly the same, with burnt orange carpet, royal purple chairs, the chrome and glass and Liberty and Justice for All. Pete Codding, with gold cufflinks shaped like the African continent, asked, "What do you know about Africa, Stephen?"

Africa? What did he know about Africa? George Morris always used to say, "One day this crazy nigger's going to get to Africa, Stephen. Marcus Garvey had it right."

"Marcus Garvey?"

"Yup," George had said. "Marcus Aurelius Garvey. He was a great man. Way ahead of his time. The first real leader of his people, a visionary. Until they did him in. He had the right idea; we all ought to go back to Africa. That's where we started. That's where we belong."

Stephen had always wondered why George wanted to go back to Africa. The Italians did not want to return to Italy, did they? Nor the Germans to Germany? Nor the Swedes to Sweden? No immigrant to America wanted to return from where they came, did they? "Why," he had asked George, "do you want to go back to Africa?"

"Why? Because I didn't choose to come here. I was enslaved to come here."

And that was not the only thing George had said. With the same passion with which he had put down Anna when she said, "Oh, but I don't see any of James Baldwin's work here," George had screamed at the professor in the literature course they both attended, "Joseph Conrad, what the hell did he know about Africa? Heart of Darkness is bullshit. Kurtz would have been psychopathic in New York or London or Paris or Warsaw." George spat out the last in disgust, the professor attempting to calm him, "Now, now, Mr. Morris, let's not use profanity in my lecture hall. I appreciate…" George had interrupted him. "Had Conrad seen no art, heard no music, observed no beauty in Africa?" George exhausted, as another student raised his hand, "Is Kurtz a Jewish name?" The professor exclaimed, "That's an interesting question. I never thought of that." He peered over his glasses, looked out into the lecture hall, saw Stephen, "Mr. Ledberg, is Kurtz a Jewish name?"

"I wouldn't know, sir. Ledberg is Swedish."

"Oh, I see."

"Do you think Rosencrantz and Guildenstern were Jewish, Herr Professor?" George Morris stood and shouted, a stand and shout which brought him immediate ejection from the lecture hall and a visit to the dean of students. Stephen had admired him for that outburst, not only because he felt it was courageous and clever, but also because George had come to his defense.

What did Stephen know about Africa?

"Nothing really. Why?"

"Because that's where Brown has gone."

"He has? To Africa?"

"Yes. Come over here. Let me show you something."

Pete Codding stood cradling his mug of coffee, warming his hands as if the day outside were not a sweltering ninety or so degrees but frigid, with ice and snow and arctic wind, not July but January.

"You see this photograph, Stephen. The President of Tanzania. Brown's gone there. He's gone to Tanzania, and we'd like you to go there and find out if and when he plans to return."

Stephen said, thinking on his late friend George Morris' exposition, to say nothing of Marcus Garvey's, "Why do we care if he's gone to Africa? If that's where he wants to be why not just leave him alone? He's free of all our legal constraints. What harm is there in that?"

Pete Codding said, "I'm astonished at you, Stephen. I don't care about the bail money we have forfeited, or any harm that may come to our reputation. But you must see how important it is for him to clear his name. He has to understand we will support him a hundred percent. He will do more damage to himself and to his people by leaving the country as he did. No, he must return. If you don't think you are up to this I am sure we can find someone else. But you've done everything we've asked of you up to now. I would hope you would take this on as well.

"Think it over, Stephen. Go home. Here, here are a few books on East Africa. Look them over. They may help you make up your mind."

And now, later that day, he was in Esther Maroon's office. After she finished her diatribe on journalism and journalists, Stephen said, "You never mentioned that Marcus Aurelius Brown lived in New Falls."

"He did? I didn't know that."

"You must have known. Pete Codding had a clipping from the paper."

"From the New Falls Sun Times?"

"Yes."

"That's so interesting. All the more reason for you to go to Africa." Esther Maroon paused, and said, "I understand Ralph Nader is your hero, Mr. Ledberg."

He flushed. "How did you hear that?"

"I have my ways. You should be proud he is your hero. He's one of mine as well."

"He is?"

She nodded. "And did you know, Mr. Ledberg, that Nader grew up in Connecticut with a man who is a well-known journalist?"

"He did? Who is that?"

"A man called Halberstam. David Levy Halberstam. Now don't tell me you've never heard of him."

Embarrassed, he said, "Well, I haven't. Who does he work for?"

"You don't read The New York Times?"

"Well, occasionally I would pick it up in the library. But out in Wichita it was not what we read."

"You see what I mean, Mr. Ledberg. I think if journalism was in your blood, Wichita, Kansas or not, you would know Halberstam. But you know Nader and it's a wise choice. In the long run Nader will outlast Halberstam. I know journalists, they don't have staying power. When Halberstam is just a footnote Nader will still be making waves. Nader would go willingly to Africa, Mr. Ledberg, Halberstam would not. The Times sent Halberstam to Africa once. To the Congo. He despised it. There was no way for him to find glory there. There are no front-page stories in Africa. So he volunteered for Vietnam. Did you know the Times actually grades and ranks its journalists by the number of front-page articles they write? So many points for page one; so many points for page two, for page three and so on. Did you know that?"

He shook his head.

"No, I didn't think so. Well, Halberstam is scoring a lot of points. He is on the front page almost every day. Do you know why?"

Again, he shook his head.

"He is writing inflammatory stories about our alleged failures in Vietnam. He undermines our troops. He claims that what he is saying is the truth. The truth? No, not the truth. Just stories which enable him to have the spotlight and score points at the Times."

"But surely The New York Times would not print his stories if they did not think they were true."

"The Times, Mr. Ledberg? I lived in the newspaper world. I was married, God help me, to the newspaper world. They will do anything to sell newspapers. Halberstam could not get out of Africa fast enough. But you... you have a once in a lifetime opportunity. Don't pass it up."

XVII

"You told Esther Maroon Ralph Nader was my hero?"

"Was I wrong?" Betty nodded at the photograph on the wall.

"No." He sat with Lefty and Betty in his stifling apartment, the window and door open, a fan barely stirring the air.

"Ah don't think you should go. Somethin' ain't right. Who cares about that nigger? Leave him be. Africa's where he belongs anyways. He's the one who tried to have me fired."

Stephen said, "You know what, Lefty, I wish you would stop using that word."

"What word?"

"Nigger."

"Nigger? Why what's wrong with that? They use it themselves. What would you like me to call 'em?"

"You could call them by their names, Lefty. They have names," Betty said.

Lefty dragged on his beer.

Stephen felt elated by Betty's interjection. He was unsure how he would have answered Lefty. Would he have said, "Well, you could use the word black, or Negro, or Colored."

"Ah told you, ah'll try. But it's damn difficult. Ah ain't really got anythin' to talk to 'em about. What with the age difference an' all."

Betty said, "Please do try, Lefty. You know we've had this discussion before. I've asked you just to tell me the name of one of the caddies. You haven't even done that yet. And as for you, young man, definitely go out there. I wish I could. Africa. What an adventure. But I'll venture to say that what you'll find when you get there is that this man, Marcus Aurelius Brown is shacked up with Catherine Reticent. If I were a betting woman I'd put all my money on that."

"You really think so?"

"No question about it. She's in Kenya. That's where he's gone."

"But it's not Kenya he's gone to but Tanzania."

"I looked it up. They're right next to each other. Yup, that's what you're going to find when you get out there. Mark my word."

"I wish I had thought about that when I was with Codding or Esther Maroon. Why didn't I think of that?"

"It wouldn't have helped. They would have lied to you. She would have lied just like she lies about that third child. That child didn't die. And to tell you the truth…"

She paused and studied Stephen carefully as he drank more of his beer, anxious about what he knew he was about to hear from this woman who both repulsed and enthralled him.

"What puzzles me is how you fit into all this? My gut tells me you're the kid Esther Maroon says died. But you don't really resemble either her or Chris Reticent. That's what stymies me. But here's what I'm guessing. When you're through with this trip you'll discover more about yourself than you will about Marcus Aurelius Brown. I'm just not sure what that will be. For now, have a good and safe trip." She raised her bottle in the air, three bottles clinking,

Stephen wondering exactly what Betty meant, anxious about what the flight would bring for he had never before left America.

A week later, Stephen boarded the airplane for Africa. As he did he noticed a coat of arms on the bulkhead. It showed a lion and unicorn standing on either side of a shield. Beneath the animals and the shield the words "Dieu et mon droit". Dieu he understood. Mon droit he did not.

His seat by the window was directly above and behind the engines. Vehicles moved about on the airfield. Red lights blinked in the dusk. A man wearing earphones, a disc-like semaphore in each hand, directed the plane from its berth.

Over the intercom a man's voice requested that seat belts be fastened. The engines outside his window whined, the plane taxied to a waiting position. Five minutes, ten minutes, twenty minutes passed. British Airways Flight 700 to London, Nairobi, Dar es Salaam, Lusaka, engines screaming now, a sudden thrust and the plane picked up speed, faster and faster, the landscape blurred, an American landscape, rushing past his window. He felt dizzy as he sat back in his seat. The plane was airborne.

He gazed down at the city of New York at dusk. Lighted jewels enveloped by a dusty rose, mauve, purple, salmon, orange sky. The plane climbed higher, turning north. The plane moved up the coast, dusk turning to night. Below him were houses. Families at home. Mothers and fathers, husbands and wives, daughters and sons, brothers and sisters.

And then they were over ocean. Blackness. Fathomless. America behind him. The ocean, England, Europe, Africa, ahead.

He awoke early the following morning. He felt cramped, his muscles sore, the inside of his mouth dry and acidy, his clothes smelling of dried sweat. He went to the bathroom and looked at himself in the mirror. He thought he looked older, his face covered in stubble, his eyes puffy. He said to his mirrored face, "What have I done? I've never left America before. I have no idea where I'm going or what I'm going to do when I get there. The only person I know is a man who jumped bail. Am I crazy? Other than Esther Maroon, who has her own selfish reasons, the only person who encouraged me to go was Betty and she is a drunk, isn't she?" Even his parents had discouraged him. "Africa, Stephen, are you certain you want to go there? Africa is a dangerous place. How will we contact you?" And he proceeded to puke into the sink.

He returned to his seat and gazed out the window. The plane was bathed in a gray early morning light. He noticed a logo stamped on the engines. An R within an R, the logo of the Rolls Royce Company.

Odd, he thought, how something as insignificant as two letters, and the same one at that, could impart a feeling of confidence. Why did that imprint buoy his spirits? He had no idea.

The plane began to descend, droplets of water dribbling across the window, the engines a gunmetal gray now, the plane making its approach to the London airport, the landing gear locking, the hydraulic flaps opening, a bump, a skid, the engines in full reverse, flaps fully extended, the first contact of a new old world.

He rode in a bus across the wet airfield to the antiseptic, fluorescent transit lounge, where he sat down and ordered coffee. He finished the coffee and walked to the telephone booth. There was not one large London directory but four separate ones. A-D. E-K. L-R. S-Z. He pulled out the L-R. Even in London there were no Ledbergs.

As he rode back across the airfield he felt very much alone. He and only six other passengers from the New York flight sat in a nearly empty bus on a damp drizzly morning. At least, he mused, emigrants hundreds of years ago had each other for comfort. Perhaps that was the way voyages into the unknown should be taken, with a group of people holding similar values and customs and dreams and fears.

He settled into his seat and watched outside the window as another, more laden bus wended its way across the wet surface.

Africa

XVIII

AN INDIAN WEARING A TRANSPARENT GRAY PLASTIC RAINCOAT placed a briefcase on the aisle seat in Stephen's row. The man took off the raincoat, folded it neatly and placed it in the bin above their heads. He took off his brown iridescent suit jacket and did the same with that. Then he slid the briefcase under the seat, catching his eyeglasses as they slipped from his nose. As he straightened up he replaced the black-framed glasses and nodded at Stephen, who returned the gesture.

The man hitched up his baggy trousers and sat down. He tried to buckle his seat belt, but it would not close around his considerable belly. He sucked in his stomach and snapped the buckle. His belly now strained against both the belt and the rumpled white shirt slowly emerging from his trousers. The man sat back in his seat, closed his eyes, placed his hands in his lap, a worried expression on his face.

He sat that way while the plane went through the same ritual as in New York. Seat belts fastened. The plane moving toward the runway. Only this being England, and this being a British Airways Corporation plane, even if it were heading for Africa, Flight 700 with those special engines and even more special lion and unicorn went straight to the head of the line. No queuing up at the airport on this island. The engines whining fiercely, Stephen sitting back in his seat, the plane gathering speed, faster and faster, the moment of weightlessness, the sound of the landing gear snapping shut, the hydraulic flaps moving ever so slightly as the plane climbed and banked.

Flying through mist, England in shadow, Lilliputian, a toy country, he thought, a painted river, toy trucks and cars, the plane above the clouds, flying in crystal blue sky, England somewhere below.

Stephen glanced at the man in the aisle seat. Perspiration covered his face, a face that was pockmarked from some long ago disease. He struggled to unbuckle the seat belt. He succeeded. Then he reached into the pocket of his trousers, withdrew a handkerchief and began to mop his face and the lenses of his black-framed glasses. He replaced the glasses and the handkerchief, smiled at Stephen and said, "I do not like it when they leave the ground and when they return to the ground. Everything else is splendid, isn't it?"

The man spoke with a musical lilt. He rolled and vibrated his R's, emphasizing the last letter or syllable in every word, as if that was where the listener should focus his attention. He spoke as if his mouth were stuffed with pebbles. Stephen attempted to discern what that material might be, but he saw nothing. It seemed that that was just the way the fellow spoke.

The man reached down and untied his shoelaces. Then with the toe of his right shoe he pushed the left shoe off. And with his shoeless left foot repeated the procedure on the right. He sighed, and said, "I am Joyanti Patel. What is your destination?"

"I'm Stephen Ledberg. I'm going to Dar es Salaam."

"The same. That is where I am going. That is where I live. You are an American, isn't it?"

"Yes. I am an American."

"You are coming out to see our game, isn't it? Oh, I shall tell you which are the best parks to go. I have seen them all."

"Well, yes, I am coming out to see the country. Everything. Not just the game."

"Everything?" He lowered his voice and whispered conspiratorially. "What else is there but the game? Since independence everything else has gone down the hill. Even the game is dying off. Poachers. The bloody government does nothing about the poachers. Before independence when these people here," he swung his arm in an arc around the cabin, "when these people were running the country the poachers would be punished plenty. But now the government is afraid. They are frightened of their shadow. I wish they were frightened of our shadow as well." He sighed.

"What do you mean?"

"They want to throw us out, isn't it? The African government wants us to leave. All of us. Muslim as well as Hindu. They do not want us any longer. They are taking away all our jobs and giving them to the African."

His face took on an expression of great worry.

"But are we not as much citizens as they? Was not I born in Tanzania? And my brother? And my sisters?

"Where shall we go? To U.K.? We do not want to go to U.K. They do not want us. To India? The African politician says we must go back to India. India is not our home. We know nothing of India. There is nothing there for us. So what to do?"

And he slumped back into his seat.

Stephen leaned back, glanced out the window and thought about what Patel had said. The Indians in East Africa did not wish to return to India. So why did George want to go back to Africa? No immigrants to America wished to return from whence they came.

Patel said, "From where in America are you coming, Mr. Ledberg?"

"My hometown is Wichita, Kansas."

"Ah, that is good. You are not from New York. If you are not from New York you are not Jewish, isn't it?

"I have heard it tell that there are more Jews in New York than in Israel. Soon there will be more Jews in Tanzania than in Israel. Soon there will be no more Jews in Israel. Do you know why?"

Stephen shook his head, wondering where the conversation was heading, but thankful it had nothing to do with his name.

"The African thinks they can drive us out by bringing in the Israelis, isn't it? They think the Israelis are helping them. They think the Israelis are training the Africans to run their retail shops. They think this is the way to drive us from business. We do not worry about that. We can always compete with the African in retail. But we cannot defeat the monopoly. You see the African government has given the Israelis the monopoly of sugar, maize, and rice. But the Israelis do not do business in the right away."

Patel leaned closer to Stephen, lowered his voice and whispered, "You know Canada Dry, Mr. Ledberg? It is American, isn't it?"

"Yes," although he was not entirely certain, else, he wondered, why was it called Canada Dry?

"My friend owns the Canada Dry plant in Dar es Salaam. He buys sugar only from the Israelis now because he cannot buy from anyone else. The Israelis demand cash on deliver. But when do they pay my friend for the bottles of Canada Dry they sell in their retail shops? When, Mr. Ledberg? To this day he has not received money from them. Is that a way to do business? You cannot stay in business that way, isn't it?

"Even my own brother is threatened by them. They have opened a store in his town. They open stores all over the country."

Stephen said, "I'm not sure I understand. Israelis are running retail stores in Tanzania?"

"No. No. The Israelis have trained the African to run the store. They call them retail cooperatives. Every time a new one is opened somewhere in the country it is on the front page of the newspaper.

It is the way the government shows the African how he advances. But we are not worried about the African and his retail shop. We can compete with him, but we cannot defeat the monopoly. If the Israelis charge us more for sugar and then do not even pay us for the products we manufacture, we cannot survive, can we? The African thinks he is being helped. He will find out he is wrong. The African will regret he ever asked the Jew in.

"You see," Patel glanced about the plane and lowered his voice even further so that Stephen had to lean across the empty middle seat to hear, "the Israelis are not fools. They are here only because they want a market for their products. They pretend to be a friend of the African but that is not why they are here. Yes. You see, Mr. Ledberg, you go into one of their cooperative shops when you arrive in Dar es Salaam you know what you will find there?"

"No."

"You will find nothing but Israeli products. Jaffa this or Jaffa that. Everything is Jaffa."

Patel leaned back in his seat and smiled. Then he began to giggle as if he had just told an amusing joke for which only he understood the punch line. But the punch line was yet to come.

"But the African does not buy, isn't it? All the African wants is beans and maize and rice."

"Well, why do the Israelis bother to put their products in the shops then? Surely they are smarter than that?"

Patel's face lit up. "Aha, Mr. Ledberg, you have asked just the right question. I wish the African government would ask such a question. Why indeed? You see, Mr. Ledberg, the Israelis are no fools. They stock their shelves with their own products for the day they will occupy all of Africa. Then the African will see. Then the African will regret they asked the Jew in."

Was Patel crazy? Stephen stared at him, studying his brown eyes to see if he could discern madness. He saw nothing but Patel staring back, his left eye slightly askew, a smile of satisfaction crossing his face.

"You may ask where I have such an idea. That is your entitle-ment." Modulating his voice again, he added, "I have heard it tell, Mr. Ledberg, that many years ago the Jews wanted Uganda as their home. They could not have it then. What they could not have then they take now. And the African is so stupid he does not see."

Stephen turned and looked out the window, past the engine, the sun glinting from the wings, to the blue sky. He was embarrassed and bemused by the preposterousness of his aisle-mate's outra-geous statements. He wondered if Patel would have agreed with the boy in college who imagined Jewish girls were more sexually active than others. Hoping to change the subject, he turned and asked, "What do you do for a living?"

"I sell insurance. I was just now in U.K. for our yearly meeting. Business is very bad now."

Patel became pensive, a sad expression on his face.

"Before independence I sold much to my own people. But now they buy nothing. They have let their policies lapse. They wait only to leave."

Patel sat back. He said, with more than a hint of desperation, "I would like to go to America, Mr. Ledberg. I would like to take my family and go to America. But it is very difficult. I hear it tell the only way to go to America is to know someone. I have a friend who knew a man in your information center in Dar es Salaam. He was able to obtain a visa. He lives in California now. California, there is a place I would like to live. But," he sighed, "you must know someone."

Patel sat dejectedly in his seat, only coming out of his funk as he looked over Stephen's shoulder and said excitedly, "Look there, Mr. Ledberg. Look there. It is Africa. See. You see, there is Africa."

Stephen turned. Between puffs of clouds he could make out be-low a vast expanse of reddish earth. Barren earth. Emptiness. He saw no trees, no houses, no roads, no lights, only a vast and empty land.

Patel said, "It is not so beautiful yet. But soon we shall see the river. Soon we will see the Nile. There is nowhere a river the same.

My brother, Mr. Ledberg, lives on Lake Victoria. Did you know that that is where the Nile begins?"

And Patel was correct. Miles below Stephen's window the geography began to change. From barren red soil to reddish brown, and from that to many shades of brown, which began to mix with sketchy patches of vegetation. And then, as if by some miracle the vegetation became thick, green, a black ribbon-like swath cut through the terrain, the ribbon twisting and turning, bending, pouring over rocks which he could not see but could imagine, winding this way and that, flowing through reeds, papyrus, swamps, desert, flowing, flowing forever toward the sea. The Nile.

XIX

THE PLANE LANDED AT NAIROBI, coming in low over miles of scrubland, with the hydraulic hum of the landing gear, the thud as it locked in place, the slight bump and skid as the plane touched down, engines roaring in reverse. Nairobi. Africa.

A yellow Shell petrol truck crossed the tarmac. Africans in white or blue jumpsuits dragged a thick hose, a black umbilical cord, from the truck and hooked it to the underbelly of the plane. Even those engines with that logo needed sustenance. A fuel that originated closer to the continent on which they had just landed, Stephen thought, than the island they had left. Without that liquid, those engines would be useless, rusted, cobwebbed, ornamentation, at best a relic of the past.

He saw people on the observation deck waving at passengers as they disembarked onto the tarmac. Flags of nations of the world waved from poles in front of the terminal building, as if they too were greeting the plane and its passengers.

Looking over Stephen's shoulder, Patel said, "It is a pity you cannot spend some time in Nairobi. Nairobi is the Paris of Africa.

I have heard it tell that if you stand in Nairobi airport or at the Stanley Hotel you will meet everyone you have ever known and everyone that is famous. Here is the crossroads of Africa. You must not miss it before you return to America."

Patel withdrew from the window and sat back in his seat. "Dar es Salaam is very nice, but it is a small village compared to Nairobi. Here there are nightclubs, restaurants, and cinemas. There is even a game park near the city. New York does not have that, isn't it? Even Hollywood does not have that."

And then as if he had hit a nerve Patel winced and said, "Hollywood. Now there is a place I would like to go. But you must know someone."

The thick black hose was uncoupled and dragged back to the yellow truck. Doors locked, seat belts fastened, the plane moved toward the runway, and this being Nairobi and there being little or no traffic, even if it were the Paris of Africa, the plane took off immediately.

They flew south. Stephen sensed Patel peering over his shoulder again and moved back to allow him a view.

"Soon the pilot will tell us we pass Kilimanjaro. Then we will know the trip is nearly finished."

And again Patel was correct. Kilimanjaro, its rounded crater covered with snow, the late afternoon light illuminating it in a pinkish glow, heavy white clouds hovering a few hundred feet below the crater, was stunning.

Stephen recalled George Morris screaming, "Ernest Hemingway, what the hell does Hemingway know about Africa? Animals and death and white hunters. What does that have to do with Africa? He's just pure bullshit. Why didn't he have that woman blow her husband's brains out in Idaho? There should be a law. No white man is permitted to write about Africa. Or better yet, any white man who does should be lynched." Stephen could not remember the name of the short story that had set George off. Perhaps, he thought, it was "The Snows of Kilimanjaro".

Kilimanjaro caused him a spasm of anxiety and not just because it brought back memories of George Morris. If Patel was
correct, the trip was nearly finished, a fact that caused Stephen
discomfort. Traveling, for him, became a suspension of time. On
an airplane or on a train or bus, no one really knew who he was or
why he was there. Even now Patel did not know the purpose of
his trip. Traveling provided anonymity. But once the plane landed
and he exited, everything would come hurtling at him as if they
had been there all along, traveling a slightly different but parallel
route. He knew it would be no different this time. Marcus Aurelius Brown, Pete Codding, Esther Maroon, Betty, Lefty, Ingy
Reticent, even, he thought, his real mother and father, all waiting
for him somewhere down there beyond his window, beyond those
Rolls Royce engines. And him wishing because of that that the
trip would go on and on.

The plane taxied to the terminal, the terminal a third the size of
the one in Nairobi.

Patel leaned over Stephen's shoulder and said, "Finally, we are
here. Look there. You see. There is my family."

Stephen looked and saw a number of people waving from the
terminal's roof but he had no idea which was Patel's. He wondered
if anyone would meet him. He felt vulnerable, alone, and scared.

He followed Patel down the gently swaying stairs onto the tarmac, a soft refreshing sea breeze caressing his body, causing the flag
atop a white-washed flagpole to unfurl; the flag two triangles, one
leaf green, the other sea-blue, the triangles formed by a black bend
itself bordered by a pair of narrow yellow stripes, the flag framed
by the deep blue late afternoon sky.

Stephen was surprised at customs to be separated from Patel.
Whether because he had just passed many hours with him, or because, besides Marcus Aurelius Brown, Patel was the only other
person he knew in an unfamiliar land, he felt a pang of anxiety as
his friend, for that was how he thought of him, was directed to the
residents' line and he to another.

The customs official said in a voice as soft as the breeze that wafted throughout the building, "Come right this way, please. There is someone who meets you."

He had no idea who would meet him. Codding had said, "Don't worry about it. We will arrange it. You'll be in good hands." As it was, the hands were those of a young man, "Juma," he called himself, dressed in a white long-sleeved shirt buttoned tightly at the cuffs and tucked meticulously into starched khaki trousers.

Juma shook Stephen's hand in a peculiar manner, Juma grasping his right elbow with his left hand, as he grasped Stephen's with great gentleness. What, Stephen thought, would his dad have made of that?

"My minister sends me to drive you to your hotel." He gestured toward a gray Land Rover parked by the curb.

"Your minister?"

"Bwana Nyarimbere. He is the minister of cooperatives."

"I see." But Stephen was puzzled. He did not understand why the minister of cooperatives would have any dealings with him.

While Juma placed Stephen's bags in the Land Rover, he walked to what he thought was the passenger's side. That is what he thought it was. But what it was was an English legacy. The steering wheel was on the right. That would be something he would have to remember. The English had left a souvenir. It would not be the only memento they forgot to bring home.

They drove on the left side of a narrow asphalt-topped road, the edges of which were covered with a fine layer of drifting sand. On the right palm trees, discarded coconuts, a beach, the Indian Ocean. On the left scattered amongst more palm trees were small one-story cement block buildings. It was the industrial area of the city. Tegry Plastics. Ideal Carpentry. Singh Ironmonger. Perhaps that was why the air was so pure. There were no smokestacks anywhere in Dar es Salaam.

They passed women walking on the side of the road, children skipping to keep up with them.

"What is in those containers the women are balancing on their heads, Juma?"

"They are debes filled with water."

"Debes, Juma?"

"They are tins, bwana. Debe is our word for those tins. Do you know no Swahili?"

"No. I don't."

"You will have to learn it."

He did not think he would be there long enough to need to do that. But he kept that to himself.

"America is far away, bwana. For myself, I have never left Dar es Salaam."

"Well, I've never left America until now, Juma."

"How do you find our country?"

"It is very beautiful."

"It will not be in a few weeks."

"Oh, why is that?"

"The rains are due any day. You have not come at a good time."

"Rains, Juma? How bad could rains be?"

"You will see, bwana."

The Land Rover moved down the airport road, the road becoming a street, entering the outskirts of the city. One and two story houses, paint peeling from their rectangular facades, iron bars on ground floor windows reminding him of his own apartment. He felt as if America was centuries away. What time was it there? For that matter, what day was it? What were his parents doing? Was Lefty out on the course? Was Betty in her classroom? Was that kid slamming an umbrella on a table? Did any of them even exist? As the vehicle moved down the crowded street, Stephen caught its name, Independence Avenue. As they passed shops with names like Naseem's or Mohamed's or de Silva's, he thought on his friend Patel and what he had said, "The African wants us to leave." Aware, it seemed, as if none had done so. They drove around a circle, in the middle of which stood the statue of a soldier on a perfectly manicured lawn. The soldier held a rifle, a bayonet fixed, that bayonet and rifle pointing toward the harbor. He wondered if invaders had come only from the ocean, or if there were similar monuments near the borders in the north, west, and south as well?

They drove around another circle, down a street paralleling the beach, Ocean Road, and stopped in front of a hotel.

Juma parked and Stephen followed him into the lobby. A porter carried his bags to his room. It was light and airy, the walls whitewashed, the sea breeze gentling through the windows. The bed was covered with a white spread; above the bed hanging from the ceiling and tied to the headboard was a mosquito net. Beside the bed a stand with a reading lamp and telephone. A desk and chair stood next to one window, a bureau and armchair opposite. On the floor a sisal mat, and suspended from the ceiling a fan that moved ever so slightly as the breeze blew through the window. The contrast between this room and the one in Houston pleased him and he reminded himself to thank Pete Codding when he spoke with him.

After Juma and the porter left he took a long, warm, soothing bath. Then, completely naked, he lay down. He felt the soft cotton material against his back. He felt clean and relaxed. He lay staring at the mosquito netting hanging above him. His limbs felt exhausted, his whole body like a weight. The refreshing breeze bathed his body; the ceiling fan turned slightly, hypnotic, the white room, the trip, his eyelids heavy, until he fell into unconscious sleep.

When he awoke it was dark outside. He searched for the light beside the bed, found the switch and clicked it on. He rose, went into the bathroom and splashed water on his face. His whole body felt cumbersome. He stared in the mirror. He thought he looked like a wreck. He hardly recognized himself. His eyes were puffy and half-closed, dark and shadowy hair grew on his face. His appearance frightened him. He urinated, dressed, and walked outside.

Everything was still. Except for his own breathing there was no sound. The night was illumined by the daylight brightness of a full moon. Was it a full moon in America as well? America seemed so far away.

He walked past the verandah where a straggle of people sat conversing, barely noticing him as he walked across the street. In front of an old church he looked up again at the sky. It awed him. Not even in Kansas had he seen anything like it. It was blue-black, saturated with millions of stars. The moon was perfectly white. It seemed to him make believe, like what a movie director would imagine a tropical night to be. Even the few clouds seemed unreal, a part of the set, as if they were hanging in the sky suspended by an invisible wire. Everything so still, clear, sharp, like a camera lens in perfect focus.

He walked past the church to the beach, the sand squeaking and entrapping itself in his shoes. Freighters floated in the calm water, their lights and the moon's beams reflected in and refracted by the sea. They were only freighters but the string of lights along their length gave them a festive look. As if they, too, were part of the movie set.

He walked to the edge of the water, the lapping the only sound he heard. Six thousand miles from home. Somewhere in America there was a lapping of water as well. The Atlantic, the Pacific, the Indian Ocean, all commingled at some juncture. Was there not a hint of America somewhere in this sea? Were not all the oceans linked? And if oceans, why not the rivers that fed them? Water and sky girdling the earth, but not continents. You could sail or swim or fly to America, but you could not walk. America somewhere out in that darkness, eons away. Although he had left America less than twenty-four hours ago it seemed to him as he stood at the water's edge that his life there had been in some far distant past.

He walked up the beach in the direction in which he saw both a red and green light moving toward a jetty. The moon was so bright it cast his shadow on the sand. He could see that the lights were attached to a ferryboat, the boat nothing more than an open flat deck plying back and forth between the mainland and a spit of land across the harbor.

He walked toward the landing and then stopped. He stopped and held his breath. Near the ferry landing sat a young woman, her arms wrapped around her knees, her knees drawn up against her, her eyes watching the ferryboat as it approached. Stephen exhaled and stood stark still. She had not noticed him. In the bright moonlight he could see her profile perfectly. She had short-cropped hair and wore a sweater over a blouse and skirt. Suddenly she jumped up and walked briskly in the direction of the ferry landing. As the ferry docked she boarded it, handing the man at the bow what appeared to be money. Then she went to the rear of the boat and stood staring out across the harbor.

Stephen moved swiftly up the beach. He had no intention of boarding the ferry, but he wanted to have a closer look at the woman. He could very well be mistaken, perhaps he was, after all it had been a long and tiring trip, but she certainly reminded him of someone he had seen in a photograph in a blue leather frame. And while it was only a photograph and he had never met her in person, the woman sitting on the sand under that full moon did indeed look like Catherine Reticent. But what the hell would she be doing here?

As he drew closer he heard the sound of the diesel engine revving, the boat moving out into the darkness of the water. He had reached a road leading down to the water's edge. He stood and watched as the ferry drew away.

He thought for a moment of yelling impulsively, just shouting at the top of his lungs, "Catherine, Catherine Reticent". But he thought that would make him appear foolish. And then the ferry was out of earshot, the night silent again.

He stood looking across the harbor much as the woman had. He stood under that star-saturated sky and wondered if he had seen Catherine Reticent, or whether he was simply imagining what he wished in a strange land, fantasizing that he had seen someone he had known only in a photograph.

He retraced his steps to the hotel, emptied his shoes of sand, and sat down on the edge of the bed. Catherine Reticent? He must be mad. What would she be doing here when she was supposed to be in Nairobi? Still, he thought, if it had been Catherine he stood a good chance of running into her again, didn't he? After all, Dar es Salaam was a small town. Certainly not the Paris of Africa, so Patel had said.

His eyes fell on the telephone and the directory beneath it. He withdrew the book, a book no more than forty or fifty pages thick, and opened it to the L's. There was nothing there for him. He did not expect there would be.

He turned to the P's. He found a long list of Patels, three with the same first name as his friend but only one with the name of his profession next to it. Then meandering, he whiffed to the R's. Catherine Reticent did not live in Dar es Salaam. She probably was not listed in the Nairobi directory either. She had not been out here long enough for that, he understood. Besides, he thought to himself, Betty had said, "Avoid her at all cost. If you run into her, run as fast as you can in the opposite direction." But what did Betty know? She was the one who had encouraged him to come to Africa in the first place.

He shut the book, undressed, turned off the light and tried to sleep, but his mind moved from the woman on the beach to the photograph Ingy Reticent had shown him. He wondered if it were Catherine Reticent, what she was doing here, sitting on the beach, waiting for a ferry, at this hour of the night?

XX

"JUMA, WHAT DOES UHURU MEAN?"

Juma had picked him up around eight the next morning. The sun had already cleared the water, causing him to squint to protect his eyes. They drove down Ocean Road in the direction he had walked the previous night.

Juma parked the car in a quadrangle enclosed by a two-story dun-colored building. Barefoot men slashed with sickles at the vast lawn between the parking area and the building. Above the entrance to the Ministry of Cooperatives was a coat of arms. Where Stephen imagined a lion and unicorn had once balanced on hind legs, an African man and woman stood. Beneath them, where "Dieu et mon droit" belonged, were the words "Uhuru na umoja".

"Freedom, bwana. Uhuru is the Swahili word for freedom."

Stephen smiled inwardly, recalling the taxicab outside of Short's office, knowing the meaning of Ltd., while Juma added without being asked, "And umoja is one."

They entered the building that reminded Stephen of the court-house in Houston in the sense that his eyesight required adjusting from the brightness of the day. But unlike the inside of that other building there were no clusters of men, only a solitary guard perched opposite the entrance.

As they walked into the minister's office, the minister stood, and gesturing with his hand, said, "I am Nyarimbere, Mr. Ledberg. Karibu. Welcome to Tanzania. Please, come and sit here."

Nyarimbere and Stephen sat on an uncomfortable couch, its wooden arms sloping downward, its back providing no support. An elderly barefooted man entered with a tray containing a tea-pot, cups, saucers, sugar, and a can of condensed milk. The man placed the tray on the table in front of the couch and backed out, bowing as he did.

"I have given up trying to tell them they need not carry over habits of the English. We are not kings or queens. But bad habits are hard to break. Would you like some tea?"

"Yes, thank you."

They sat bolt upright on the uncomfortable couch for that was the only way they could drink their tea without spilling it. After a moment Nyarimbere said, "So you have come out to persuade this Brown chap to return to America?"

"I have."

"I wish you good luck on that."

"Why good luck? You don't think he will come back?"

"Perhaps. He may stay here as long as he wishes. We have many émigrés living here who have escaped the injustice of their countries. We have no problem with that. When would you like to see him?"

"As soon as I can."

"We will arrange it. We will have him come to your hotel. It will be simpler that way."

"What do you mean by that? Why would it be simpler?"

"Why? He lives a bit out of the way."

"He does? Where?"

"Well, there is a bit of land across the harbor. You would have to take a ferry to reach it."

"The ferry down the road from here?"

"The very one. You have seen it?"

"Is there an American woman who lives there?"

"An American woman?"

"Yes. Last night when I was walking on the beach I thought I saw…"

"Someone you know?"

"Well, not exactly."

"How do you know she was an American then?"

"Well, I sort of know her, if it was her. It's not important. But I would prefer to go to see Brown where he lives."

"We'll manage it then. Perhaps you will run into her when you are over there. Why don't you take the next few days and explore our city. Anything you may need Juma will see to it. Pete Codding is our friend. We will help you in any way we can. Juma will arrange for you to have a car. We will meet again after you have visited this Brown chap."

They stood and shook hands, then Stephen walked down the hallway and out into the bright sunshine. Those barefooted men still slashed at blades of grass, Stephen wondering why they were not using lawn mowers, discovering later that there were few lawn mowers in Africa. Labor was cheap and plentiful, the more people cutting lawns, he was told, the more prosperous the nation.

He knew which direction he wanted to go, up Ocean Road toward the ferry landing. Was it possible that Betty was correct? Were Catherine Reticent and Marcus Aurelius Brown lovers? Was that child, Adam, in Betty's class theirs?

He walked up Ocean Road, the morning warmer than before, his underclothes sticky and uncomfortable, thinking that perhaps the breeze last night blew only during the late afternoon. To his left were more government buildings, the President's palace, glaringly white, a building which he discovered later had been rebuilt by the British after they leveled an earlier German one, which they destroyed by shelling from ships anchored in that very harbor, past a hospital also German built but spared the ravages of the earlier bombardment. The British gunners were meticulous in their accuracy. He walked until he reached a fork in the road. A narrow asphalt strip led to the ferry landing.

There were automobiles lined up waiting for the ferry. Heat waves shimmered from their roofs. The sun was so bright that its reflection off the water forced Stephen to squint and cup his hand over his eyes as he watched the ferry approach.

He stood in the sweltering sun as the ferry made two complete passes. Then he retraced his steps down Ocean Road, past the ministry of cooperatives, a glance showing him that those bare-footed men were still slashing at the grass. He walked on past the hotel toward the center of town, hearing in the distance a rhythmic clicking. Da da da dada da. A Morse code. Where was that coming from? He saw a man in a white robe, an embroidered cap on his head, his left hand swinging a chain at the end of which was a copper tray and on the tray demitasse cups, a coffee urn, how did he manage not to have them fall off? in his right hand two cups, castanets clicking one against the other, da da da dada da.

Further on, was the aroma of burning wood and roasting meat. An aroma that reminded him of home. Pangs of homesickness swept over him, thoughts of his dad roasting meat and his mom boiling corn on the cob, his gastric juices pumping, mouth salivating, an emptiness in his stomach, to say nothing of his heart.

Men stood selling peanuts, cashews, oranges, bananas, even ears of roasted corn that he discarded into a wastebasket after discovering the kernels were neither tender nor sweet but mealy and starchy.

He walked on, past curio shops owned by Indians, elephant tusks, wooden sculpture, grotesque figures like the carving in Pete Codding's office. Past jewelry stores and fabric stores, rolls of brightly colored materials, yellows and blues, crimsons and chrome yellows, blues and olives, all sorts of patterns, arabesque, herringbone, floral, all owned by the Indians of East Africa. He wondered where the African retail stores were that Patel had mentioned, the stores that contained Israeli products and the Africans trained by the Israelis to run them. He wandered into a bookstore and bought a local paper, walked on down Independence Avenue wondering if he would run into either Catherine Reticent or Marcus Aurelius Brown. He passed the statue of the soldier, the soldier still facing the harbor, a fierce expression on his face, his left leg forward, knee bent, bayonet in place, rifle ready. If that statue could speak, would it tell him if it had seen Catherine Reticent or Marcus Aurelius Brown?

XXI

Stephen drove slowly up Ocean Road toward the ferry landing. It was Sunday and there were few other people about. Even so, in the car Juma had provided, he drove with some trepidation. He still had not mastered driving on the left. It was not so much the straight-aways but turns, particularly the rotaries or round-abouts that gave him trouble. He wondered why, if the Tanzanians had their own coat of arms, they could not change which side of the road they drove on as well. If they were so intent on shucking all English influences why not do it by driving on the right, which as far as he was concerned was the correct side of the road?

He drove past the government buildings, the buildings empty, ghostlike, the grass growing with impunity, the atmosphere hot and humid. He made the right turn that led to the landing. There he parked the car and boarded the ferry. He was anxious about seeing Brown again. How would he welcome him? What would Brown say? What if Catherine Reticent were there? Still, Stephen looked forward to the meeting. In some peculiar way he thought of Brown as a friend. An American meeting another American in a foreign country.

Brown's bungalow was about a quarter of a mile from the ferry landing. The small cottage sat nestled at the edge of a line of coconut palms, light brown fibrous husks resting on the white sand. Stephen knocked on the door. He heard movement inside. He imagined Catherine Reticent was there as well. Would she answer the knock? Brown, himself, opened the door.

Marcus Aurelius Brown, dressed in cut-off jeans, a white tee shirt and sunglasses, stood barring the doorway.

"Aren't you going to invite me in?"

"I didn't believe the minister. I didn't believe they'd send someone all this way. For what?"

"Can I come in?"

"Help yourself."

Brown sat down in a rattan chair and lit a cigarette while Stephen settled on a leather hassock, bits of straw protruding from its seams. They sat in silence until Stephen said, "I'm here to try to find out when you might be coming home."

"Home? I am home."

"I apologize for that. I guess I didn't mean exactly home. I meant back. They want me to find out when you think you will return to America."

Brown did not answer.

"I'm not here to bring you back. They just want to know your plans."

Still Brown remained silent.

"I guess they feel they put up a lot of bail money."

"I didn't ask them to do that."

"Is that what you want me to tell them?"

As Stephen awaited an answer, he glanced about the room thinking he might notice evidence of Catherine Reticent. He saw nothing. No framed photographs. No clothing. Nothing in that room, at least, to provide any clue that Catherine Reticent had ever been there. Perhaps that had not been Catherine Reticent on the beach. Perhaps, he thought, I was never on that beach. Perhaps it was the nonsensical suggestions of a drunken schoolteacher that put the thoughts in my head.

"Tell them anything you want. I don't really care."

"May I use your bathroom?"

"Be my guest."

Stephen imagined he might find evidence of Catherine Reticent there. But he discovered nothing, until he washed his hands and noticed the water draining slowly, discovering strands of light brown hair clogging the drain. That does not prove anything, he thought. It could be anyone's. Nauseous, he thought it could even be Anna's.

Returning, he said, "You lived in New Falls, Pennsylvania once. I live there myself now."

"I did?"

"And I found out by accident that Moses Short gets a check from there every month. Is that a coincidence?"

"I wouldn't know. Moses gets a lot of checks from all over."

"But you did live in New Falls once?"

Brown did not answer.

"But doesn't it make sense that someone who knew you in New Falls sent that money?"

Still Brown remained silent.

"You know the way I discovered you lived in New Falls was by reading an article in the New Falls Sun Times. It was about your arrest in Houston. Someone on that paper remembered you. Do you know anyone who works for the paper?" Stephen hesitated and added, "Or anyone connected to the family that owns it?"

He thought he had done that well. He was proud of himself.

Still Brown said nothing. He sat in the chair, smoke curling from his cigarette, those sunglasses pointed in Stephen's direction as Stephen silently damned all sunglass manufacturers; the reason he never owned a pair, thinking people wore them not as protection, but because it was cool. It was cooler still to push them atop head when not covering the eyes. He wondered if General MacArthur wore them because he thought they enhanced his image and did not give a damn what protection they afforded from the sun.

"How would a nigger know anyone on that paper?" Brown punctuated the silence and buzz in Stephen's brain. "What do you think I left that town for? Why do you think any nigger in his right mind would leave? The only ones who can't are too old or too dumb. They pick up jobs at the golf club or washing dishes in a restaurant. You think I wanted to do that for the rest of my life? You think I wanted to carry around some white man's golf clubs?

"Let me tell you something. My mother was a beautiful and intelligent woman. You know what she did for a living? She cleaned houses. And when she died, did any of those rich honkies give a damn? Shit, no. She worked right up to the moment she born me and nobody cared. Do I know anyone in that town? I don't even want to remember that town."

With a disgusted expression he inhaled his cigarette, blew the smoke into the room, and then crushed the cigarette in an ashtray.

He was lying. Stephen was certain of it. But why? What difference if he acknowledged Catherine Reticent? Why the secrecy?

Stephen considered confronting him, telling him about the woman he saw on the beach the night he arrived as well as the matted hair clogging the sink. But he rejected the notion. Brown would only deny it, wouldn't he? And with those sunglasses how could Stephen hope to guess what he might be thinking?

As he stood to leave he said, "So I should tell Mr. Codding you're not going to return at all?"

"Tell him whatever you want."

Brown's tone of voice ended the meeting as it began. Though Stephen knew he could never be a close friend, he had hoped that there might be some common ground on which they could meet while he was in Africa. Brown's statement and inflection made it clear there was not.

XXII

It was a week after he had called Pete Codding to inform him that Marcus Aurelius Brown was not coming home. He sat in the early evening on the verandah of his hotel waiting for Nyarimbere, a gin and tonic in hand, the glass beaded with humidity, the gin relaxing him, taking his mind from the mosquito bites on his legs and the rash under his armpits. He gazed at a scattering of sailboats tacking for home, a lone water skier skidding sheets of spray as he zoomed in and around the freighters. Each day the humidity had become more oppressive. The atmosphere was like a sponge absorbing water or a rubber balloon held under a faucet. Pregnant. Heavier and heavier.

Codding had said simply, "Go back. Try again. Keep after him." Stephen, frustrated said, "Does Brown know Catherine Reticent?"

"What? What did you say, Stephen? I think we have a bad connection here."

"I said, does Brown know Catherine Reticent?"

"Why are you asking?"

So he told him.

"You think you saw Catherine Reticent? Have you ever met her?"

"No, but…"

"Then how can you possibly think you saw her?"

"I've seen a photograph."

"A photograph? If you saw Catherine Reticent, Stephen, she was probably there to interview Brown for the Nairobi paper. If you saw her."

At midnight? She was there to interview him at midnight, Mr. Codding? That's what he wanted to say. But he hesitated and the moment passed.

"And by the way," Codding added, "the minister might ask you to help him on another project. We have no problem with you doing that. Nyarimbere is important to us. We will assist him in any way that we can. But your primary job is Brown. If there is any change in his plans, Stephen, call me immediately."

Nyarimbere arrived and they sat on the verandah together, the minister sipping Coca-Cola, lime and ice. Stephen wondered if it was the light as the sky grew darker in the dusk, or only his imagination but each time Stephen moved his head slightly, the skin on Nyarimbere's forehead seemed to change color, from brown to dark brown and back again. It reminded him of brushing his hand over tufts of carpet at home. He could not recall George Morris' forehead ever changing shade. Perhaps, he thought, it was simply the gin and tonic.

Nyarimbere said, "Now that you have met with Brown I wonder if you would consider doing us a favor as well?"

"Mr. Codding said you might."

"Yes. It is a delicate problem. It requires the utmost discretion. I feel ashamed I must even discuss it with you. You see, we have a problem with some of our retail cooperative stores in a little town called Buhaya on Lake Victoria."

"Really? I heard about those on the airplane flight out here."

"You did? How is that?"

"I sat next to an Indian. He told me about them."

"Really? I would have loved to be a fly on the wall and listened to that."

"Well, actually, he said…"

"No, no. You need not repeat what he said. I can imagine. But I am certain he did not go into the history of the Indian duka owner in East Africa, did he?"

"No. No, he didn't."

"I am certain he did not tell you that for years they controlled the retail trade out here. I'm also certain that he did not tell you that at critical moments, droughts, poor harvests, and the like, they held maize or rice or other foodstuffs from the market in order to drive up prices."

"No, actually he never mentioned any of that."

"I imagine not. You know, we do not wish to drive the Asian trader from Tanzania, Mr. Ledberg. There is a role for him still. But if they decide to pack it in, well, we shall not shed any tears. You see, the Indian trader has earned himself the unenviable reputation as the yahudi of East Africa."

"The yahudi?"

"The Jew, Mr. Ledberg. The Indian trader is the Jew of East Africa. I hope I have not offended you. If you are Jewish I meant no harm. Many of my friends are Indian. It is only the trader who has …"

"No. I am not Jewish. I…" Stephen was confused at the minister's virulence, given what Patel had said also about the Israelis assisting the Tanzanians in establishing their retail stores. But he was unable to finish his thought as Nyarimbere interrupted.

"No, I did not think so. Ledberg is Swedish, is it not?" Nyarimbere sipped his Coca-Cola that had become more water than syrup as the ice cubes melted, a slight smile of satisfaction on his face.

"Yes, it is. How did you know?"

"I make a study of names, Mr. Ledberg. You show me the name of a Tanzanian or Kenyan or Ugandan and I shall tell you to which tribe they belong. I have been to Sweden. The Swedish are our friends. Yes. I thought I was not mistaken. I thought Ledberg a Swedish name. It is important, for our purposes, that you not be a Jew."

It had become dark. The lights strung from bow to stern on the freighters anchored in the harbor made them appear as if a party was in progress, but he could neither see people nor hear music. The night sky was filled with stars. The moon was as bright but not as large as on the first night. The verandah was filled with people drinking and smoking and huddled in conversation. An occasional automobile moved down Ocean Road.

"Why is that?"

Nyarimbere glanced around, lowered his voice much as Patel had on the flight and said, "You see it is the Israelis who manage our retail cooperatives. It would not have done for us to send another Jew even if you had been from America. The members of the cooperative are up in arms. They are saying the products they want are not in the stores. They are saying money is missing. They are saying the shopkeepers give items to their friends. And they are saying," Nyarimbere lowered his voice even further so that Stephen had to lean closer to hear, "the Israeli who manages the stores, this Jacobson, has hired only women shopkeepers. He is the only one in the country to do so. He is married of course. But still, there are rumors."

Nyarimbere finished what was left in his glass, an expression of great sadness and resignation crossing his face.

Stephen wanted to say, so let me get this straight. Are you suggesting that this man, this Jacobson, is sleeping with his staff? But he did not. Instead he asked, "But why me? Why not the police?"

"No, that would never do. We do not wish the glare of publicity. All we want is for you to keep your ear to the ground, so to speak. Make your impression. We will inform Jacobson that you are an American graduate student undertaking a study of the cooperative movement. Yes, that is what we will do. I will personally contact

Jacobson. What is so embarrassing is that we need your help at all. But perhaps it is our own fault. Perhaps we have been too subtle for our own good."

Nyarimbere turned to beckon a waiter, who had not ventured far from the minister's side since he had sat down. He ordered another Coke, and much to Stephen's delight asked the waiter to bring peanuts – groundnuts Nyarimbere called them – and cashews.

"Do you know, Mr. Ledberg, may I call you Stephen?"

"Of course."

"Do you know, Stephen, the meaning of uhuru na umoja?"

"Yes, actually. Juma told me."

"Did he? What exactly did he say?"

"Uhuru is the Swahili word for freedom. Umoja is the word for one."

The minister sighed. "Almost correct. Uhuru is the Swahili word for freedom. Umoja, however, is the word for unity. Moja is the word for one. Adding the letter U makes it unity or togetherness. Yes, we have been too subtle for our own good. Like Juma, some of our people do not understand the difference. Some think uhuru means they may do whatever they please. Steal, pilfer. Perhaps our mistake was taking our motto from yours."

"Ours? From America? What do you mean?"

"Do you know the national motto which is on the great seal of your nation?"

"In God We Trust, you mean."

"No, no, no, Stephen. That is what all you Americans think. I have no idea where you come by that. E Pluribus Unum. Out of many one. Have you any idea how many tribes we have? More than your thirteen colonies, I can tell you that. We have no choice. How could we grow if we allowed each tribe to go in whichever direction it wished?"

Of course it was E Pluribus Unum. How stupid could he be? What was he thinking? But did it mean what Nyarimbere thought? Did it mean from the thirteen colonies to one country, or from the many to the individual? After all, if America was about anything it was the individual. Anyone, he had been taught, could become president of the United States. He doubted the same was true for Tanzania. What was the origin, he wondered, of the phrase, E Pluribus Unum? In God We Trust. How could he have been so stupid?

"Have you ever seen a contest between racing shells, Stephen? When I was at Oxford the crew races turned everyone out. They were very beautiful to watch. The girls dressed in spring finery, men were in straw bowlers and school colors. I was a Balliol man myself. There was Christ Church, Merton, St. Edmund, but I was a Balliol man. It was great fun. But what impressed me most was the race. Each man in the shell had to pull exactly in the same rhythm as the others, otherwise there would be no chance to win. America is a country that can afford the luxury of the individual. Nchi, our word for nation, will be here long after you and I have departed and long after the memory of tribalism has faded. Nchi is so important that we sing its praises at every opportunity. I would be pleased to sing you a verse or two."

And before Stephen had a chance to say, no, that's all right, as he did not wish for the minister to embarrass himself or to draw the attention of other guests on the veranda, to say nothing of telling him he had heard the analogy of crewing once before in a newspaper publisher's office, Nyarimbere began to sing. He sang in an exquisite tenor voice, which surprised Stephen because he never imagined Nyarimbere possessed such a gift. So impressed was Stephen by the voice and the joy it exuded that he did not mind the other guests ceasing their conversations to listen.

"Oh, ohhhh Nyerere, ya jenga nchi, Nyerere ehhhh, Nyerere ohhhh.
Oh, ohhhh Tanu, ya jenga nchi, Tanu ehhhh, Tanu ohhhh."

Nyarimbere paused. "We praise the president, then our party. Jenga means to build. If you decide to take on this project in Buhaya, Stephen, we would sing your praises as well. It would sound like this."

But instead of Nyarimbere's gorgeous tenor Stephen was stunned by another voice, one he knew too well, shouting more than singing, "Oh, ohhhh Shorrrt yajenga nchi. Moshes Short ehh-hh. Moshes Short ohhhh. Shshshshsh." Moses Short was laughing, blowing air from the oblong opening at the side of his mouth.

Jesus Christ.

Angry and disgusted, Nyarimbere turned in the direction from which the ugly disturbance had come. Moses Short dragged an empty chair, sat down, and said, "Sho good to shee you again, Mishter minishter.

"Sho, Mishter Ledberg, I hear you have been peshtering Mar-cush Aureliush."

"I haven't been pestering him. Mr. Codding asked me to talk with him."

"You're on my continent now, Mishter Ledberg. Ishn't that right, Mishter minishter? Shshshshh."

Nyarimbere did not acknowledge Short's presence.

"I wouldn't go around ashking queshtionsh about my pershonal bushinessh, if I wash you."

"I haven't asked…"

"You haven't? I'd shay ashking where checksh come from ish pretty pershonal, wouldn't you, Mishter minishter?"

Short rose, snuffed out his cigarette, shook Nyarimbere's hand but not Stephen's and headed toward the black-and-white check-ered cab that had pulled up in front of the hotel.

"How do you know that man?"

He told him.

"That man, Stephen, is not to be trusted. Think about what we have discussed. The country would be forever grateful if you would assist us in Buhaya."

XXIII

ON THE FOLLOWING DAY THE SKY SHATTERED. The balloon burst. The water broke. Sheets of warm tropical rain fell, sometimes so heavy and thick that the opposite side of the street could not be seen. Window wipers were useless. Water inundated the car. People scampered across streets, heads covered with newspapers or umbrellas or banana leaves. But nothing protected from that onslaught. The only thing people could do, the only protection one had, was to wait until it stopped, which it did as abruptly as it began, only to commence again a half hour or hour later. The odd thing was it could be pouring at one end of Independence Avenue and ten blocks away, the sun would be shining. The water evaporated as swiftly as it fell. A cycle that went on and on. It would not have been so bad if the humidity had broken. But if anything it just got worse, exactly like the rash under his armpits which had spread to his groin.

It was during one of the downpours that he lost sight of Marcus Aurelius Brown and Catherine Reticent. He had been hanging around the ferry landing hoping he would see them. They were driving a light green Peugeot sedan. Why, he wondered, am I following them? There is nothing to be gained. Brown is not coming home. Is it to prove Betty was right? Is it to prove that Adam is Brown and Catherine Reticent's child? Or is it to prove to Pete Codding that it was Catherine Reticent on the beach the night I arrived? Or, he wondered, is it some warped sick connection to Anna and George? But George is dead and Anna is the past, isn't she? He did not know the answers to any of those questions as he followed the couple down Independence Avenue, the rain pounding the roof of his car, the carpeting dank, musty, the windscreen fogged, the Peugeot making a sudden right, no signal, into the section of town known as Kariakoo.

Through narrow streets, bending left and then right. Up side streets and alleys. Men, women, children, dogs, chickens, cats, rats, rotting refuse strewn about. Burning wood and perfumed smoke. The Peugeot nowhere to be seen. What had become of it? How had he lost them? The streets led always back to a large empty lot, a piece of land on which cows grazed in the pouring rain.

The cows stood, water dripping from their saturated hides; heads bowed as they mooed and munched. Stephen was intrigued by something hanging from one cow's mouth. He rolled down the window. One sodden bovine chomped on a limp, soggy piece of newsprint. Stephen left the car, his shoes squishing, the cow gazing at him, newspaper hanging from blubbery lips. Stephen reached to recover the newspaper, the cow moving away but not before Stephen could determine that it was an edition of the East African Standard. Cows in the major city of the country, in the center of Kariakoo, ingesting windblown copies of old newspapers. What sort of milk, he wondered, did that produce?

When he returned to the hotel, Joyanti Patel called, "Will you join my family for dinner this evening? It would be an honor. Here is how you find us, Mr. Ledberg. I have told my family all about you. My wife is very excited. She has been shopping all day. You must not disappoint."

"This is wonderful, Mr. Patel. I will see you this evening. By the way, how did you find me? How did you know to call this hotel?"

"There are only a few hotels Americans would stay, isn't it, Mr. Ledberg. We have tried them all."

XXIV

"My family and I are so pleased you have honored us, Mr. Ledberg. Come in. Come in."

Patel was perspiring as he ushered Stephen into the apartment. Except for the slippers on his feet he could have been in an airplane either taking off or about to land. His apartment, however, unlike an airplane, felt like an oven in which all sorts of exotic ingredients, none of which were familiar to Stephen, were cooking. The aromas permeated everywhere, as if a harmattan had swept through the kitchen gathering up not sand but spices which triggered gastric responses in his stomach and which caused him to become famished.

"What are the extraordinary aromas?"

"They do not please you?"

"No. No. No. I've never smelled anything like them. They have made me quite hungry."

Patel smiled. "Yes. Soon you will taste the dishes of my wife and her mother."

"I can't wait."

So silent had she been and so intent was Stephen in trying to please Patel that he did not realize there was another person in the room until the young woman setting the table moved her arm, causing the bangles on her wrist to jangle. Stephen turned in her direction and saw her back, a long thick dark braid against the powder blue dress, which was worn over what he thought were pajama bottoms, but which he knew were not.

"Come, Jasmine. Meet my friend from America. This is my niece, Mr. Ledberg. This is Jasmine."

She wore a mauve pink flower in her jet-black hair and a sensual expression on her face. He felt suddenly as if the floor were falling away, as if the room were bending, physical objects warping.

Patel said, "Jasmine is visiting since a few weeks. It is her school holiday. Soon she must return to school. She finishes and goes to university. Perhaps Jasmine goes to university in America. Isn't it, Jasmine?"

She blushed. Stephen wanted to protect her from her uncle's blather but he could think of nothing to say, offering feebly, "Where do you live, Jasmine?"

Patel said, "My brother lives in Buhaya, Mr. Ledberg. Buhaya is on Lake Victoria, many miles from here. It is a long journey from Dar es Salaam."

Buhaya? Wasn't that the town Nyarimbere wanted him to visit? And hadn't Patel said on the plane the retail cooperatives had opened in his brother's town? Jasmine lived in Buhaya?

"Mr. Ledberg, is something the matter?"

"No. I am fine."

"Here, then, this is my wife's mother. She has just now told me the food is prepared. Come. Come to the table. You are our guest of honor. You must sit here."

In the middle of the table Patel's mother-in-law had placed a large platter of steaming rice upon which lay pieces of bright red stained chicken. On another plate still more rice, saffron colored, decorated with tissue-thin strips of what appeared to be silver foil. In yet another dish, fillets of fish floated in a cream sauce and beside it a stack of round crusty bread. Condiments sat in white porcelain dishes. Stephen was wondering what had become of Patel's wife, when she entered carrying what turned out to be dessert, a plate of curled sticky-looking fried dough and a solitary pomegranate on a silver tray.

"Mr. Ledberg, this is my wife."

"It is my pleasure. Joyanti has told me much about you. Have you eaten Indian food before?"

"No. I haven't."

"Allow me then to tell you what are the dishes."

Before she had an opportunity to continue, Patel interrupted her and, pointing to the chicken, said, "This is tandoori chicken. It is my mother-in-law's specialty. And this is lamb biryani, my wife's special dish. And this, this is Jasmine's favorite, is it not Jasmine?" which only made her blush. "It is fish, tilapia from her beloved lake. Which would you prefer first?"

"I shall try the fish first."

Stephen bit into the fish. The white tender flesh melted, the flesh bathed in rich coconut milk, a subtle garlic flavor, a slight hint of cloves. It was sublime, as if he were consuming the nectar of some god, or rather, he thought, some goddess.

He said, "This is extraordinary. I have never tasted anything like it."

Patel said, "Aha, you see, Jasmine, Mr. Ledberg likes your dish as well."

She blushed and smiled. A smile that overwhelmed him. He felt as if nothing existed in that room but himself, Jasmine, and that smile.

"Come, Mr. Ledberg, you must try my mother-in-law's chicken."

What was chicken to that smile? But he had to admit it was the most succulent, most tender, spiciest chicken he had ever eaten.

"How do you make this? It is simply delicious."

Patel's wife said, "We use many spices, Mr. Ledberg. We grind coriander and cumin and cinnamon, iliki…" She stopped and peered quizzically at her husband who said, in that particular manner of his, rolling and vibrating the R, "cardamom". His wife continued, "Yes, cardamom, and cloves and chili peppers and garlic and anise. All these we grind together and mix with yogurt and the juice of a lime. The chicken is skinned and then the mixture is brushed on. The chicken sits that way for hours. And then we bake it. It is served only on special occasions."

Now it was his turn to blush. He glanced at Jasmine. She smiled again. He felt exhilarated.

Patel said, "You must have some of the condiments with the lamb. Here, try this lemon achar. It is delicious."

"No, no, Joyanti, you must not ask him to eat the pickle. It is too sharp."

Hesitantly, Stephen placed a sliver of the pickle alone in his mouth. He felt a spurt of saliva flow from the glands under his tongue. Something in which the pickle was preserved caused that spurting. He felt the heat of the condiment burn the roof of his mouth, his tongue and gums.

Mrs. Patel said, "See how he is sweating, Joyanti. You need not eat any more if you do not wish, Mr. Ledberg."

Her husband said, "The sweating is good for you, isn't it? It is ancient India's way of cooling you. That is why in the south of India more spices are eaten. They increase the rate of sweat. It is India's way to air condition. You are feeling well, yes?"

"I am fine," Stephen answered, wondering if the spices would ease his rash and admitting to himself he would eat everything at that table so as to please Jasmine.

"Now you must try the sweets," Patel said. "They are Jasmine's favorite." Again she blushed and smiled. If only he could tell her how her smile affected him.

The jalebis tasted like an American doughnut fried in cheap oil. The seeds from the pomegranate on the other hand were tart. The pomegranate was sliced in half, then in smaller sections, sliced to get at the seeds, crimson, pulpy. Jasmine picked the seeds from the sliced fruit, sucking them, her mouth puckering from the tartness, her expression now affecting him in another way.

It was then, at the completion of the meal, that he thought he had the answer to why Joyanti Patel spoke as if his mouth contained a foreign substance when in fact it did not. His host withdrew a small carved teak box from a drawer at the cabinet behind him.

He opened the box and took from it a metal implement that he placed on the table. Beside it he placed a leaf, a round brown nut, various powdered spices, and a little jar of what looked like Elmer's glue but Stephen discovered later was a paste of lime. Then Patel smoothed out the leaf as one would straighten a bed-spread, picked up the metal instrument which turned out to be a nut chopper, chopped up the nut, opened the jar of lime paste, smeared the creamy substance on the leaf, sprinkled the ground spices over it, and finished by spreading the chopped nut carefully over the whole concoction. Then he rolled up the leaf, inserting the wad into his mouth. Betel nut. A habit acquired by Joyanti Patel and how many other men – but not women – at a young age. A habit, which, Stephen thought, could account for his friend speaking as if his mouth contained a foreign substance.

Patel, his voice muffled by the plug of the betel nut, said, "You wish to try, Mr. Ledberg?"

Stephen shook his head and, turning toward Jasmine, asked, "So, Jasmine, you have only a week of vacation left. What will you do in that time?"

Patel shifted his chaw and said, "She will go to the cinema, isn't it, Jasmine?"

Her aunt said, "Do let Jasmine speak for herself, Joyanti."

Stephen desperately wanted to go with her to the movies. But what would they say? What did he know about their customs? How would they respond if he said, I've never seen an Indian movie? I'd love to go, too. Would he be teased? But who would tease him?

Who would make him feel as if what he felt was evil? Jasmine's aunt? Her uncle? The mother-in-law? Or Jasmine herself?

"I've never seen an Indian movie. I would love to go with all of you if that is possible."

He held his breath while his hosts exchanged glances – what did they mean? – a foreign language spoken, Jasmine blushing, Stephen imagining he had been gauche, until Mrs. Patel said, "Jasmine may go to the movies if she wishes, Mr. Ledberg. And you may join us if you wish."

Excited and relieved he asked, "What is the movie about?"

"They are highly romantic. Jasmine likes the romance, Mr. Ledberg." A teasing smile broke over Patel's face. Again Stephen felt protective and angry and responsible. But he need not have worried. Jasmine's very innocence was protection enough.

She spoke finally, a soft, shy voice, filled with a sultry, languid sexuality, a slight English accent, "The movie is very beautiful. There is a new one on Tuesday." She glanced at her aunt.

Who said, "Yes, we could all go Tuesday. My mother enjoys them as well." She smiled and translated for her mother who nodded her head approvingly.

It was as simple as that. Tuesday next they would all go to the movies.

XXV

HE LEFT THE APARTMENT ECSTATIC. Sheets of warm rain soaked him. A few hours ago he could not wait for the rains to cease, and now there was something about that drenching, the tropical rain dripping from his forehead, trickling into his eyes, which caused him to feel manly. Even the itching had ceased. Was it the magic of the food or the presence of Jasmine Patel?

He started the car. The windshield wipers cleared the glass for only a fraction of a second, the headlights reflecting off the downpour. He drove slowly, unable to see where he was going, clearing the condensation on the windshield with his hand, thinking about Jasmine Patel, as the rain pelted the car, hammering the metal roof. What was that he had felt when he saw her? Was it love? Was he in love with Jasmine Patel? Here's where I get onto Ocean Road, isn't it? He smiled to himself, wondering if he had been influenced by her family so swiftly, thinking the trip to Africa was not futile. Betty's advice was well taken. If he had not come he would never have met Jasmine Patel. He peered intently through the windshield, wiping it clear, trying to see where he was heading.

Then, as he was driving, focusing on the road, the downpour ceased. Just stopped completely. No drizzle or light rain. The night was dark and heavy. He rolled down the window. The wheels of the automobile rolled through deep puddles, he thinking on Jasmine, pulse throbbing.

What was that? The front wheels struck something. And another and another. The sound frightened him. He slowed the car, the automobile sloshing through a large flooded area. A figure jerked in front of the headlights. A shadow, an animal, hopping, springing, my god, they were frogs, a multitude of frogs bounding wildly in all directions. He was terrified of hurting the frogs, but even at that slow speed he could not avoid them. Where had they come from? Where were they going?

He did not stop. He drove through and over them, muffled thudding sounds striking the slow moving car, splaying bodies beneath the wheels. Jesus. Death. That odd sensation in the pit of his stomach and then his groin. Don't think about it, just drive on. Get to the hotel. But what did it mean, was it some sort of omen? Or were those frogs simply jumping for joy now that the rains had finished?

Tuesday came and the theater was packed. It seemed to Stephen as if the whole Indian community in Dar es Salaam was at that cinema. A movie in which a man with a gimpy leg chased after the maiden of his choice, trying desperately to seduce her, dragging that leg behind him, limping, singing wailing songs at the top of his voice. The maiden with downcast eyes, avoiding not only her would-be seducer's torrid glance but also his outstretched hand, always sprinting from his grasp at the last moment, running through fields, herself singing high-pitched songs, diaphanous cloth appearing from nowhere, pinks, reds, oranges, blowing in the obviously man-made wind, the hero hobbling in mad pursuit. The hero dying finally, the heroine bending over, touching him, exclaiming her love, her undying, unsullied, limpid love.

Just about everyone in that dimly lit auditorium was sobbing, except Stephen, who had a splitting headache, who thought it was one of the worst movies he had ever seen, and in spite of all that thought he should tell the Patels how much he enjoyed it. Perhaps, he thought, that was why the hero never seduced the heroine. He had not agreed with her family enough.

Mrs. Patel said, "Did you enjoy it, Mr. Ledberg? It is a shame there was no English translation."

"Yes. I did. I didn't understand everything of course."

"I don't think you liked it." Jasmine's statement caught him off guard.

"Well, Jasmine, I didn't enjoy it as much as you and your family because, as your aunt said, I did not understand much of the dialogue. But I certainly enjoyed going with you and your family. And I hope I will have a chance to see all of you again before Jasmine returns to, it's Buhaya, isn't it, Jasmine?"

She smiled and nodded.

Two days later he found himself walking on Ocean Road with the whole Patel family. It was at sunset. An hour, now that the rains had ceased when the whole Asian community, grandmothers, grandfathers, daughters, sons, fathers, mothers, sisters and brothers strolled up and down Ocean Road, every now and then stopping to gaze out over the Indian Ocean, gazing, staring, thinking, wishing, longing – for what? They did not want to return to India, did they?

He strolled beside Jasmine, her body like a magnet. She wore a light blue sari, a blue halter, gold bangles on her left wrist, that sensual expression on her face.

They walked down Ocean Road, the blood red sun setting in the west, the sand white, the water lapping, the coconut palms, the coconuts, the aroma of roasting meat and burning wood, shish kebab and coffee and maize and oranges and bananas and cashews and groundnuts for sale, da da da dada da, the rains finished, everyone outside again, a breeze blowing in off the water, off the Indian Ocean.

Stephen recalled what Nyarimbere had said about the Asian community, particularly the traders. They are the yahudi of East Africa, if they want to pack it in, it would not bother us, and Stephen imagined all those strolling families as refugees. Displaced. Disowned. Nowhere to go. Nowhere to live. He thought how easy it would be if the African government really wanted them to go home, to go back to India or Pakistan. How easy it would be to deport them. Why, all they had to do was wait for a movie to begin, and then surround the theater, herding the audience like cattle prodded through a tick bath into idling trucks. Or better yet, wait until dusk. Wait until now. Then roll a fleet of LST's onto that beach, right onto that white sand, herd those strolling families past the coconut palms, into the open iron jaws, full steam ahead, across the Indian Ocean to the tip of the sub-continent, depositing those families from whence they came. And then, proudly, the African government could draw an imaginary line through the middle of the Indian Ocean, you call your half the Indian Ocean and we'll call ours the African, or Tanzanian, or Kenyan.

What if everyone did that? What if Marcus Garvey was right on? And not just about his own people? What if every immigrant group returned from whence they came? An epic film covering millions of years run backward from the present to the distant past. A vortex sucking up today and depositing it amongst faraway yesterdays. What then? Would the Irish return to Ireland and from there to Germany and France? And the Italians to Italy mixing and marrying Visigoths, Huns, Etruscans, even the above Celts? Even the Native American back to … Siberia? What about that? Cochise would have a long trek. Pocahontas an even longer one. Traipsing across North America, back to the Bering straits, back to Asia, from whence they came. If only they had known. Go home. Everyone cleared out. America empty. And not just of people but even of plants and animals. Everything returning from whence it came until the planet was naked, a sphere spinning through space, order through gravity, until even that gave way, hurtling back from whence it came. He thought himself mad to be thinking such things as he strolled down Ocean Road with Jasmine Patel in the city of Dar es Salaam, Tanzania, the ocean exquisite, the aroma of roasting maize and chunks of meat causing him to feel famished.

He said to Mr. Patel, "I have to go to Buhaya."

"What? What did you say, Mr. Ledberg?"

"I have to go to Buhaya."

"Why? Why do you have to go to Buhaya?"

The family paused, formed a semi-circle, suspicious, looked to Mr. Patel, waited for Stephen's explanation.

"I have to meet an American there. I am flying. Perhaps Jasmine would like to fly as well."

The moment he said it he knew he had made a mistake.

"No. No. It is out of the question, Mr. Ledberg. Jasmine will not fly with you. She will take the bus."

"I want to fly. Why can't I? I have never before been in an airplane. Please, auntie, uncle, let me fly."

"No. You cannot, Jasmine. You will return as always, by bus."

The Patels stared menacingly at Stephen, he embarrassed, imagining he had destroyed any opportunity to court Jasmine, clumsy, berating himself, ruining whatever fantasy he imagined.

The following day he called Nyarimbere and said he would go to Buhaya. He would take him up on the job he wanted done. He would find out all he could on this Jacobson fellow. He would report to Nyarimbere periodically on whatever he found.

"That's excellent, Stephen. Excellent. What made up your mind?"

"Before I go I would like to see Brown once more. I would like to see if he has changed his mind."

"I'm afraid you cannot do that."

"Oh? Why is that?"

"He is no longer here. He has gone."

"Gone? He's gone? Gone where?"

"We don't know exactly. He has just gone."

XXVI

THE MORNING HE LEFT was much like the day he had arrived. The sky was an infinite blue, the burnished heat of the blazing sun stunned him. A breeze stroked the green and blue, black and yellow-striped flag flying atop the whitewashed flagpole.

The pilot's hair was the color of an African sunset, grayish clouds at his temples. His aviator-style sunglasses reflected Stephen's image and reminded him of the skyscrapers in Houston.

"You Ledberg? Let's go then. Plunk yourself next to me."

He did not realize anyone else was on the plane until the pilot turned slightly and shouted, "You all right? We're going to take off now."

Stephen turned to see whom the pilot was addressing. He saw no one. He was about to say, I'm fine, when he heard from the last row of that small plane, "Itsh okay. I'm ready. You can take off now." Jesus Christ. Moses Short. Why hadn't Nyarimbere warned him? Was Short going to Buhaya as well?

The engines vibrated, coughed belches of white smoke. The small plane taxied to the head of the runway. The pilot revved the engines, the plane heading toward a stand of palm trees, barefooted children in tattered khaki shorts standing under the palms, waving. The plane gathered momentum, the wheels free, the plane airborne.

From the air, Kariakoo did not seem like a maze at all. From the air it appeared inconsequential, a few narrow streets ending in the bush, the vacant lot with the grazing cows not at the center as he had thought but off to one side.

The plane flew north following the coastline. He could see the ferry moving across the water and he could pick out Brown's house, solitary, empty. The water violet, aquamarine, deep blue; the ocean framed by that slash of sand and the endless horizon. Then the plane banked and headed west.

The pilot stuck out his hand, "Name's Hadley-Smith. You can call me Ian."

"Is the man in the back going to Buhaya as well?"

"Him? No. I'm dropping him off in Arusha. Why?"

Stephen, relieved, said, "I know him."

"You know him? He's a bwana mkubwa. A big shot. I always fly him when he's out here."

"Why is he sitting in the back?"

" He's terrified. He hates to fly. He always thinks the plane is going to crash. He'll wretch before the trip is over."

"Why doesn't he drive, then? He could do that. He could have someone drive him. He owns a taxi service out here."

Hadley-Smith shrugged. "I know, but it's far safer to fly than to drive. Once you're outside the city, it's all a game of chance. At the least the roads will destroy your car. At the most they'll destroy you. He's smart. He knows that. He'll put up with a little discomfort.

"You said you know him. How do you know him?" Hadley-Smith asked.

"I was doing a project for school. I had to go to Houston to find out why one of his clients was not out on bail. I met him then."

"Well, I admire the bloke. Yours are so different from ours. I mean, look down there. Yours are not sitting in a bloody manyatta covered in flies and drinking cow's blood. Now are they? Eh?

"Why I've heard yours were flying fighters against the jerries. Whoo. Can you imagine what jerry thought when he saw a black face swooping out of the sky? I bet he peed in his trousers... or worse. It'll be bloody generations before ours will be piloting an airplane, I can guarantee you that."

The plane was wending westward above a circle of huts, an indolent plume of smoke rising from one.

"No, it will be a long time before any of them can do what that bloke in the rear has going for him. A clever man. He's got this taxi business. Pretty near a monopoly there. He's big in Dar, Nairobi, up here in Arusha. And he's got his bird business. That's why he's flying to Arusha. He meets with the ex-pat who traps for him. They ship all sorts of birds to the continent. They do just fine as long as the ex-pat keeps his mouth shut."

"What do you mean? Is it illegal?"

"Illegal? Trapping? No, no. But I've heard the ex-pat bragging when he's had too much to drink. Seems they stuff more birds in the boxes than they're allowed."

"I don't get it."

Hadley-Smith looked annoyed. "You're only permitted to ship a certain number of birds a year. Evidently, they ship out many more. False invoices, some may die in transit. They have to cover that. Give one document to customs, mail the real one. Have a bank account. God knows where."

"Can he hear us?"

"Him? Nah. Even if he wasn't sick he couldn't hear us. Too much noise in this plane."

"How does he get away with it, sending more birds than he's allowed?"

Hadley-Smith shrugged. "The customs people are too lazy or they're paid off. Who wants to count all those birds? You never count the tablets in an aspirin container do you? How do you know there is really a hundred? Suppose there are only ninety-nine. A bloody huge profit you can make on that, eh? Anyway, no one gets hurt. Granny has her pet African bird. She has someone to talk to, gets her through the winter. Everyone's the better for it."

The plane droned on, Stephen wondering if pharmaceutical companies would dare do that, thinking that no one gets hurt except the birds, recalling the ones in Short's filthy office, wondering why he never heard them sing.

"Look there, Ledberg. Bloody Kilimanjaro. You ever see that? Bloody beautiful, that is.

"All right now, hang on. We're going in."

The plane landed and taxied to the small terminal. Short staggered from the plane, his shirt plastered with particles of puke. He stumbled to the black-and-white checkered cab, the driver helping him in.

After refueling, the plane was in the air again, flying due west above miles of plains, ahead the first blemishes in what had been a perfectly spotless sky. Clouds unlike any Stephen had ever seen. Thick, billowy, anvil shaped clouds that gave him an uneasy feeling. As if, if they flew anywhere near them he and Hadley-Smith and that tiny airplane would be vacuumed up, vanished from the face of the earth.

Hadley-Smith headed straight for those clouds. He made no attempt to avoid them. Closer and closer, Stephen sitting, staring, all but hypnotized.

And then Hadley-Smith flew the airplane into them. Stephen held his breath, not wanting to appear frightened but frightened, imagining they were heading into a darkness from which they would not emerge.

Hadley-Smith shouted, a grin on his face, "Just a bit of fun really. Hope you don't mind. Wanted you to see that even clouds, like everything else out here, are only a state of mind. If you had seen these anywhere else you wouldn't have given it another thought. But here they frightened you, didn't they? They frightened me, too, for a long time. It's Africa. Even clouds take on a meaning of their own. Now black clouds, that's another thing. But these are a piece of cake. The only thing that can happen if you're piloting is that you might lose all orientation. I've known fellows to come out of one of these flying upside down. But that's all. A piece of cake really."

The plane dove through the mist into the sunshine, Stephen relieved he knew where he was.

Hadley-Smith shouted again, "Those clouds only form over the plains. We're nearing Serengeti now, so keep your eyes open. Plenty of game around."

Stephen peered out the window hoping Hadley-Smith had no more unrequested side trips up his sleeve. He saw no animals. But Hadley-Smith did.

"There, Ledberg. Look there. My god, that's a sight. Thousands of them down there. Never get tired of seeing that. Let's go have a closer look."

The plane banked, allowing Stephen to spot the animals, the plain teeming with zebra. Zebra kicking up dust as the plane disturbed them, wild black and brown and white striped animals galloping across the plain, attempting to escape that noisy winged bird.

"Exciting isn't it, Ledberg? I never get tired of seeing it. You ever see anything like that before? I bet not, eh? That many zebra in one place."

Not zebra, but zebra skins. He had seen a lot of zebra skins in one place. The plane banked again as Hadley-Smith shouted, "Over there, Ledberg. Look over there. Thompson's gazelle. Beautiful, eh?"

They were very beautiful. Hundreds of graceful, lean, muscular bodies. A light brown, down textured skin, a wide black stripe running the length of the body. A body hurtling across the plains, trying to escape their intrusion, at the apogee of their leap they were momentarily airborne, suspended in space, floating really, perfect grace, every bone, muscle, nerve, fiber focused in that one motion.

"As long as I live, Ledberg, I'll never tire of seeing that. That's why I never leave this country. Not the most beautiful woman in the world can do to me what that herd can do."

Had that herd made Hadley-Smith's knees buckle? The floor give way? Did Hadley-Smith dream of herds of zebra and gazelle while Stephen was kept awake by images of Jasmine Patel?

The airplane continued heading west, across the plains, flying over bush, scrub, acacia, occasional outcroppings of great boulders. Stephen had the distinct impression that they were heading deeper and deeper into the center of that vast continent. Not dark but sunlit, not black but filled with color and grandeur and endless horizon. He thought of how America at one time was as empty and vast and endless, and that flying from either coast toward its center, if that had been possible two hundred or even one hundred years ago, might have placed him, interestingly enough, near what is now Wichita, Kansas, a flight in which he would more than likely have spotted, or had pointed out to him, herds of buffalo, antelope, elk, and bighorn sheep.

"There is no continent like this one, Ledberg. There are days up here, I swear to god, I can see surf breaking on the west coast. It's a bloody miracle. No dolly can touch that."

Stephen scanned the horizon to see if he, too, could make out the Atlantic Ocean, his eyes widening and his pulse accelerating as he thought he did glimpse water.

"Look, Ledberg. Look there. There it is."

Was that the Atlantic Ocean? Was it possible? He squinted to see if he could make out surf cascading on sand.

"Look at that, eh. Ever see anything like that? Right here in the middle of the bloody continent. Think what that did to Speke and the others when they saw it for the first time. A bloody miracle right here in the center of Africa. Fucking Lake Victoria."

"What is that black cloud doing suspended over the water?"

"That cloud, Ledberg? That cloud tells you the rains are due any day up here."

"Rains? There are going to be rains here as well?"

Hadley-Smith smiled. "Ledberg, those rains in Dar were nothing. Those were showers compared to what you're going to have here. My friend, when it rains here, the only way you can get in or out is by lake steamer. Although god knows why anyone would want to get in."

The plane was flying over endless water, occasionally passing dots of islands. Hadley-Smith avoided that black cloud, that cloud was far to their left and behind them. And now he could see the other side of the lake.

"That's our destination, Ledberg. Buhaya. Not much of a place. What do they have you coming up here for? You never did say."

"I'm studying the retail cooperative movement up here. It's for a graduate thesis."

Hadley-Smith grunted, "Well, there it is. Buhaya."

They had crossed the edge of the lake and were flying over a small town. Single and double story buildings lined two parallel dirt roads that were intersected by an asphalt-topped road running from the town to the airport. And high above the town, looking over it, protecting it, jutting out over the lake was a series of cliffs.

The plane banked and made its approach, the landing strip, like those two parallel roads, made of dirt. Stephen could see a large cream-colored automobile racing up the road toward the airfield, the car paralleling their approach to the runway.

Hadley-Smith whistled. "Fancy. You certainly know the bwana mkubwa. A Rolls no less."

And then their view was blocked by a stand of trees, the plane moving lower and lower, until Hadley-Smith touched down perfectly.

XXVII

He extended his hand and said, "I'm Stephen Ledberg."

The man said, "Ya, nice to meet you, Mr. Ledberk. Jacobson. Abraham Jacobson. You haf a nice trip?"

And before he could respond Jacobson said, "So please to get in," Jacobson gestured with his hand, a hand that had made no attempt to shake Stephen's.

Stephen settled into the leather covered seat thinking the ostentatiousness of the automobile was slightly out of place. Ingy Reticent's office was one thing. Pete Codding's another. But here in the bush?

Jacobson pulled the door shut, the inside of that air conditioned automobile like a vacuum, sealed off, the interior sleek, plush, an aroma of leather permeating the air, an environment which gave Stephen an uncomfortable feeling.

Jacobson said, "This is Deos. He does all the drifink here. Ve vill go first to the showroom, and then Deos vill drife you to the hotel. Go ahead, Deos."

The landscape was different from the coast. Groves of banana trees lined the road. The trees were scattered around the small plots of cultivated land. Set back behind the trees and gardens were houses with tin roofs.

As he sat thinking how uncomfortable it must be in those houses at the height of the day, wondering why the roofs were built from tin, a dog scampered onto the road directly in the car's path. Deos did not brake or swerve, he made no attempt to avoid the dog. Stephen's own foot thrust hard against the floor, his hand flashing instinctively in front of his face. He heard and felt a thump, the car continuing on, as Deos waved his hand in the air, a gesture dismissing the incident.

Stephen glanced over his shoulder. The dog lay on the ground twitching, then righted itself, struggling to its legs, and hobbled off.

No one said anything, the inside of the car silent. Jacobson gazed nonchalantly out the window. The automobile sped down the asphalt road. They had just hit a dog, hadn't they? It wasn't his imagination, was it? How come neither of them reacted? What was the matter with them? What was he getting himself into? The car hurtled down the road, approaching a roundabout, slowing down, taking the second road, Uhuru Road, and pulling up in front of a long low building.

Jacobson said, "Come, Mr. Ledberk, follow me."

They entered a large, airy showroom at the farthest end of the building. Rows of goods on metal shelving faced the plate glass window. Two men, Africans, stood, bowed, and greeted Jacobson. A woman, an Indian, did the same.

Jacobson headed straight for a glass-enclosed office to the woman's right. He closed the door, walked to his desk, and said, "Sit, Mr. Ledberk." He gestured to the chair beside the desk. "Before you meet the others I vant to haf some thinks straightened vith you." He paused and studied Stephen's face. "I do not belief in pretend-ink, Mr. Ledberk. I know vy you are here. Ya, I know that. I see you are surprised. But ve do not haf the best intelligence in the vorld for nothink. God, he created the vorld in sefen days. But ve, ve vin a var in six. Who vould belief it? Who has heard of such a think? And vy? Because ve haf the best intelligence. I know you are here not to study. But I do not care. I vant to tell you vy I am here these three years. Then ve vill understand each other, yes?"

Yes. No. Jacobson was leaning toward Stephen, his arms resting on the desk. On his left arm were numbers which startled Stephen, a tattoo, blue ink, the sevens crossed in the European manner, and above the numbers were letters not all of which he could make out. Arb ma frei. The tattoo sitting in a charred field similar to the damage on his father's hands. Jacobson leaned so close Stephen could smell onions on his breath, see the pore from which a single hair grew on his nose.

"You know your American Precedent Lincoln? Abraham Lincoln? You know him?"

Jesus Christ. Abraham Lincoln? Yes, he knew Abraham Lincoln, thinking on the portrait in the kitchen, his parents, Wichita, Kansas, America. Did any of it still exist? Abraham Lincoln?

"Ya, vell vonce I vas interested in comink to America so I study your precedents. This man Lincoln vy is he the only von vith such a Chewish name? Vy?"

What? Was Jacobson mad?

"You did not think Lincoln can be Chewish? Ya, it is true. Lincoln is a Chewish name. But more, vy the Abraham? Vy he haf my name?

"So I think this Lincoln must be vone of us. A Chew. So I read about him. And I find he did not luf the schvartza so much. You know vat is schvartza, Mr. Ledberk? The people here are schvartza. Ya, and this Lincoln did not luf them so much I find out. I vonder to myself vy he vait so lonk to free them. Vy he did not do it the minute he become precedent? Vy? You know, Mr. Ledberk?"

He knew. But why bother educating Jacobson? Lincoln was a Jew? If he believed that he could believe anything.

"No? I tell you then. He vas a politician. He vas a shrewd Chewish politician. He vait for the right moment. He vait for vhen he make the most impact. Then bang, he free the schvartza. He need the French. He need their guns and ammunition and food. And that is vy ve are here, Mr. Ledberk."

It was? Stephen had no idea what the hell Jacobson was talking about. What he did know was that he had just butchered a good part of American history to fit whatever crank theory he thought he was expounding.

Stephen said, "Well, you're wrong about Lincoln."

"Wronk? Vas he not a Chew?"

"No, he was not. But that's not what I'm talking about. He would have emancipated the slaves during his administration, civil war or not. He didn't do it immediately because he was scared he'd set off the very war he feared."

Jacobson said, "You are wronk. If there vas no cifil var the schvartza they vould still be slafes. And your Precedent Lincoln he vas a Chew. He had the face of a Chew, the beard of a Chew, the nose of a Chew, and the name of a Chew. You know ven he free the schvartza? No? September twenty-second, eighteen sixty two. You know vat is this date? It is the veek of Rosh Hashanah. You know vat is Rosh Hashanah? You are a Chew, Ledberk, yes? No? Vy he do it then? Vy that date and no other? Vy the generals vonder vy he vant to valk to the rifer? You haf a rifer in Vashington, yes?"

"Yes. The Potomac."

"Yah, the Potomac. Vy your Precedent Lincoln throw bread into the Potomac River? You don't know? To feed the ducks? No. Because he vas a Chew.

"You Americans think you know eferythink. You know nothink. Abraham Lincoln vas a Chew and he free the schvartza because he need somethink from the French. And he free them on Rosh Hashanah. It vas a deal. The same vy ve are here. And now I explain to you the deal."

Stephen was puzzled by the reference to Lincoln's tossing bread into the waters of the Potomac River, but more importantly he expected the deal, after all Jacobson had said, to be momentous, some deep intricate Machiavellian strategy. But it was not. What it was, was Jacobson explaining simply that if he were overseas longer than two years he could return to Israel – Isriel, he called it, turning the a into a long i – with any luxury item he wished. A car, a radio, a tape recorder, a toaster, anything, and he could not be taxed.

"Ya, they do not tax me. And vhile I am here I lif like a kink. And I haf the power of a kink." He paused and stared, an intimidating stare, which Stephen imagined meant, and don't you forget it.

"I hate this country, Mr. Ledberk, but I make the best of it. Soon I leaf. But until then you leaf me alone, I leaf you alone. Now that is vy I am here."

Jacobson relaxed a bit and continued, "Others are here for their own reasons. The kibbutzniks who do the irrigation projects, the farmink, they are younk, adventurous. That is vy they are here. And also because they too can brink in luxury items when they return home.

"Ya, I see you do not belief me. You who haf efery think in America. Ve do not, Mr. Ledberk. You know how much is a radio in Isriel? You vould not belief. A simple transistor radio in Isriel it costs ofer a hundred dollars. Ya, you are surprised. Vell, I buy one here and there are no taxes on it. I brink it in duty free."

He paused again and stared. That stare penetrating, wanting to see if Stephen had taken everything in up to now, which he had but not necessarily accepting all of it, or even most of it, as gospel.

"You know vy is Isriel here in Africa?"

He knew why Mr. Patel thought Israel was in Africa. Patel would have said because the Israelis want all of Africa as their home. Why Patel had said, at one point the Israelis wanted Uganda as their home.

"Actually, I don't know why Israel is here."

Jacobson smiled, a sinister smile which Stephen took to mean, you are such a naïf, Mr. Ledberg. You know nothing of the world.

"Isriel is here, Mr. Ledberk, because they vant foreign exchange. You think because they vant to help the African? They could not care about the African. You think because they vant votes in the United Nations?" He stared again. "Ve do not care about the United Nations. No, the Isriel government is here because they vant foreign exchange. Efen if it is only shillinks. Those shillinks are backed by British sterlink. Ya, if you go to our godown, you vill see vy the Isriel gofernment is here. The retail shops are a gift. You think ve care about them? Vat can these Africans buy in retail shops? They buy a little oil, some flour, beans, rice. That is all. Ya, you go to the godown and you vill see. Nails, paint, tires, irrigation equipment. All made in Isriel. You know how much it is if ve supply to paint all the gofernment buildinks? You know how much it is if all the gofernment vehicles they drife on Isriel tires? You know? That is vy ve are here."

Jacobson paused again, as if he were about to conclude. He stared as if he were about to conclude with a point he wanted completely understood. He need not have stared, his speech was emphasis enough. His speech and that number and those words on his left forearm were enough to hold Stephen's complete attention.

"So you see, Mr. Ledberk, I do not care vat you find or who you tell. You cannot hurt me. I haf serfed my time. I am ready to go home. My vife she vants to go home. She has hated efery minute out here. Ve haf a son in the army. Ve vant to go back. Ya, ve are ready to go home." He slumped in his chair and closed his eyes, then opened them. "Ya, now I vill introduce you to efery-one. Come."

XXVIII

THE TELEPHONE JOGGED HIM. Stephen had fallen asleep, a deep sleep, the sort of sleep he often wished for at night. His right ankle rested on the lower part of his left leg. His right arm was crossed over the left, arms resting lightly upon his chest. It was a position in which he rarely slept at night, but a position in which he always slept in the late afternoon. And although there was no way to verify it, he always imagined because of the deepness of the slumber, it was the position and hour in which he had slept the soundest nestled inside his mother's - whoever she was, wherever she was - uterus.

The telephone rang again. At first he thought he was in his room at home and had overslept. Then through the haze that only such a deep sleep can cause, he realized he was in his hotel room in Buhaya.

He picked up the receiver. The voice on the other end said, "Bwana, dinner is served." He inquired about the time. "Seven o'clock, bwana." He thanked the voice and replaced the phone.

He lay on the bed, his mind lethargic, thinking about all that had happened since the morning.

After Jacobson's harangue, a discourse that left Stephen wary, thinking he would stay as far away from Jacobson as possible, Deos drove him to the hotel. The hotel was a dun-colored structure with a red tile roof, white smoke rising from the chimney, the air filled with the aroma of burning wood, an aroma which caused him a pang of homesickness, strangely enough not for summer cookouts but for fall burnings. Leaves raked, piled, and set ablaze. Those feelings provoked, he thought, by the smell of the burning wood and the row of pines, the first such pines he had seen since he arrived, which shaded the driveway of the hotel. The pines and aroma and the fact that it was almost the end of September were a combination stirring some internal biological clock to alarm. A clock that would have been set off in America by chilly nights, crisp days, the changing of foliage, the beginning of a new school year. A combination that evoked that nostalgia, a tremendous appetite for a McIntosh apple, and thoughts of his parents.

He had set his bag on the hotel's verandah on which a number of tables and chairs faced the lake. Then he walked across the immense lawn stretching between lake and hotel, the lawn dotted here and there with rusty croquet hoops, remnants, he thought, of better times.

The lawn ran down to the lake's edge. A row of tall dark barked, green-leaved trees grew at the rim of the lawn. He stood under them looking out over the lake, eyeing that black cloud. He thought about Hadley-Smith and what he had said about Speke and the others who saw the lake for the first time, how awed they must have been by finding this body of water in the middle of Africa. Was it possible, he thought, that there were fish or snails or amoebae today whose ancestors had inhabited that lake over a century ago. What information had they passed down through generations about that solitary, oddly clothed, pale skinned man,

John Hanning Speke, which the present generation must now take for granted.

A rustling in the branches of the tree above him interrupted his reverie. He looked up to see a figure leaping from branch to branch. It was a monkey, who dropped to the ground at his feet.

The monkey had blue eyes and silver colored hair, the backs of its hands lightly touching the earth. The monkey moved slightly and Stephen caught a glimpse of another flash of blue, this time toward the monkey's rear. My god. The monkey had blue balls. A silver-haired blue-eyed monkey with balls to match, staring at him. Those black-barked, darkly leaved trees were alive with silver-haired blue-balled monkeys.

What had Speke thought of them? Had Speke brought one home? A gift for the queen. He smiled as he imagined Speke presenting that monkey, "Your Majesty, I have named the lake for you, and return with this memento", Speke bowing, backing out, leaving the monkey blinking, shivering, wondering why it was so frigging cold, and who the plump overdressed woman was who was sitting above everyone else as if she were in a tree.

In the lobby of the hotel was a child, a young girl who played on an oriental carpet, reminding him of Adam, the half-caste child in Betty's class at the Bridle Street School. Not because she had an angry expression on her face, on the contrary, it was soft and radiant and warm, glowing like the lights against the wood paneling, but because she was about Adam's age, a half-caste herself, her eyes blue, her skin tawny, her light brown hair frizzy.

What Stephen found disconcerting was that the child, Nectarinia she called herself, the daughter of the owner of the hotel she said, that girl with the exotic name playing on the rug caused such an empty feeling to surge through him. A feeling bordering on loneliness and despair. What had caused that? The child? Jacobson? Or the realization that he had no idea where Marcus Aurelius Brown was and that he had failed to alert Pete Codding that Brown had left Dar es Salaam for god knew where, to say nothing of the fact that he, Stephen, was really in Buhaya not because of Nyarimbere's request to gather information on Abraham Jacobson but only because of Jasmine Patel.

He had found his room in the hotel, lay down for a nap, and had fallen into that deep slumber. He lay a while longer and then when a wave of loneliness swept over him he forced himself from the bed and went downstairs.

He felt self-conscious as he entered the dining room because aside from the three waiters at the far end, he was the only other person there. He thought of retreating, to return later when others would be dining, but one of the waiters said, "Sit wherever you wish, bwana." And he approached with a menu.

Stephen sat at a table set for two, the china, silverware, glasses, linens, napkins immaculate and arranged just so. He glanced at the menu and wondered why the waiter bothered with it at all. Unless he declined a course he would eat mock turtle soup, cucumber salad, roast chicken, savory, dessert, coffee or tea.

He felt odd as he sat at the table eating alone. He wondered what time the other guests were going to eat. It never occurred to him that there might be no other guests. It never occurred to him until a man approached his table.

"I'm Peter Lewenberg, Mr. Ledberg. I hope everything is satisfactory." He held a pipe in his hand. "Do you mind if I join you?"

Understanding instinctively that the man was the owner of the hotel he said, "Not at all." Stephen held out his hand toward the empty chair. "And feel free to smoke if you wish. It won't bother me."

Peter Lewenberg glanced at his pipe. "Oh no, I never smoke anymore. It upsets my mother too much. She says it reminds her of my father. So I don't smoke any longer."

"Your hotel is very beautiful."

"Thank you. My father built it over fifty years ago. Those were the good old days I'm afraid. There were all sorts of people coming out here then." He paused and sucked on the pipe.

"There were always people coming through, officials of one sort or another. There used to be quite a community of Europeans living here. But now as you can see things are quite different. I would not mind this," he swept his hand over the room, the pipe stem homing in on each empty table, "because we have some money saved and there is always the occasional guest like yourself. But we wish to stay and I worry that we may not be allowed to do that. I worry that we may have to leave. I would not look forward to that."

"Why should you have to leave?"

Lewenberg sighed. "We are worried, Mr. Ledberg, that the man who met you at the airstrip is going to give us a bad reputation. We have been here for over fifty years but in all that time we have never had to cope with a situation like this."

"I don't understand. Perhaps I'm missing something. I…"

Lewenberg interrupted him, explaining with a simplicity that shocked him, "We are Jews, Mr. Ledberg. We have never tried to hide that."

With that statement Lewenberg lowered his soft, vulnerable, blinking eyes, drawing back in his chair as if he were prepared to ward off a blow.

Stephen noticed Lewenberg's fingers frantically turning the pipe over and over, the stem circumscribing a circle. Fingers and hand which Stephen had an impulse to touch and quiet, an impulse, which, had he followed it, might have had its desired effect. Instead he did nothing.

"I don't know everything Jacobson is up to, Mr. Ledberg. Nor do I care to. But I do know, and so does everyone else, that he is treating the Africans badly." He lowered his voice, "He sleeps with any woman he can find. And he sleeps as often as he can with his shopkeepers. They are free to pass any number of goods to friends and relatives. The members of the cooperative are very angry. If there is an explosion I worry that it will spill over to us. When we heard an American was coming up we were hopeful. There have been rumors for months that Dar was going to send someone. We thought perhaps you were going to take Jacobson's place. But then," he glanced out of the corner of his eye, "I saw your name and became apprehensive. You see, I did not think it would do to send another Jew even if you were an American."

"Well, I'm only here to study the retail stores. It's for a graduate thesis I have to write. And Ledberg is not Jewish, anyway. It's Swedish."

Lewenberg blushed. "You understand I have nothing against the Israelis. Only Jacobson. Even now my mother is in Israel. She goes every year at this time. And if it comes to that, if we should have to give up everything we have built here we will return to Israel."

"Is that where you are from?"

"No. Not at all. Both my father and mother grew up in Germany. But there is nothing left for us there. All that is left in Germany is dead family and stolen property. I love Israel, Mr. Ledberg, but the Israelis should never have sent Jacobson here. The Israelis should have chosen better."

A statement that brought the conversation to an abrupt halt.

Feeling uncomfortable with the silence, Stephen said, "I met your daughter earlier today."

"My daughter?"

"Yes. She said she was your daughter."

"Oh. Nectarinia you mean. She's not my daughter. No, she tells everyone that, but she's not my daughter."

"Oh, I'm sorry. I thought…"

"No, that's all right. How were you to know? No, she is the child of a girl who used to work for us. The father was just passing through. The girl went back to her people and asked if we could care for Nectarinia. You see she couldn't very well take a child of that nature home. Out here a half-caste is an outcast.

"So my mother and I care for her and she tells people we are her parents. Which is still another reason to worry if we must pick up and leave. I can't imagine what will become of her."

"You wouldn't take her with you?"

"No. If it came to that we'd have to leave her."

Perhaps, Stephen thought, that was it. Perhaps that was what caused the earlier feeling of despair. That he sensed beneath the girl's words a kindred spirit.

"And her father? What became of him?"

"Her father? Who knows where he is. He was here for a few months. Nectarinia is almost six. He came through and stayed here while he was doing some work with birds. That's how she came by her name. Nectarinia is the name of a family of birds. Sunbirds in layman's terms. They are quite common out here."

"Was her father trapping birds?"

"As a matter of fact yes. Do you know him?"

"No. No, I don't." He told Lewenberg of the conversation in Hadley-Smith's airplane.

"Do you think it could be the same man?"

"Possibly. It might be the same chap. He's never returned."

"So whoever it was doesn't know about Nectarinia?"

"No. They wouldn't would they?"

"Have you told Nectarinia about her real father?"

"No, we have told her nothing. Why go out of our way to stir up anguish?"

"But she knows her real mother?"

"She knows we are not her parents. We have told her that. But being a child she has taken it into her head to adopt my mother and myself. That's why she tells everyone she is my daughter."

Stephen wished to say, And you have done nothing to discourage that? Instead he asked, "Her real mother never visits?"

"No. They have had no contact for some time. She lives a good distance from here. It is not easy for her to travel."

"But what will you tell Nectarinia when she grows older? Will you help her locate her mother?"

"If she wishes that. My own feeling is that unless the mother decides to leave this region she will do nothing to claim Nectarinia."

"You really believe her mother will not try to contact her?"

Lewenberg shrugged. "It is not uncommon out here. Besides, Nectarinia has a home as long as she wishes." He paused. "Or as long as we are here."

He sucked on the pipe while Stephen thought about Nectarinia and wondered when, not if, but when, she would want to locate her real parents. When that time came she would have an easier task than he did. Even if Lewenberg did not choose to tell there must be others who knew her mother. Her mother would be easy. It was her father who was the problem.

Lewenberg said, "Tell me, I don't suppose you know anyone here?"

"As a matter of fact I do."

"Oh, yes? Who is that?"

"When I was in Dar es Salaam I became friends with an Indian family. The Patels. Mr. Patel has a brother who lives here. He owns a retail store. Unfortunately, I don't know his first name. He has a daughter. Jasmine…"

"Of course. Their duka is on Jamhuri Street. You are fortunate to have friends. You will need them over the next few weeks."

"Because of Jacobson?"

"No, I wasn't thinking of him. Although come to think of it, that, too. No, the rains are due any day now. It's the worst time to be here. Have you a pair of rubber boots?"

Stephen shook his head.

"No? Well, you'll need them once the rains begin. What size shoe do you wear?"

Stephen told him.

"Well, that's close enough. I'll have an old pair of mine sent up to you. If there is anything else we can do, just let me know. As you can see my staff is not overburdened. I should really let some of them go, but I can't bring myself to do that. Most of them have been with us for years. Most have been here since my father."

He placed the pipe in the pocket of his cardigan, stood and said, "Now if you will excuse me. I hope I have not imposed."

"Of course not."

"I'll have those gumboots sent up to your room."

He turned and left, leaving Stephen to finish his coffee and to ponder not just the conversation but also everything that had happened since he stepped off that airplane.

XXIX

DEOS DROVE HIM TO THE RETAIL SHOPS the following morning. Except for that distant black cloud, the day was clear and sunny and warm.

They drove west on the asphalt road, the truck trembling, packed tightly with burlap bags of rice, beans, maize and flour, cases of beer, soft drinks, detergents, powdered milk, the road switching without warning from asphalt to dirt, the truck, like those gazelles in Serengeti momentarily airborne, then slamming hard onto the dirt road. The truck was rumbling, shaking, rattling, the load in back pushing them, hurling them down the dusty, corrugated potholed road.

Stephen sat anxiously beside Deos, studying the road ahead, his fingers mentally crossed, hoping no animal would saunter into their path.

A few miles from town they passed a wooden barn-like building, a sign above the door reading: PEOPLES FOOD COOPERATIVE GODOWN. He recalled Jacobson's words, "You think ve care about the retail shops, Mr. Ledberk. Ve do not care. Ya, you go to the godown. You know vhat you vill find? You vill find nails, paint, tires, irrigation equipment." The warehouse had a large metal padlock clearly visible on the front door.

They passed other wooden buildings, doors wide open, men working on automobiles or buses. And then all signs of industry ended, the road running through endless bush as far as he could see. The blue sky stretched over and around them, the road a brown scar through the landscape, the truck shaking, leaving a cloud of brown dust in its wake.

Stephen smiled to himself as he thought of the chain of events that had brought him here. Ingy Reticent did not appreciate his story on the highway into New Falls, but Stephen thought he could certainly write a lengthy piece on the need for a new road into and out of Buhaya. Hadley-Smith had been correct. It was far better to fly out here than to drive. What was the life span of an automobile or truck in the African bush? he wondered.

"How far is it to the shop at the agricultural research center, Deos?"

Deos shrugged. "About twelvi miles."

"You do this every day?"

Deos raised one finger in the air.

"Once a week?"

"Yesi. Once a week. But now the rains come. Deos drive every day. Deos not drive in rain. Roadi wash out. Deos deliver everything now."

The shop at the agricultural research center was nothing more than a hole in the wall. But Sarah, who ran the shop, was voluptuous. She was tall, full chested, her hair combed out like a wire brush; her eyes large, almond shaped, dark brown, seductive. She wore a French blue colored skirt and a white short-sleeved scoop-necked blouse, her long dark arms contrasting with the bright French blue and silver of the bangles on her wrist. She seemed to him brazen, provocative, and yet, when she shook his hand she was gentle, delicately touching her right elbow with her left hand. He thought Jacobson had chosen well. The store was filled with men.

He helped Deos unload the truck and after Deos finished drinking a beer and talking earnestly with Sarah, he and Deos drove back to the store in town, Stephen hoping that the beer had not obfuscated Deos' driving.

The shop in town was at the far end of Uhuru Road. It was run by a woman who was bending over behind the counter as they entered, her back to them, her flowered skirt hiked to her thighs, the backs of her legs fleshy, showing what appeared to Stephen to be swirls of currents as if a fish had flashed its tail creating a series of eddies on that soft, caramel colored skin.

When she heard them enter, the woman straightened up and turned around. She was a half-caste and she had one of the most beautiful faces he had ever seen. Her breasts swelled above the low-cut, loose fitting blouse. What was that he was feeling in his groin? He knew what.

Deos said, "Thisi Dolores."

She quickly brushed her hand over her skirt, shaking hands, her voice soft and shy, the voice, he thought, of a young child. Her manner was the opposite of Sarah's. Her manner but not her beauty. He thought Dolores even more beautiful than Sarah. Yes, Abraham Jacobson had excellent taste. That would go into his report to Nyarimbere. But were they both sleeping with Jacobson? Why would they do that? They didn't find him attractive, did they?

When Deos drove him back to the showroom, Abraham Jacobson was at his desk.

Jacobson said, "Shut the door, Mr. Ledberk. So how do you find the hotel? It is beautiful, yes?"

"Yes."

"And you haf been gifen the best room, yes?"

"Well, I don't know if it is the best but it is more than sufficient for me."

"Ya. You haf met Lewenberk?"

"Yes."

"Yes, he is a good man Lewenberk. I haf arranged eferythink vith him. If there is anythink you need you ask him, yes? If he doesn't gif vhatefer you vant you tell me, ya?"

"I am sure he will provide me with anything I want," Stephen said, momentarily catching sight of the tattoo.

Jacobson paused, stared, his lips slightly parted. "So. You haf met Dolores and Sarah, ya?"

Stephen nodded. "Yes."

Jacobson smiled. "So you vould like to sleep vith them, no?"

The question caught him so off guard that he sat with a blank expression on his face.

"Ya, Mr. Ledberk, they are beautiful. Very beautiful. I haf good taste, no?"

"Yes."

"That is vy I haf chosen them. They attract business. But they are not to sleep vith. You know vy not?"

Stephen shook his head, wondering if Jacobson was going to say because they were his.

"Because you should nefer shit vhere you eat." Jacobson stared at him, the tattoo visible, the sevens with lines through them, silence in that office, Stephen paralyzed by Jacobson's words. "Ya, Mr. Ledberk, stick vith your little Hindu girl. Leaf Dolores and Sarah alone."

Jesus Christ. How did he know that? What sort of legerdemain had Jacobson just performed? Was the Israeli intelligence service that good? Why did they care?

"You are blushink, Mr. Ledberk. Ve know eferythink. And vy? Because ve are Jews. Go to her now. Go. I do not need you here."

Stephen Ledberg walked down Jamhuri Street in a state of confusion. Nyarimbere had sent him, he thought, on a wild goose chase in which the only ones, it seemed, who could catch the goose were the Israeli intelligence service. Jacobson was not sleeping with Dolores and Sarah. He would not break his own rule, would he? Besides, Stephen could not imagine either Dolores or Sarah sleeping with Jacobson. They were young and beautiful. Jacobson was old and fat and obnoxious. Of course, Jacobson did have the power of the boss, doing the hiring and firing. And, he thought, if either Sarah or Dolores refused to sleep with Jacobson, he supposed he could fire them. But could he get away with that in Tanzania? He might be able to get away with it in Israel, but he doubted he could do that here. No, he thought, Nyarimbere and Lewenberg, the owner of the hotel, did not know what they were talking about. He thought of what Hadley-Smith had said about the clouds over the Serengeti. In Africa people see clouds and imagine danger. Jacobson, he thought, was like those clouds. People projected onto Jacobson the very things they feared in themselves. If Jacobson knew so much about him, Stephen thought, perhaps he could tell him where Marcus Aurelius Brown had gone. Or better yet, who Stephen's real parents were.

He stood in the afternoon sun outside the Patels' duka. He had not telephoned. His plan was to drop in casually, say he was walking around town only to find himself in front of their duka. He entered and saw a man and two women sitting behind the counter. The man stood and asked, "May I help you?"

"Yes. My name is Stephen Ledberg. I met your brother Joyanti Patel in Dar es Salaam. He told me I should look you up when I got here."

Had it not been for the frightened expression on his face, the man whom Stephen thought must be Jasmine's father would have been handsome with his thick black hair and smooth tawny skin and without his brother's poor eyes, pockmarked face and heaviness. Stephen could see where Jasmine had attained some of her beauty.

"Mr. Patel said he would write you. Jasmine knows me."

The man looked at the two women. The younger woman whom Stephen took to be Jasmine's mother said, "Jasmine will be home from school soon. Would you like a Fanta?"

"A Fanta will do."

He felt foolish as he sipped the orange soda. Had Jasmine never mentioned him? He should have telephoned. Even in America he would not have just dropped in. How inconsiderate of him.

"I don't want to take up any more of your time. Can you just tell Jasmine I was here? I'll come back later."

Jasmine's mother said, "No. No. Wait. Jasmine will be right along. Aha, here she is now."

Jasmine was startled to see him. "You should have given us warning."

"I know. I'm sorry. It was stupid of me."

Jasmine introduced him to her parents and her grandmother, and then speaking a language foreign to Stephen they became quite animated, moving about, shuffling chairs, all of which made Stephen even more self-conscious.

"I don't want to bother you…"

"It's all right. They are just now preparing chai. You will stay and have some."

Jasmine wore a gray colored skirt, white blouse and maroon jacket, her brown legs for the very first time visible, a birthmark on her left shin.

"How was your bus trip?" he asked her.

"It was fine."

"The bus trip from the coast is long and arduous," her mother added. "But Jasmine loves to visit my brother-in-law and Dar es Salaam offers so much more than Buhaya. You have seen how small is the town."

"But it has a movie theater."

"Yes, but it is open only on Friday, Saturday and Sunday. It shows only old movies. It is not like the cinema in Dar es Salaam. It does not show the new films." Her mother then asked, "And where are you residing, Mr. Ledberg?"

"Stephen. Please call me Stephen. I stay at Lewenberg's Hotel. It's a pretty glorious place."

"Yes. It is one of the few luxuries in Buhaya. How long will you be visiting?"

"I'm not sure actually."

"What is it you are here for?" Jasmine's mother continued to pepper him with questions.

"I'm here to meet another American," Stephen said, thinking it unwise to tell them he was connected in any way with Abraham Jacobson. If the Indian community's intelligence was the equal of Israel's, so be it.

"But I have an idea. Why don't you all come to tea at the hotel one day? After everything Mr. and Mrs. Patel did for me in Dar es Salaam, I would like to return the favor."

Jasmine smiled at him and he knew instantly that they would accept.

"It would have to be on a Sunday," her mother said, "and only Jasmine and I and my mother will be able to attend. Mr. Patel must mind the store."

"Oh, I am sorry you cannot come, Mr. Patel." Turning to the other three he said, "Well, what about this Sunday, then?"

"That would be fine."

"Wonderful then. Around three?"

"Yes. Three is fine."

He left the duka ecstatic. He did not care about Abraham Jacobson. As far as he was concerned Jacobson could sleep with whomever he wished as long as it was not Jasmine Patel. What Jacobson did was none of his business. Nor was it any of his business where Marcus Aurelius Brown was. Who cared if Brown and Catherine Reticent were lovers? It was almost as if his past had ceased to exist. And Sunday he would spend time with Jasmine Patel.

XXX

HE SAT AT A TABLE ON THE VERANDAH while Nectarinia spun an open umbrella on the lawn. She was playing a game, singing quietly to herself.

He sat watching and wondering if he would have an opportunity to be alone with Jasmine, or whether his plight would be similar to that of the man with the gimpy leg in the Indian movie. Would Jasmine always remain an arm's length away?

He had concocted a plan, a simple but fragile plan. He would ask her to go for a walk. What he feared was that her mother would say, "A walk, Mr. Ledberg? That's a fine idea. My mother and I and Jasmine would love that. Where had you in mind?"

How would he respond? "Haven't you heard, Mrs. Patel, three's a crowd? To say nothing of four? Or even too many cooks spoil the broth? Burn the rice pulao?"

As it turned out he need not have worried, he did not have to plead his case. As it turned out the English tea did it all for him.

He saw Jasmine and her mother and grandmother turning the corner of the building, the three women dressed to the nines. Dressed not as if they were going to have tea on the verandah of Lewenberg's hotel in the town of Buhaya on the west side of Lake Victoria, but at Buckingham Palace or Windsor Castle, or even the Taj Mahal.

Jasmine was not a schoolgirl today. She wore her light blue sari, the sari wound tightly around her, draped just so over her shoulder, revealing the smooth brown skin of her neck and collarbone, the collarbone curving from the hollow of her throat toward her slender shoulders. Her long black hair was draped loosely down her back. On her wrist were a half dozen bangles, which jangled each time she moved her arm. And on her face an expression of pure innocent delight. Her beauty stunned him.

He had ordered a special tea of tiny sandwiches and cakes. Delicate English sandwiches. Crustless bread slathered with butter. Cheddar cheese with mango chutney, watercress with cucumber, tiny wedges, delightful morsels, sandwiches and cakes and Darjeeling tea.

They sat on the verandah looking out over the lake, Nectarinia playing on the lawn, Mrs. Patel nodding in her direction, speaking a foreign language, the only word Stephen catching being Lewenberg's name.

"What did you say, Mrs. Patel? What about Nectarinia?"

"It is nothing. I have just now told my mother she is the daughter of the owner of the hotel."

"No. I'm afraid you have that wrong, Mrs. Patel. She is not his daughter."

"Whoever told you that? Of course she is his daughter."

"Mr. Lewenberg himself."

Jasmine's mother smirked knowingly, that smile implying Lewenberg did not tell the truth. Was it possible? Stephen felt defensive of Lewenberg, but he did not respond.

They sat on the verandah, Jasmine's mother and grandmother wolfing down the sandwiches, a waiter bringing another platter, the two women moving on to the cakes.

"Would you like to go for a walk, Jasmine?"

"A walk? Where?"

"I thought just down to the lake. Is that all right with you, Mrs. Patel?"

Stephen held his breath, not daring to imagine what he wanted to hear, planning an alternative if this initial foray failed, realizing as Jasmine's mother shoved another cake into her mouth that she had no intention of going anywhere until every last cake and every last sandwich was devoured. Mrs. Patel implored them not to go far. Thank god for the sandwiches. Thank god for the cakes. Thank god for the English tea.

They walked across the lawn, past Nectarinia who paused for a moment to follow them with her eyes, Stephen not wishing to break the mood even to acknowledge her presence, as Jasmine's bangles jangled, the swish of her sari brushing gently the grass.

Stephen did not glance back. He did not look back for fear he would catch Mrs. Patel's eyes and she would realize the enormity of her appetite.

They stood at the shore, the water lapping near their feet, Jasmine staring out over the lake; Jasmine looking, he thought, at that black cloud hovering far in the distance. She had a perplexed frown on her face, her brow furrowed as if there were something she did not understand. He imagined she was waiting for him to do something, to give them direction and, noticing a path to their left, he suggested they walk that way.

She followed him, the path winding among the trees circling the lake, the hotel out of sight, the lake on their right, woods to their left.

They walked down the path, the only noise the jangling of bangles and the swish of the sari. In that stillness it seemed that the bangles could be heard for miles. Like a cowbell. And it occurred to him that perhaps that was their purpose. To let the two women gorging themselves on the verandah know where Jasmine was at any moment.

And what would happen if the jangling ceased? Or became only intermittent? What would those two women do when they could no longer hear that tintinnabulation? And what would they think?

They came to a boulder set back from the lake. "Why don't we rest for a bit, Jasmine?"

He had not realized until that moment how long her hair really was as she sat beside the boulder gently gathering it to use as a cushion.

"What are you thinking?" he asked her.

"I would have liked to fly with you. I have never been in an airplane. What is the lake like from an airplane?"

"It is like an ocean. The water just goes on and on."

"Yes, one day I shall see that. An ocean. Yes, I could see how it might appear. My uncle always feels so responsible for me. They never let me out of their sight. You can see my mother does not mind."

He wanted to say, So it is not the sandwiches. Instead he said, "I hope one day you will fly. You can come to America. I will show you around."

"My uncle wants to go to America. It would be difficult for me. I have been nowhere. There is so much I don't know. We are so different. We come from different worlds. I feel so stupid sometimes.

"Once when I was in Dar es Salaam I saw a hideous thing growing from an American boy's mouth. I thought it was a tumor. It terrified me. That poor boy. Suddenly the tumor exploded. I thought it was skin he had all over his face. I was crying and he was laughing. I didn't know it was bubble gum until my uncle told me."

Stephen, who was jealous of the boy, laughed.

"Don't laugh at me."

"I'm sorry. I didn't mean to hurt your feelings. You never knew what bubble gum was?"

She shook her head. "Can you teach me to blow bubbles?"

"Of course. Does your father sell bubble gum?"

"He sells no chewing gum. He thinks it is a disgusting habit. But I would like to try bubble gum. What does it feel like to chew this gum?"

"What does it feel like? Huh. I never thought about that. What does gum feel like? It's sticky. But it doesn't stick to your teeth. I chew it for the sugar and the flavor."

"What flavors?"

"Peppermint, spearmint, and others."

"Yoohoo. Jasmine. Oh, Jasmine. Yoohoo."

They glanced at one another and smiled.

"Your mother."

She nodded.

He touched her hand. Already he had been more successful than the hero in the film.

"Will I see you again?"

"Of course."

XXXI

AND THEN THE RAINS CAME. Hadley-Smith was correct, they were different from the ones in Dar es Salaam. They did not even begin the same way. Except for the black cloud there was no buildup, no forewarning, no humidity. No one even noticed that cloud close in.

It happened at night. It just started teeming, so hard that the noise woke him. Sheets of rain thundered against the roof, slashing against the window, striking the windowsill, splashing his chest as he gazed out and saw only blackness and heard only the rain. Dawn came and it was still pouring. And along with the torrent were clouds. Large heavy billowy clouds that were whitish at the fringes, grayer toward the middle, and pitch black at the center.

Those clouds hovered over the lake and the town and the hills beyond. And it turned out that some of those clouds were not celestial, but filled with lake flies. Thousands of gnat-like flies that moved with the rain clouds over the town. Flies in his nose, his eyes, his ears, his food. Flies so thick that sometimes he could not see the opposite side of the street. What he could not figure out

was that the few times the sun did break through, the flies disappeared. Where did they go? Had the sun devoured them? And then
the deluge would begin again, clouds passing in front of the sun,
and magic, the flies were everywhere.

Everyone just accepted it; the torrential rains and the flies and
the quagmire the rains made of the roads. That first rainy morning he found outside the door a pair of knee high rubber boots.
Compliments of Mr. Lewenberg. He tried them on and found they
fit perfectly.

At dinner that evening Lewenberg approached his table. "May
I join you?"

"Of course."

Lewenberg carried a bottle of cognac and was in better spirits
than at any other time since Stephen had arrived. What was different?

"I've brought you a little after-dinner schnapps. I thought you
could use it in this weather." He clapped and called for two glasses.
When they were brought he poured some cognac in each. He raised
his snifter and said, "To the end of the rains." Stephen smiled and
repeated the toast.

"The gumboots fit?"

"Yes. Perfectly, thank you."

"Well, there's no sense in buying a new pair unless you know you're
going to be here a long time. Believe it or not the rains do stop."

"You seem pretty happy. I would have thought the rains…"

"I love the rains, Mr. Ledberg. For me they are a great equalizer.
They treat everyone the same. No one can go outdoors and if they
must it is as uncomfortable for them as for everyone else. And if
one remains inside one knows he is not alone. Everyone is in precisely the same situation. Yes, I've always enjoyed the rainy season
while others have deplored it.

"You need not worry because it is your first and for a while at
least it will be something of a novelty. But I have known men –
and women – who have found the rains a terrible ordeal. In the
old days most people tried to take their leave at this time. But

of course not everyone could. Usually the lower level person-
nel remained. It can be a frightening experience to find yourself
suddenly in total isolation, the only way out by a lake steamer,
which does not come every day, nor even arrive when it is meant
to. Our only contact with the outside world in those days was
the wireless. That and the lake steamer. In the old days those
who remained would go down to the pier no matter what hour
the steamer arrived. They would stand under umbrellas in little
groups watching the loading and unloading, occasionally talking
to whichever passenger was brave enough to come on deck. Some
even went aboard for a meal. They would pretend they were in a
restaurant in Paris or London, anywhere but Buhaya. They would
order quantities of wine and champagne and celebrate until they
were forced to leave. Yes, the long rains have been known to affect people in rather strange ways.

"But tell me, you've been here a bit now. How do you find Jacobson?"

"Jacobson?" He said the name by reflex, his mind still focused
on Lewenberg's reminiscences of the past.

Lewenberg nodded. "Yes, Jacobson."

"He's okay."

"Well perhaps you will discover differently in a few weeks."

"Why?"

"There will be a cooperative meeting soon. The members will
speak their minds."

"Well, so far I have heard no one speak ill of him. He's not
someone I might get close to, but I think it is more his personality
that accounts for all the rumors."

"Rumors, Mr. Ledberg? I don't think they are rumors. You will
not hear anything. But I hear many things. Even my mother hears.
On her trips to Israel she has heard many things."

"What kinds of things?"

Lewenberg glanced at him as if to say, Can I trust you? And
then, deciding either to confide in him or unable to help himself,
said, "Jacobson was sent here as a punishment. My mother was

told that before he came he worked for a grocery chain in Tel Aviv. She was told that there was money missing and Jacobson was sent here."

"Wait a second. You're saying that Jacobson stole money from a grocery store he worked at and was sent here as punishment? Why send him here? Why not arrest him?"

Lewenberg shrugged, sipped some cognac and said, "Who knows? Perhaps no one else would come. Buhaya is not Dar es Salaam. They needed someone. They had this on him and they gave him a choice. Africa has always been the refuge of such choices. Men have come here for centuries to escape their past. It is no accident that the French foreign legion originated in Africa. Livingston, Speke, Burton, even Caesar and Napoleon were driven as much from something as toward whatever it was they hoped to find here. So why not Jacobson? You yourself have told me that he hates it out here."

"Yes, that is true. But I still think you're being hard on him. To be frank I'm not fond of him, but I won't believe those things until I have more solid evidence. I still think it is his personality that is responsible for people's feelings toward him. He's been through a lot, you know. You've seen the number and words on his arm I suppose?"

Lewenberg gazed at him, sad, yellow brown eyes looking across the table. He said, "Yes, I know about that number and those words. But does it give him license to do whatever he wishes? If he was in such a camp would that exonerate him from immoral actions of his own?

"I would think not. I would think to the contrary. I would think that that experience would lead him to be tolerant and not exploit other people. As it is we have heard the number is not real."

"What? What are you talking about? How can you say such a thing?"

Lewenberg continued, never hesitating, "Perhaps I should mention nothing. As you say there is no proof. But then there is no proof that he was in a camp except for that number. And as for the words, do you know what they mean? No? Well, they are arbeit macht frei. Work makes you free. They were the first words the Jews saw upon entering Auschwitz. No one else who survived Auschwitz has those words on their arm. Why does Jacobson? No, I do not think Abraham Jacobson was anywhere near the camps."

Now it was Stephen's turn to stare across the table. "I don't believe it. No one would purposely have his arm tattooed so people would think he was in a concentration camp. How could you think such a story was true?"

Lewenberg shrugged again. "Anything is possible. A man can do anything. As grotesque as it may be it is not unusual. Man has always twisted such things for his own perversion."

"But what possible reason could he have?"

Again Lewenberg shrugged, this time reaching into the pocket of his cardigan to withdraw his pipe. He placed it in his mouth and said, "Who knows? Perhaps if he did avoid the camps he feels guilty now. Perhaps it is an entrée to a job. Such things are common in Israel." He shrugged again. "I do not know. But I do know it is not the first time someone has done this. Nor will it be the last. Even here I worry about these things. Do you know the slogan of TANU?"

"The political party?"

"Precisely. Very good. How did you know that?"

"The minister sang me a song about their exploits."

"Did he tell you their motto?"

Stephen shook his head.

"Uhuru na kazi. Do you know what that means?"

"Uhuru is freedom. I thought it was uhuru na umoja."

"That is the country's motto. No, uhuru na kazi means freedom and work. I find it chilling."

Lewenberg stared at Stephen, causing him to feel uncomfortable. Then Lewenberg stood and walked out of the room leaving Stephen alone and confused. Uhuru na kazi. Arbeit macht frei. Jacobson was never in a concentration camp? What, he wondered, did that mean?

XXXII

The hall was packed for the cooperative meeting. Men, women, children, babies. A brown black sea. And in the front of the room facing them, Jacobson, Deos, Dolores and Sarah.

Puddles of water settled near resting umbrellas or wet coats, the air rancid, an aroma like curdled milk and stale farts, the room reminding Stephen of the recreation hall at summer camp, a gloomy rain tattooing that wooden roof, everyone singing Pack up your troubles in an old kit bag and smile, smile, smile.

There were no smiles in this audience. The women, mainly the women, were jumping to their feet, angrily pointing fingers first at Jacobson, then at Dolores and Sarah, who was dressed in a long black skirt stretching to her ankles, and a white blouse topped with a peter pan collar – where had they found those clothes? – her eyes slits. She wore a haughty expression, looking as if she was about to spit in those women's faces. He thought if Jacobson was attempting to put on a show he had forgotten to provide Sarah with a pair of sunglasses. Dolores was dressed identically, embarrassed, eyes averted, studying the floor. And Jacobson, well, Jacobson was bored, listening to Deos as he translated every time one of the women opened their mouths. Deos saying, "They liki you, bwana. They happy with the shops. They happy with Dolores. They happy with Sarah." Jacobson nodding, arms crossed, that tattoo visible, a tattoo Stephen did not believe had been inscribed for any reason other than the one for which millions of others had died, Jacobson nodding and saying, "Tell them thank you from me."

What, he thought, was going on? Why was Deos telling Jacobson one thing when clearly the opposite was true? Was everything completely turned around out here? Did angry expressions and jabbing fingers signify peace and happiness and satisfaction?

Which was exactly what the man standing in the back of the room wanted to know. A man Stephen had not noticed before. A white island rising to the surface. A very familiar man. My god, what the hell was he doing here? The man in the seersucker jacket and khaki trousers was Ralph Nader, wasn't it?

Nader here? In Africa? So far from the beaten path? Esther Maroon said Nader would have come to Africa when she was discussing that journalist, whatever his name was, who wrote for The New York Times and who had lived in the same town as Nader. Nader addressed Jacobson, the tide changing, "I'm very excited by the participatory nature of this meeting. But I don't understand why you are ignoring these people. It is obvious to me, if it's not to you, that they are very angry."

Stephen's heart was swelling, exultant, even as Jacobson stared in his direction as if to say, So now vhat? This is a friend of yours? And then beckoned him over.

"Who is this? Vhat does he vant?"

Stephen explained. He explained not what he wanted but who Nader was and when he finished Jacobson said angrily to Nader, "You vant to discuss? I discuss with you later, Mr. Nadler."

Embarrassed, Stephen corrected him.

"Ve talk about this later, ya?"

"No," Nader replied, "I think it should be discussed openly and above board. I don't want to be the only person who hears it. I'm only a guest. These people are members of the cooperative."

There was a silence, everyone awaiting Jacobson's reply, the rain drumming the roof, the room damp and humid and uncomfortable.

Jacobson, disgusted, said, "Listen you, whoever you are, Noodler, Nadler, you come out here stickink your nose in people's affairs you don't know from vhere you talk. You go home who is left? Me. I am left. Let me tell you somethink, Mr. Consumer Expert, these people are ankry because I put into their stores thinks besides beans and rice and oil. Vhat do they know? You think they can make a profit on that? You are crazy. You vant I should show you around, okay, tomorrow I show. But tonight you shut up, ya? Okay?"

Stephen expected his hero to counterattack but he did not. Instead he sat down, the meeting hall quieted, the exchange between Nader and Jacobson taking the edge off. People were subdued, even the crying of babies had ceased, the loudest sounds the silence, and the deluge pounding the roof.

Jacobson took advantage of the lull by ending the meeting, sweeping from the hall, Deos and Dolores and Sarah at his heels.

Stephen, on the other hand, waited for Nader, and as he left introduced himself.

"Mr. Nader, I'm Stephen Ledberg. I'm an American. You are a hero of mine. If there is any way I can help I'd love to do that."

"Really? You know who I am?"

"Of course. Unsafe At Any Speed had a great impact on me. I'm an investigative journalist because of you."

"Really?"

They sloshed through the mud and muck toward the hotel, Nader holding an umbrella but offering none of its protection to Stephen, who cared not a whit, exultant at Nader's presence. He thought his parents would never believe his fortune.

"You're staying at Lewenberg's Hotel?" Nader asked.

"I am."

"I am as well. Well, let's get there my friend. Then we'll have a talk over a Coke."

As it turned out they did not talk over a Coke but a game of darts.

"Wow, the English are fantastic," Nader said. "Look at that dartboard. You want a game?"

"Well, I've never played before."

"Neither have I."

Stephen thought, as the game began, that if Nader had never played before he was damn lucky, as Nader's throws hit the target nearly every time whereas Stephen's missed the round corkboard more often than not, his darts striking the wall above or around the target, ricocheting off, ending on the floor, their points penetrating the wood.

"You interested in making a small wager?" Nader inquired.

"I'd rather not. As you can see I'm not very good."

"Me neither. A bet just makes things more interesting."

"If you want."

They bet fifty East African cents per point, Stephen losing handily, Nader toeing the line aggressively, accusing Stephen twice of having stepped over it, not counting those throws, as it happened two of the very few which made him points.

"Do you know why I'm here, Stephen?"

"Not really."

"I'm here to collect data to analyze consumer movements all over the world. Some day we hope there will be an international consumer movement with a central bank of computers feeding information constantly all over the globe. It will be similar to Interpol but we will do our own policing.

"If an American drug company tried to sell something here in Africa which is prohibited in America we'll know about it. What we hope to establish is an international network of ombudsmen. If there is a complaint, against this Jacobson say, why the ombudsman will contact his counterpart in Israel who will in turn contact whoever the elected official is responsible for the Israeli consumer movement or even better Jacobson's direct boss. There would be nothing more effective to short-circuiting bureaucratic layers. It may sound utopian, but we are not that far off. Each day brings us closer to our goal. Someday there will be no more consumer exploitation. Someday everyone, regardless of nationality, religion, or even sexual inclination will have a voice in their own affairs. So whatever you can tell us would be most helpful."

Enthusiastically Stephen told him everything he knew, nuances, rumors, and all. He left nothing out. He told him what Nyarimbere had said. Had Nader met Nyarimbere? He had. He told Nader his impressions of Jacobson, including his cockamamie story about Abraham Lincoln, which he thought Nader would laugh at, but instead Nader said simply, "Really. Really. He thought Abraham Lincoln was a Jew?"

He told him he did not think Dolores and Sarah, the two women in the front of the room, slept with Jacobson but he had no proof. He told him about the padlocked warehouse outside of town and Jacobson's boast that that was the Israeli goal, to supply paint and tires and irrigation equipment to the Tanzanian government. He even told him about the number and words on Jacobson's arm and that Lewenberg did not believe they were real. And when he finished, exhausted, Nader said, "You've been a great help, Stephen. You should think of working for me when you return home. You interested in doing that?"

Stephen, his heart swelling, pulse pounding, said, "Absolutely. I would love to do that."

"Great. Oh, one last thing. If I asked you to work over a weekend and you had a personal matter to take care of, which would you attend to first?"

"I don't understand. What do you mean?"

"Well, suppose your father was ill. Would you go to the hospital or to the office?"

Why was Nader asking that question? Was there a trick here? What was going on? Would the job now depend solely on how he responded? Why would Nader ask the question if he did not want him to say, why go to work, of course, Mr. Nader? That would be the answer Nader wanted, wouldn't it? But that would not be the truth. Maybe you told a fib to secure the job? But suppose Nader was testing him. Wouldn't everyone want to see their father first? Wouldn't Nader? That was it. Nader was testing his truthfulness. Everyone would see their father first. So that is what he told Nader.

"I admire your honesty, Stephen. Yes, I admire your honesty."

Stephen felt that that statement was about to be followed by a but, but it was not. Instead Nader threw a dart with passion and precision and, Stephen thought, anger and disappointment, striking the target dead center.

"Game over, Stephen. Big day tomorrow. I'm going to bed."

Stephen sat at the bar upset and confused. Should he have told Nader what he wanted to hear? But that would have been dishonest. Never tell a lie, that's what his father always said. You tell one lie you'll have to tell a hundred more until you'll forget what you lied about in the first place. A calculus of lies. Who cut down the cherry tree, George? I did, dad.

"What's the matter with you?" Lewenberg had a bundle of newspapers tucked under his arm.

He told him.

"That man's a hero of yours?"

"Yes."

"He'll be lucky to get out of here in one piece from what I hear."

"Why? What do you hear?"

"He's angered the wrong people by his antics tonight."

"You sound as if he angered you as well."

"He has."

"But why? He challenged Jacobson. He brought things out in the open. Isn't that what you wanted?"

"Not this way. This man leaves tomorrow. Who is going to pick up the pieces?" Lewenberg withdrew the newspapers under his arm and said, "Here. I have no use for these right now. You might as well read them. Just leave them downstairs when you finish."

Stephen lay on his bed skimming the newspapers but his mind was more focused on the turmoil the evening had brought. Lewenberg and Jacobson had said the same thing. But were they correct? Had Nader come and left a mess? What about the way he had treated Stephen? Why did the one question determine whether or not Stephen would be offered a job? Couldn't Nader see how well he understood the situation, wasn't that what was most important? Would someone else have answered differently? Maybe. Maybe someone who did not care about his father. Maybe someone who knew Nader expected that answer. Maybe... until he noticed a photograph in The Daily Nation. What the hell? Was it possible? Not possible. He read the caption. "First Kenya Open Golf Tournament." The photo was grainy. He reread the caption again more carefully. "Mama Kitabu, popular chanteuse appearing nightly at the River Road Club, sings national anthem at Muthaiga Golf Club."

He looked at the date of the paper. It was over two weeks old. He studied the photograph again. Was the man missing a left arm? He could not really tell but it certainly looked like Lefty. What the hell was he doing out here? If it was Lefty, Stephen wondered if he was still here. He would love to see him, but he had no idea how to contact him unless he went to Nairobi. And why not? Jasmine's uncle had said it was the Paris of Africa. He studied the photograph again. Yes, by god, that was Lefty. Suddenly he was feeling a lot better about himself. Was that because of Lefty? Or only because he had a plan which gave him some direction? Who would have dreamed when he woke up this morning that Ralph Nader and Lefty would be in Africa? He knew why Nader was here. But what in the world had brought Lefty?

XXXIII

HE KNOCKED LIGHTLY ON THE DOOR. There was no answer so he knocked again. Still no answer so he knocked a little harder. He heard nothing. He twisted the knob and the door opened. He hesitated, peered in and cried, "Mr. Nader? Mr. Nader?"

The room was in shambles. Clothes strewn about, the bed unmade, a suitcase opened on the floor. Stephen could not help himself. Old habits were hard to break.

The suitcase contained nothing out of the ordinary. Some autographed copies of Unsafe At Any Speed. An old Princeton Alumni Weekly. Fruit of the Loom underwear. Arrow shirts. Ties from Tie City. A cache of hotel size toothpaste and soap. But beneath the clothes was a manila envelope. He picked it up and looked inside. It was stuffed with newspaper clippings. Were they stories about Nader? No, they were stories from The New York Times written by David Halberstam. About the Vietnam war. They were stories that contradicted what the military commanders had said, stories critical of the leaders of South Vietnam. There were stories about the

American soldiers fighting the war. Why had he never seen these before? How could Esther Maroon have thought they were trash? Of course The New York Times would never have printed these if they did not trust Halberstam. But why did Nader have them in his suitcase? So absorbed was he that he did not hear Nader enter.

"What the hell are you doing?"

"Oh, I'm sorry. I knocked on your door to say goodbye and found it open. I shouldn't have come in."

"No, you shouldn't have. I could have you arrested."

"Well, you've been such a hero to me. I feel so badly about the way things went last night…"

"What's that in your hand?"

"This? They're articles by a New York Times reporter, David Halberstam. On the war. I'm sorry. Here."

"By a New York Times reporter? You don't know who David Halberstam is?"

He shook his head. "The first time I heard his name was when Esther Maroon mentioned him."

"Esther Maroon? You know Esther?"

"I do."

"You must be the only American who doesn't know who Halberstam is. Didn't you tell me you were a journalist? How is it possible?"

"We don't get The New York Times in Wichita, Kansas. But why do you have all these old clippings of his?"

"That's none of your business."

"I'm sorry. Oh, I remember now. Esther Maroon told me you both grew up in the same town."

"Esther told you that? What else did she say?"

"She told me you should be my role model. Not Halberstam."

"She did?"

Nader's face brightened, as if a teacher had patted him on the head. "You really want to know the truth?"

Stephen nodded.

"I keep these because eventually they disintegrate. I enjoy watching them turn to dust."

"I don't understand. You don't like…"

"The truth is he's always been my nemesis. He has always tried to be one step ahead of me. He has always rubbed that in my face. Here, let me show you something."

Nader unzipped a pocket of the suitcase and withdrew a small envelope containing a number of two-by-three photographs, headshots of a severe looking bespectacled longish-faced man with a short haircut.

"You know who this is?"

"Halberstam?"

"Yes, Halberstam. They're mug shots. The Times takes them of all their journalists when they go overseas. He always referred to them as morgue shots. He was trying to impress me. He always said they'll use them for his obit if he dies overseas.

"But do you know how I came by so many? No, of course you don't. He stayed with me the night before he left for Vietnam. When I returned home after he left, I found them tucked in mirrors and frames, inside books, under my clothes, even taped to the bathroom mirror. He has always tried to one up me.

"We competed for everything. I wanted to go to Harvard so badly. But they chose him."

"Well, Princeton's not exactly…"

"Princeton's not Harvard. The Daily Princetonian is not The Harvard Crimson. He even stole the only girl I have ever loved. When we were in fifth grade. Amanda Bernstein. He was supposed to be my friend. But he stole her from me. He probably doesn't even remember. He probably never thinks of her. But I do. And do you know where she is now? She lives in Toledo, Ohio. She is married, she married a dentist. Do you know what they named their first child? No, of course you don't. She named her first child David. I bet her husband doesn't even know why."

"You've kept in contact with her?"

"No. But people in our class keep me informed. And I will tell you this. One day the Viet Cong may put up a statue of Halberstam in Hanoi because his articles have as much to do with helping them win the war as they do. But I guarantee you this. When all is said and done, Winsted, Connecticut will erect a statue of me, not him. Now get out of here. I have to pack and leave."

XXXIV

"THE RAINS GETTING TO YOU?" Lewenberg asked.

"This you mean?" Stephen brought the glass to his lips.

"Yes. Schnapps before dinner? You want to get tipsy?"

"Actually, yes."

"What is going on?"

"I don't know. I feel I've destroyed any chance I may have had to work for Ralph Nader. Not only did I answer his question incorrectly, but I barged into his room this morning."

"You did? Well, you shouldn't have done that. But he did not say anything to me about it. I shouldn't worry if I were you. What was the question he asked you?"

He told him.

"I would have answered it exactly as you did. I would have seen my father first and then gone to the office. Why do you think it was the wrong answer?"

"Because of the way he reacted. He was angry. I'm certain it is not what he wanted to hear."

"Well, why would you want to work for him then? You don't need to work for that kind of person."

He thought Lewenberg did not understand. After all, Lewenberg was not an American. How could he understand how important it would be to work for Ralph Nader?

Changing the subject, Stephen said, "Do you remember you gave me a stack of newspapers last night?"

"Yes, of course I do."

"Well, it turns out that I saw a photograph of an old friend from home in one of them."

"Really? What's wrong with that? It wasn't an old girlfriend, was it?"

"No. It seems there was some sort of golf tournament in Nairobi. He was there."

"Is he a golfer?"

"No, he's actually a caddy."

"A caddy? Well, he must have been caddying for someone."

"That's possible. Do you play golf?"

"Me? Play golf? First, there are no golf courses for miles. You would have to go to Entebbe, Uganda for that. And to put it bluntly, it is not a game that Jews would play."

"Oh. Why is that?"

"Have you ever heard of a famous Jewish golfer? Golf is a game alien to us. Few Jews grew up anywhere near a golf club. I can assure you if there had been a famous Jewish golfer the Jewish community would know."

"Seeing my friend's photograph set off something in me. I'm not sure what it is."

"You're homesick."

"Perhaps, but it's more. You see in a way I'm out here because I was fired from my job as a journalist covering a story about a golf course."

"Why were you fired?"

"I don't know."

"What was the story about?"

"Well, it's a little embarrassing. There is one hole on the course that is so short the golfers can hit the green from the tee. Some golfers may be lucky enough to make a hole-in-one."

"A hole-in-one?"

"Well, most golf holes are so far away they require the player to hit the ball three or four times or more before it goes into the cup. But this hole is so short it only requires one shot. My boss, the publisher, wanted to find out why so many women were hitting their shots directly into the cup. And it's what we found out that was so disturbing."

"And what was that?"

"I'd rather not go into the details. But what we found was that the women did not really hit their balls into the cup. The caddies put them there."

"My god, they were cheating. But why?"

"That's the thing. When the women discovered they had made holes-in-one they… well, let's just say they … disrobed, and the caddies…"

"My god. You Americans. Were they sacked?"

"Sacked?"

"Were those blokes sacked? I would have sacked them on the spot. If one of my blokes did something like that they would be sacked instantly." Lewenberg picked up his glass of cognac and drank half of it.

"That's another thing. They were never fired, but I was."

"How is that possible?"

Stephen shrugged. "I don't know. Perhaps they didn't want to bother with training new caddies."

"Did he publish the story?"

"No."

"Then why did he have you do all that work?"

" I just don't know."

"Well, now that you have brought up this deplorable subject, what about the shopkeepers?"

"The shopkeepers?"

"Yes. Jacobson's shopkeepers. What about them?"

"What about them?"

"Have you asked them if they have been sleeping with him?"

Lewenberg's directness embarrassed him.

"Ask them? I would never do that."

"Why not?"

"Why not? Would you like me to ask you such a personal question?"

"I would not mind. I have nothing to hide."

"Well, I'm not going to do it."

"Then what will you tell the minister when you return to Dar es Salaam?"

"I'm not going back to Dar es Salaam. I'm going to Nairobi."

"Nairobi?"

"Yes, I'm going to find my friend Lefty. I'm going to see if he is still in Nairobi."

"But how will the minister learn of your impressions here?"

"I will write him a report."

Lewenberg picked up his glass of cognac and emptied it. "What will you put in your report?"

"I will certainly tell him about the way Jacobson treats the coop members. I will suggest that Jacobson be replaced. He wants to go home anyway. I am sure the minister will hear the same from Nader."

Lewenberg glanced at him quizzically. "Nader? He has gone to Nairobi as well. He will never return to Dar. No, a report will never do. A report they will file and forget. If you do not return to Dar, nothing will change. It has always been that way up here."

"It has?"

"Yes, it is because of the lake."

Lewenberg sucked on the stem of his pipe, removed it, and set it on the white linen tablecloth. "The lake acts as a baffle," he said. "It absorbs everything. Unless the people in Dar actually see you, we do not exist."

He paused. "If only the lake had worked as a baffle from the rest of the world as well, my father might be alive today." An expression of immense sadness crossed Lewenberg's face.

"What do you mean?"

"If only my father had not glimpsed snatches of what was going on in Europe. If only mail from his cousins had not stopped. If only we had not had a wireless. If only the occasional refugee had not filtered through with stories of what the Germans were doing to the Jews. If only… But this is inappropriate. It is the past. I should not be telling you these things. I don't know why I am."

"No, no. Go on."

Lewenberg studied Stephen's face, an attempt, Stephen felt, to determine if he could handle what he was about to hear. Then, concluding either that Stephen could or just that he had all ready gone too far, Lewenberg said, "The more my father heard of these things the more disturbed he became. He barely slept. If not for my mother the hotel would have wasted away. Every waking hour my father consumed the Torah."

"The Torah?"

"Yes. Surely you are familiar with the Torah? I know you said you are not a Jew but still… The Torah is the first five books of the Old Testament. Surely you are familiar…"

"No, I am not."

"That is not possible."

"It's true."

"But surely you have heard of Genesis and Exodus. Everyone…"

"Genesis. Yes, of course, Adam and Eve. But no, not really Exodus."

"How is that possible?"

Stephen shrugged. "I went to church with my parents. But except for the music, I am embarrassed to say I am ignorant of these things. I barely listened to the minister. I found it boring. I never took religion courses in college nor have I ever read the Bible."

"How is it possible to go through university and never read any of the Bible? What sort of education is that?"

"You are right. I agree with you. It is embarrassing. But why don't you tell me what it was that your father was looking for in the Torah."

"I don't know if I should."

"Please. I would like to hear and it is helping me forget myself."

"No, no. I think given the circumstances I ought not to do that."

Stephen drank from his glass, set it down, and said, "Really, I am a journalist. There is nothing you might say that would offend or surprise me."

Lewenberg thought, twiddled with his pipe, and said, "For years we went as a family to the hills overlooking the plains to watch the annual burning of the grasses and the shrubs. But now my father went alone save for the Torah.

"He sat there all day and watched the flames and listened to the dry grass snapping in the hot air, the smoke spreading for miles. He sat there until the sun set and the very next morning he would return to stare at the charred earth. He did that day after day until the first green splinter of grass appeared. Then he never went again.

"He wandered around the hotel and the lawn and the edge of the lake. He muttered to himself. He wasn't addressing anyone. He was just speaking to the air. 'I understand it. I understand it now.' 'What, papa? What do you understand?' God is a coward. God is a bully.' 'Papa, stop it. You are frightening me. It is blasphemous what you say.' 'Only cowards and bullies need to test people. Why threaten Abraham? Why test him? If you are God what is the need of that? Babel was no threat to God. Why scatter them to the four corners of the earth? God is so insecure. If he is a God why is he so insecure? Perhaps it is because of Jacob.' 'What, papa? What is because of Jacob?' 'It is Jacob who has caused us to be cursed. Why wasn't Jacob punished? Was Jacob in a camp? I understand now. It is so clear.' 'What is, papa? What is so clear?' 'Adam and Eve were not the first displaced persons. God was. Who had tempted him? Who had scorned him? Who had bullied him? From what corner of the universe was he flung?'

"My mother and I were beside ourselves. She cried constantly. One day my father began ransacking the hotel's kitchen screaming nazi, nazi, nazi. I thought he was hallucinating, that he thought there were Germans somewhere in the kitchen. My mother understood. He loved coconuts. He was looking for a coconut. It was not the season. You see the Swahili word for coconut is nazi.

"I was relieved. I thought he is coming to his senses. But then all my hopes came crashing down at Yom Kippur."

Lewenberg was parched. He finished his cognac in one fling, picked up the glass of water and swiftly drank that. Stephen realized they had eaten nothing. He wanted to order dinner but was afraid to interrupt Lewenberg.

"You see for years we held religious holidays at the hotel. The few Jews who lived within driving distance would come. If we did not have a minyan we asked the staff to join. They did not mind. But they minded that day.

"The service was proceeding as usual when suddenly my father stood and shouted. Alhamdu lilahi. Inshallah. Mungu akijalia. Baruch hashem. Baruch atoh adonoy. Dia dhuit. Buichos le Dia. Wenn es gottes Willen ist. Se dues quiser. Where was all this coming from? It terrified and embarrassed me. I didn't know what to do. My mother was hysterical. The staff looked as if they wanted to bolt. The others, well, the others tried to ignore him."

"What do all those phrases mean?"

With an air of despair, he said, "They are all the same, in many languages. God bless. God willing. God is great. Neither my mother nor I knew he understood all those languages. Where had he learned Portuguese? Where had he learned Celtic?

"But the oddest thing was, he spoke each sentence as I have just done and he spoke them backward as well. At first I thought it was gibberish. Then I understood. How was that possible? From what madness had that come?

"Early the following morning he took the Torah from the Ark, walked down to the shore, climbed into a rowboat, and rowed out onto the lake. My mother ran after him. I followed. She was screaming, Samuel, Samuel, what are you doing? Come back. Have you gone mad? Then such a terrible thing. He threw the scrolls into the lake.

"My mother collapsed. She lay there motionless. I didn't know what to do.

"When my father stepped on shore he said, God works in mysterious ways not because he is a mystery but because he is devious. Esau. That was his last word. The very next day he was dead."

Lewenberg's mouth turned down as if he were about to cry. But he did not. He drank a long draught of water.

"The doctor said he had had a brain aneurism. But we will never know for certain. But here's the odd thing," he took a deep breath, "three days later the largest tilapia ever seen washed up on the shore. Inside this great fish was the discarded Torah."

With those words Lewenberg began to sob. He brought his hands to his face in a feeble attempt to hide his emotions.

"It's alright."

"Forgive me. You are the first person in all these years. I feel so foolish. Please excuse me."

"It's alright." Stephen reached over to touch Lewenberg's arm but was startled when he rose suddenly.

"Wait here. I will be right back."

While Stephen sat turning the story over in his mind, he recalled the day he and his parents had attended an all-star high school football game. The most valuable player, holding high his trophy, exclaimed, "I want to thank my mom and my dad and my dog." Everyone snickered. Stephen's mother leaned over and said, I know that boy. They should leave him alone. He is dyslectic. He meant to say God.

Stephen had thought about that. It had never occurred to him until that moment that there were words which, when pronounced backward, spelled other words. Why was that? And was it the same in other languages? After that football game he had spent weeks poring through the dictionary searching for such words, wondering what it meant – abut, flog, laid, pots, snip, loot, rood, teem, lag, tar, pans, raw, mood, omen, spit, mad, warts, ward, wed, drab, jar. He even wondered if some sort of commercial word game could be constructed. But he soon ran out of words, became frustrated, and gave up. None were as interesting or as powerful as dog, he thought, although sore and live came close.

Lewenberg returned with a scroll, the paper starched, scaly, with streaks of blood, patches of dried mucous. The waiters began to move restlessly, glancing at one another.

"You see how they talk amongst themselves. They are superstitious. They think this caused my father's death."

Delicately, he unrolled the scroll.

"See."

Although the water from the lake had damaged the parchment, Stephen could make out two names obviously inked in. One, Jacob, was blotted with a line drawn through it. Alongside, in large capital letters, the name ESAU, which strangely had been untouched.

"Your father wrote these names?"

"Yes. He should not have."

"How do you explain that the name Esau is not damaged?"

"How indeed. Do you know the story of Jacob and Esau?"

Stephen had begun unconsciously to hum to himself when Lewenberg first mentioned Jacob. Now he realized it was a tune from his childhood. We are climbing Jacob's ladder, soldiers of the cross. Did Lewenberg know the song? Was that the Jacob Lewenberg's father was referring to?

Lewenberg shook his head. "I cannot imagine why anyone would write a song about that man.

"After my father's death, at every free moment I pored over the Bible. All of it. Both the Old Testament and the New. No story can match that of Jacob and Esau. It has taken years to understand. It is so convoluted. If you wish I will tell it, and after the telling see if you would write a song about Jacob."

Stephen nodded, feeling faint from hunger. He glanced at his watch. They had been sitting and drinking and talking for over two hours.

"Jacob and Esau were twins. God had said to Rebecca, their mother, the first will serve the younger. Esau was born minutes before Jacob. Esau was a hunter, a man of nature, a lady's man, while Jacob, well, Jacob was a mama's boy. He stayed home, close to his mother's apron. He was the apple of his mother's eye, as you Americans would say."

Lewenberg paused and drank, Stephen thinking they were both becoming quite drunk.

"I was a little like Jacob. I was never adventurous. I suppose in a way I was a mama's boy as well. And you, Mr. Ledberg, were you a mama's boy?"

Stephen felt himself blush.

"No, I don't think so."

"Well, one day Esau came in from a day of hunting. He was famished."

As am I, thought Stephen.

"Jacob had cooked a huge pot of lentil soup. Esau wanted some."

That did it. The mention of food was overwhelming. He interrupted Lewenberg to ask that they order something.

"Oh, how rude of me. I apologize." He called over one of the waiters.

"Will sandwiches do?"

"Anything will do."

Lewenberg asked for chicken and roast beef sandwiches with mango chutney and a plate of cheese and crackers.

"Now where was I?"

"The lentil soup." And Stephen smiled.

"Oh yes. Esau asked his brother for some of the soup. And do you know what Jacob said?"

"No."

"Jacob said, I will give you some in exchange for your birthright. He wanted everything Esau, as the oldest child, would inherit, land, riches, in exchange for a bowl of soup."

"And did Esau agree to that?"

Lewenberg stared again at Stephen and nodded.

"Would you give up your birthright for a bowl of soup, Mr. Ledberg, or even a roast beef sandwich?" he asked as the food was placed on the table.

Stephen wanted to say, I just wish I knew what my birthright was, but instead he shook his head, "I have to admit I was ravenous, but I am not sure I would sell my birthright for food, even a roast beef sandwich as good as this. Why did Esau?"

"I have thought about that question for years. Why would he do that? Maybe he understood that it was his birthright and all it entailed which kept his relationship with Jacob from becoming a loving one. If Jacob wanted material things let him have them.

"Esau was a remarkable young man. He did not care about frills. He did not care about trappings. They did not concern him. He was a young man who knew himself. But there was one thing he did care about."

"What was that?"

"His father's blessing. One day when Isaac, his father, was old and blind he said to Esau, Go out into the fields and kill some game. Return and cook me my favorite meal and I will bless you.

"Rebecca overheard what Isaac said. She went to Jacob, told him what she had heard and said, Go out to our flock. Kill two kids, put on your brother's clothes. I will cook your father the meal he wants before your brother returns. You will serve it and he will bless you.

"Jacob said, But he will know it is not Esau by the sound of my voice. And suppose he wants to touch my skin?"

"Touch his skin? I…"

"Yes, Esau had hair that covered his body while Jacob was fair-skinned. So Rebecca said, Take the skin from one of the kids and wrap it around your arms and the back of your hands."

"But why was Rebecca doing this? I understand Jacob was her favorite," for a moment Stephen thought of Ingy Reticent admiring his youngest daughter's photograph, "but it seems to me Rebecca is…"

Lewenberg interrupted him. "It is what my father saw. Oh, he saw so well."

"What did he see?"

"He understood that Jacob had told Rebecca about Esau's birthright."

"He did?"

"Yes. He understood that Jacob would want his mother to be proud of him. It was the first time he had ever accomplished anything so daring. Proud as a peacock, feathers unfurled, he strutted in to tell his mother.

"But Rebecca was horrified. She did not share his pride. Rebecca saw the enormity of his folly."

"I don't get it."

"You will. When Esau returned to discover his father had blessed Jacob instead of himself, he went into a rage. Had he found Jacob he might have killed him. But Rebecca had heard Esau screaming that he was going to kill Jacob and she sent Jacob on a long journey to her brother's home. And here, Mr. Ledberg, is more proof of Jacob's inadequacies."

"Why is that?"

"Jacob fell in love with Rachel, his uncle's youngest daughter."

"He fell in love with his cousin?"

"Yes. In those days they were not aware of the dangers. Rachel's father told Jacob he could marry Rachel if he worked for him for seven years. When that time expired, Jacob demanded Rachel. Oh, such a story."

Lewenberg's body sprang to life. His eyes widened. He became animated. His words flowed strongly.

"The morning after their nuptial night Jacob discovered it was not Rachel with whom he had slept, but her older sister Leah."

"What? What are you talking about? How is it possible he slept with the wrong woman? That is in the Bible? I don't understand."

"Precisely. How is it possible that Jacob, who lived with his cousins for seven years, did not know it was not Rachel but her sister Leah with whom he coupled? How?"

Lewenberg's lips were quivering.

"Some say because Leah was veiled. Veiled, Mr. Ledberg. But unless they were physically identical, unless they were identical twins... Oh, Esau would have known. Esau would have known the woman who came to his bed was not Rachel. Esau would have ranted and raved. He would have smelled it was not Rachel. Oh, such a story."

Stephen recalled a group of classmates at college bragging that if you put a paper bag over their heads, all women were the same. The crudity and cruelty had curdled his stomach, making him ill, wondering why he felt so devastated by that remark – why couldn't he join in their merriment? – as they slapped each other on the back and laughed. Was that the derivative of that inanity? Jacob and Leah?

"What did Jacob do?"

"He accepted his uncle's explanation. I could never permit my youngest daughter to be married before my eldest. Work for me another seven years and you shall have Rachel. Why if that man had said that to Esau..."

"But the saga continues, Mr. Ledberg. Jacob finally returns home. He marches back followed by a huge entourage. As he approaches the land in which he was born he sends ahead a group of men with cattle and gifts to make certain Esau will do him no harm. Oh, such a story. And here is what my father fathomed. Esau, upon seeing his brother, runs to him with outstretched arms. He hugs and kisses him. And do you know what Jacob said?"

Stephen shook his head.

"Jacob said, I see in your face the face of God. Now do you understand, Mr. Ledberg? Now do you grasp what my father and Rebecca understood?"

Stephen felt foolish. What was it he was meant to see? He shook his head.

Lewenberg seemed again on the verge of tears, but this time Stephen felt they would not be tears of sadness but joy.

"When Esau gave his birthright to Jacob, Jacob became the eldest and Esau the youngest. Jacob was meant to serve Esau. That is what Rebecca saw. That is what Rebecca understood. The only way to correct that, she hoped, was with Isaac's blessing. Oh, don't you see. Abraham, Isaac, and Esau, Mr. Ledberg. That is who the patriarchs were meant to be. If what my father saw is correct, and it is, to say nothing of Rebecca's terror, then Judaism is flawed. Is it because of Jacob there were pogroms? Is it because of Jacob there were concentration camps? Is it because of Jacob that the world hates Jews? Would things be different if Esau had been the third patriarch, as he was meant to be, and not Jacob, a man who attained the position through guile and weakness?"

Tears poured from Lewenberg's eyes, his body heaving, tears caressing his cheeks. But there was no sadness on his face, only joy. Joy accompanied by music. Music? Stephen had imagined he heard music when Lewenberg began his tale of the twins. But the music had become more defined. Where was it coming from? Was he so drunk and so tired that he was imagining music? Even the waiters were crying. Tears of ecstasy were soaking their long calico gowns, washing over their feet, those feet no longer chalky and scratched, but shades of glorious brown, brown, he thought, a darker shade of pale. In that dining room there was no heart of darkness, only an ocean of tearful joy and majestic music while rain pounded the earth outside.

"You hear it? I can see from your expression that you hear the music too. It is alright. It happens each time I think of the truth of the story of Jacob and Esau. I just have never told anyone before. I have not even told my mother. Do you know what the music is?

"No? Beethoven. Usually it is only the opening notes to the Ode. But tonight it goes on and on. I can see that you hear the kettledrums and horns and strings. And now the voices." Lewenberg's eyes were shut, his head like a baton moving with the music. "I often wonder if those opening notes were written for Esau. Was that who the deaf Beethoven was celebrating? Esau, Mr. Ledberg, was a better man than Jesus Christ."

"He was?"

"But have any parents ever named their child Esau? If they have I would like to meet them."

His eyes still shut, his head conducting the final movement of the symphony, he continued, "Do you know the story of Christ and the fig tree?"

"No."

Lewenberg opened his eyes, withdrew a pouch from his pocket, retrieved his pipe, opened the pouch, plucked a pinch of tobacco, stuffed it into the bowl, a waiter brought a box of matches, the tobacco lit, "A few weeks before his death Christ awoke famished. In the distance he noticed a fig tree. He approached it but saw there was no fruit. It was not the season. And do you know what he did? He destroyed the tree."

"He destroyed the tree? Jesus Christ destroyed a fig tree? I don't believe it. Why?" The story reminded Stephen of another tree, George Washington's cherry tree, and he wondered if Jesus Christ's father had asked him, who destroyed the fig tree, son? Had Christ answered, I did, father?

"Why indeed?" Lewenberg shrugged. "Christ had a tantrum. He was like Nectarinia when she is hungry and wants her food instantly. She throws her spoon to the floor."

Lewenberg puffed furiously on his pipe, the tobacco's aroma neither as sweet nor as distinctive as Reticent's, Stephen thinking the blend lacked even a hint of latakia.

Lewenberg settled into his chair, neglecting the cognac, concentrating on the music and the story.

"Have you ever read Dostoevsky's The Brothers Karamazov, Mr. Ledberg?"

"No."

"No? Well, neither had I until one of my guests brought it to my attention. It was Stone who pointed out for me the story of Christ and the fig tree. Stone said there is a chapter in The Brothers Karamazov titled The Grand Inquisitor.

"In that chapter it is Dostoevsky's conceit that Christ returns to earth, is arrested, and is interrogated by the Grand Inquisitor. Stone said Christ refused to answer any questions either because he did not wish to incriminate himself or, more likely, Stone thought, because the Inquisitor asked the wrong questions and because the Inquisitor was more intent on his own bravado. Like most egoists, Stone said, the Inquisitor only wished to talk about himself. Stone said if Christ returned to earth today, he would have just two questions to ask. Christ, he said, would most likely not respond, but Stone would ask them anyway."

Lewenberg paused, finished his glass of water, and re-lit the tobacco in his pipe.

"Stone pretended I was Christ. He said, you knew, didn't you, when you destroyed the fig tree, that you had committed a crime? You tried to cover it up, didn't you, by pretending you had performed a miracle? See what you can do, you said, when you have faith. You can destroy trees, move mountains. Faith, Stone said to me, what does faith have to do with killing a tree? Why, he said to me, imagining I was Christ, did you not admit you had made a mistake and bring the tree back to life? You could have done that. You had the power to do that. Perhaps, he said to me, your mind was on other things. You knew your death was imminent. It is excusable to make a mistake under such pressure. Luke excuses you. Matthew and Mark write the story as it happened but Luke, Luke understood the pressure you were under and changed the story. He understood historians would not view the parable of the fig tree favorably. He changed it completely. It is all right, Stone said to me, to admit your fallibility."

Stephen said, "Matthew, Mark, Luke, they were…"

"The recorders of Christ's life."

"Did you tell this Stone person about Jacob and Esau?"

"No. I had not yet understood what it was my father had discovered. As you will see I wish I had."

"Then what was the second question this Stone would have asked Christ?"

"Oh, yes. Still pretending I was Christ he said, At the end, when you were on the cross, you uttered two conflicting statements, My God, my God, why has thou forsaken me and the other, forgive them, father, for they know not what they do. Which, Stone asked, was the truth? Perhaps, Stone said, they are both true. It is fine, he said, for you to admit that. It would make you more human. But you must answer the question. If you doubted yourself at the end that is all right. Perhaps we all doubt at the end.

"By this time I was beginning to feel very uncomfortable, as if I were Christ. It terrified me. I found myself under enormous pressure to answer Stone's questions as if I were defending Christ. I wanted Stone to cease. Finally, I asked him to stop.

"The odd thing is that the story does not end there."

"What do you mean?"

"Many months later I received in the post a copy of The Brothers Karamazov. Stone had sent it. I turned straight away to the chapter."

"The Grand Inquisitor?"

"Precisely. Actually, Stone had failed to mention the most important part of the story."

"He had? How is that possible?" Stephen imagining there was not much more of importance the author could have added.

"After the Grand Inquisitor finished with Christ, after Christ had sat unwavering in his silence, do you know what he did?"

"What? What did he do?" Stephen imagining Christ had spoken finally.

"He stood. Christ stood and walked over to his inquisitor and …" Lewenberg paused, filled his lungs.

"And? And?"

"Kissed him."

"Kissed him? Jesus Christ kissed the Grand Inquisitor?"

"Yes. Christ kissed the Grand Inquisitor."

"Just like…"

"Exactly. Just like Esau does Jacob."

"So, wait, you think Jesus knew the story of Jacob and Esau?"

"Precisely. Of course he did. Jesus knew the Torah backward and forward. He would have known the story of Jacob and Esau."

"So you think Jesus' teachings grew from Esau's example?"

"I do."

The music had ended. The only sound in the room was of the rain falling outside.

"But who is this Stone person who put you through all this?"

"Isidor Feinstein Stone. A Jew. He is an American journalist. Surely you have heard of him?"

"Isidor Feinstein Stone? I. F. Stone. Do you mean I. F. Stone? That Stone? He was here? In Buhaya? The I. F. Stone who writes a newsletter?"

"Precisely. That one. He was with his brother-in-law and their wives. They came to view the lake. He called himself Izzy."

"I. F. Stone was here? That's just amazing. Who is his brother-in-law? What was his name?"

"I do not recall his name. He was very handsome. A barrister, I believe. But he was no match for Stone.

"I suggested to Stone that perhaps if there had been journalists, like himself, in Christ's day they would have recorded the truth. He scoffed at me. A journalist, he said, a journalist would have gotten it wrong."

"Stone said that?"

"But you are a journalist, I said. Why do you demean…"

"I am not that kind. I work for myself. No one tells me what to cover. No one edits me. I have no need for advertisers. Somehow, he said, I think the journalists would have missed something, or not asked the right questions, or even if they had it right, been edited wrong or maybe even someone would have decided it wasn't a good enough story. And then he said something that haunts me to this day."

"Which was?"

"He said the most difficult truths to know are our own."

"What did he mean by that?"

Lewenberg shrugged. "I'm not sure."

"You didn't ask him?"

" No, I didn't. But I know one thing," Lewenberg pointed the stem of his pipe toward Stephen. "Stone would have asked the shopkeepers if they were sleeping with Jacobson."

Lewenberg's transition confused Stephen. How had he gone from Jacob and Esau and Christ and I. F. Stone to the shopkeepers?

"No. I don't think so," Stephen said. "I don't think Stone would have done that. He told you he was not that kind of journalist. He researches. I have read that he is the only person in America who actually goes through the nation's budget line by line. He discovers where money is wasted. He finds senators or congressmen who have appropriated funds for pet projects of their own. I read that each congressional office subscribes to his newsletter, that he makes more money from them than anyone else, because he has done their work for them. He is not a journalist in the everyday sense of the word. No, I. F. Stone would not have asked the shopkeepers that question."

Lewenberg puffed on his pipe. "Perhaps you are right. I remember his telling me he wanted to learn Greek."

"Greek? Why did he want to do that?"

"He said that one of the things that bothered him ever since he was a young man is why the Athenians murdered Socrates. He said one of the things he hoped to accomplish before he died was to find that answer. He felt he could only do that by learning Greek. Perhaps you are correct. Perhaps Stone would not have been interested in the shopkeepers. But I know someone who would."

"Oh, really? And who is that?"

"Halberstam. David Halberstam. He would have asked that question."

Stephen looked at his watch. It was almost two o'clock in the morning. Jacob. Esau. Christ. Beethoven. Stone. Halberstam. Was he dreaming?

"I suppose you're going to tell me he stayed here as well?"

Lewenberg nodded. "When he was stationed in the Congo. He stayed here for a few days."

"You know he was a friend of Nader's. They grew up in the same town."

"Did he? Well, Nader can't hold a candlestick to Halberstam. I wish I had had more time to talk with him. He made one remark about Africa I shall never forget."

"What was that?"

"He said Africa's progress should not be judged by the number of roads or schools or dams built, but in the freedom of our journalists. The success of a nation, he said, can be measured by the number of independent newspapers. The more the merrier. Yes, I wish I had had more time to talk with him."

"Why didn't you?"

"He was preoccupied."

"Preoccupied?"

"Yes. He was with the most beautiful African woman I have ever seen. I often wonder what became of her."

Lewenberg gazed off into the distance, his pipe in his mouth, his body erect.

"Yes, I often wonder what happened to her."

"Were you in love with her?"

Lewenberg's head snapped back. He stared unblinking at Stephen.

"No, no, no, no. I was never in love with her."

He looked at his watch. "It is late, very late. You will have to excuse me."

He stood, gathered the scrolls. He glanced at his glass of cognac. Stephen noticed a lake fly floating on the surface, the fly motionless, either dead or dead drunk. Lewenberg picked up the glass, drained the remains, lake fly and all, excused himself again and departed, leaving Stephen exhausted and drunk, but not so exhausted and drunk that he was unaware that something miraculous had occurred. But what? What was it about the evening that caused him to feel something had changed within? He did not know.

XXXV

WHEN HE AWOKE THE FOLLOWING MORNING the rains had ceased. The day was glorious. Birds were singing. Crows were crowing. The sky was a deep blue, the sun bright and warm and glowing. Nectarinia was playing in the sunshine, rolling various colored croquet balls over the lush and verdant lawn. The lake was still and calm. The black-barked dark green leafed trees looked strong and content. The silver-haired blue-balled monkeys frolicked in the branches. In the dining room, the only evidence of the previous night was the salt stains beneath Lewenberg's chair and in the places where the waiters had stood. It was as if Lewenberg had exorcised pain that had tormented him for years and the earth heard and gifted him beauty. It was a day when Stephen was to have lunch with Jacobson, the first time he had been invited to his house. Jacobson invited him, Stephen thought, because he knew Stephen was soon to leave.

Deos drove them out the west road. Stephen had not expected Jacobson to be in the car as well. Jacobson was silent. He gazed out the window, the number and words visible, the origin of that tattoo a mystery, only two people knowing the truth, the man who wore it and the person who inscribed it.

Just before the west road changed from hardtop to dirt, Deos made a right turn, the secondary road climbing the hills overlooking the town. The automobile climbed in low gear, twisting, turning, the lake behind them, endless, an ocean, impossible to tell where water ended and sky began.

Deos made a left turn down an even narrower path, stopping in front of a chalet style house built into the side of the cliffs. To their left through the trees Stephen could see the lake, the water dappled by the noonday sun.

He entered the house with Jacobson who went immediately to an empty bookcase, empty except for several audio devices including a Uher tape recorder, on which he pushed a button. A sexy, voluptuous, velvety voice quivered, "Birds do it, Bees do it, E-ven ed-u-cat-ed fleas do it, Let's do it, Let's fall in love".

"Ya. Eartha Kitt. You haf heard of her, yes?"

"Yes."

"I luf that voman, Ledberk. Vhat I vould not gif to meet her." Jacobson stared into space, his mouth partially open, his rotten teeth visible, Eartha Kitt echoing through the carpetless house.

Jacobson led him into the dining room, a dining table in front of a picture window that had an unobstructed view of the lake. As they entered, a gray hued parrot in a cage by the window screamed, "Errrk, shalom, shalom. Errrk, Doobie, Doobie, Doobie." At that moment a huge dog bolted into the room and jumped at Stephen, knocking him to the floor. The mastiff stood over him growling, his genitals gently swaying back and forth.

Jacobson shouted, "Shev, Doobie, shev. Shev." The parrot squawked, "Shev, Doobie, errrk, shev." And as the dog sat on Stephen, genitals pressing against genitals, Eartha Kitt was belting out, "While tear-ing off – A game of golf – I may make a play for the cad-dy; But when I do I don't fol-low through 'cause my heart belongs to Dad-dy. Yes, my heart be-longs to Dad-dy, da-da, da-da-da, da-da-da-dad…"

Images of caddies thrashing on the green and sounds of cups clicking like castanets along Ocean Road in Dar es Salaam flashed through Stephen's mind as the mastiff sat licking his face. Jacobson was struggling futilely at the dog's collar and the parrot screeched as Jacobson's wife entered the room. She barked one word – the dog's name – and the mastiff began to whine and back off. He slunk beneath the dining table and lay down, his expression one of servitude and sadness.

Stephen stood and straightened himself, and as he did he could see immediately why Jacobson might have wanted to sleep with Dolores or Sarah, or any other woman for that matter.

Mrs. Jacobson was the most unattractive woman he had ever seen. She was as wide as she was short, rolls of undulating fat visible beneath the tent-like dress that feebly camouflaged her body. His mom and dad always used to say about girls who were overweight, "she has a wonderful personality".

She does? Jacobson's wife did not. Jacobson's wife was bossy, domineering, complaining. "Turn that disgusting woman off. These olives are no good. The cucumbers are not the kind I wanted. I can't teach that boy anything," as an African entered with glasses of iced tea.

And Jacobson, well, Jacobson responded to her every beck and call. Not willingly, but he always responded, closing his dull, brown eyes momentarily, then opening them, a look of loathing on his face.

Lunch was hard-boiled eggs and tomatoes and lettuce and onions and cold meats and a bottle of South African wine. Lunch was Jacobson gulping food as if there were no tomorrow. And lunch was the parrot screaming, as soon as they were served, "Errrk, schvartza, schvartza, shalom, errrk," the mastiff growling beneath the table, Jacobson jumping up and placing a cover over the parrot's cage, the parrot silent, as silent as the mastiff and the three people eating lunch.

Shattering the uncomfortable silence Stephen asked, "Do you know the story of Jacob and Esau? What do you think about Esau?" Would he never learn? Why had he asked that? Was he showing off? See, I know something about Jews and Israel.

"You are testink us? Are you crazy?"

"No. I'm sorry. I didn't ..."

"So he killed his brother. So vhat. Such thinks happen."

"What are you talking about? He killed his brother? You are the one who is crazy," Mrs. Jacobson shouted. "You are such a nincompoop. Even the Torah you do not know. Killing his brother you are talking Cain and Abel," Mrs. Jacobson was screaming at her husband.

"So it vas the story of sellink him into slafery."

"Oh my God. What are we going to do with you? You want this young man to think you are so stupid? That was Joseph. My God. You are ignoramus. Esau." Turning to Stephen she said, "He was a whoremonger. Esau was a schmuck." She swiftly returned her gaze to her husband, who averted his eyes, glancing about the room.

She turned back to Stephen. "Why do you ask?"

Before he could answer, not that he had an answer, or even say that's not what I heard about Esau, Jacobson lifted his forearm. "So vy you always eye the writink on the arm? You nefer see such a think before?"

Stephen shook his head.

"You vant I should tell you from vhere this came?"

Stephen nodded.

"You haf nefer heard of the holocaust?"

"Yes. Of course."

"So that is from vhere it came."

"But Mr. Lewenberg told me…" As soon as he said it, he knew he should not have.

"Lewenberk? Vhat he say?"

Stephen was paralyzed.

"Vhat? Vhat he say?"

"Well, he only said that he knew of no one else who had words, only numbers."

"Lewenberk said that? I fix him. Of vhat does Lewenberk know? He vas here in the jungle vhile all that vas goink on. He knows nothink. I vill fix him."

"I didn't mean to get him in trouble. I…"

"Vhat he think that Lewenberk? That I put these vords there myself? Is he crazy? From vhere he know? It vas an experiment. Ve vere guinea piks. The others they are dead. But me… I haf tried eferythink to erase these vords. Ya, eferythink. I haf seen doctors and scientists. I haf seen eferey doctor and scientist in Isriel. Ve scrape the skin. Ve burn the skin. Ve transplant the skin. The vords and numbers, they nefer leaf. I am left vith scars and the Germans' ink. The scientists and doctors in Isriel, they tell me they see the ink has seeped into my bones, ya, my bones. They vant to know how this ink vas made. They try eferythink. They vant to produce this ink. Do you know how faluable is this indestructible ink? But they haf no answer."

No answer. Who could find answers? No one else has those words, Lewenberg said. The others are all dead, Jacobson said. Who was right? From where would answers come? Arbeit macht frei. Work makes you free. Who was the brilliant marketing genius who thought that up? Some proud advertising whiz strutting around, like Jacob, guess what I just did, mom, or dad, they are using my idea for their campaign. To say nothing of the Tanzanian one. Uhuru na kazi. Freedom and work. But wait a second. Hold on. Was it possible? How could that be? Had he not read somewhere, Stephen thought, before he came out, that Tanzania was once known as Tanganyika and was not Tanganyika once controlled by the Germans? It was possible, wasn't it? Stranger things have happened. Could not someone in the family of the German who thought up arbeit mach frei have left behind the genetic imprint on someone in Tanganyika, who in turn gave birth to the Tanzanian who created uhuru na kazi? Was it possible, he wondered, that whoever thought up those pithy phrases were related to each other?

"So your Lewenberk knows nothink. But you, Mr. Ledberk, I teach you somethink. You haf seen the cash registers ve use in the stores, yes? You know from vhere they come, yes?"

"They're National Cash Registers." Stephen recalled the pride he had felt when he noticed the words National Cash Register Co. Dayton, Ohio inscribed on metal plates attached to the machines.

"Vy should you Americans haf all the fun? You haf nefer been to our godown, yes?"

"No."

"In America, they call it a varehouse. Vy they call it a varehouse?"

"I don't know actually."

Jacobson reached into his pocket and withdrew a set of keys.

"Here. I let Deos drife you. Then you vill see for yourself vy ve are here. Then you vill understand."

Jacobson ushered him to the door and into the car. Later, Stephen would recall that he had never thanked either of the Jacobsons for the lunch.

They drove to the barn-like building. Iron bars protected all the windows. Only after Stephen had opened the padlock did he realize Deos was not coming with him. Deos promptly fell asleep in the front seat of the comfortable automobile.

The warehouse was filled with goods. From one end of that earthen floor to the other were tires of all sizes, paint in different sized cans, plastic piping, refrigerators, canned goods, cucumbers, tomatoes, jams, fruits. Jaffa this and Jaffa that. All made in Israel. He thought Jasmine Patel's uncle was correct. Perhaps the Israelis did want to occupy all of Africa.

Shafts of sunlight pierced through the cracks of the wooden slatting, dust particles floating in the glimpses of light. At the far end a ladder led to a balcony, the balcony built around the perimeter of the wall. He walked toward the ladder amazed at the quantity of materiel stretched over the floor. Who, he thought, was going to buy all this? What would become of it?

He stopped to open a refrigerator and as he did he thought he heard a scuffling near the entrance. He held his breath. He thought he heard whispering. He yelled, "Deos, is that you?" No one responded. He yelled again. "Hello, who's there?" He heard nothing but the drumming in his ears.

From behind a stack of tires a man holding a baseball bat ran toward him. Another man followed with a blade in his hand. Oh, shit. He ran, turning over Israeli products. Pulling them, tossing them in his pursuers' path. The baseball bat was gaining, not a Jackie Robinson model, handle too narrow, a hand on his shirt, the shirt ripping, Stephen turning, warding off the bat with his forearm. Frightened. His right hand was a fist hurtling toward that brown face, teeth caving in, roots pulling loose, how easy it was, never did that before, blood trickling, ruby-red, rich, satiny. Blood on brown skin startled him with its beauty: viscous, regal, pumping through veins. It seemed wondrous. Like gold, oil, diamonds, copper, and coal. Oh, shit. His shirt tore free, the baseball bat was dropped, the second man was closing in, Stephen streaking toward the ladder.

He reached it and began to climb. His foot slipped, shit, the blade smashed at the rung below his heels. He was scrambling, frightened to death, the blade poised for another swipe.

He reached the top and looked around for anything to hurl at that man. He picked up a gallon of paint and threw that. And another and another, cans of paint cascading, crushed, tumbling open, gallons of white and sky blue paint mingling, his pursuer covered in blue and white paint, were there no other colors? His assailant dropped the weapon, giving up, retreating, leaving the field of battle, returning from whence he came. Stephen stood, gazing down, breathing sharply, shaking, was it over? Was he the king of the mountain?

He noticed something strange and magical and mysterious – what was that music? – music again? – not Beethoven this time. He shook his head, blinking – was he dreaming? Were two blue triangles gliding toward each other, one upside down, the other correct side up, sky-blue molecules of paint sliding across the surface of the white paint spread over the earthen floor? The music was soulful, sad, piercing, coming to a crescendo as the triangles joined, overlapped, locked, a six pointed star. The star of Bethlehem?

What was the music? Where had it come from? As he descended the ladder, slipping on the paint covering the lower rung, the heels and toes of his shoes were covered by the sky blue and white paint. He picked up the blade. Shit. It was sharp. It sent a shudder through him to his groin. He found the baseball bat, an Adirondack. A Ralph Kiner model. What the hell was it doing out here? What were the men after? What was that beautiful music? He hoped he could remember the melody in order to hum it later to someone who might know it.

He ran to the car where Deos was still asleep. Was that possible? He woke him. Had he heard nothing, seen no one? Deos shook his head, looking at him as if he were mad, him with his shirt torn, bat and blade in each hand. Deos glanced quizzically at his shoes.

"Take me to the police station, Deos. Right now."

Deos shrugged, started the engine and drove back to town, to a small one story building with bars on all the windows.

Stephen had been in a law enforcement office only a few months before. That one had gray metal filing cabinets and a fat crew-cut gray uniformed man crammed into it. This space seemed much larger because it had only a desk and a few chairs. Behind the desk sat a slight, thin, balding man, this one also gray uniformed.

"Yes, bwana, can I help you?"

Stephen told him what happened, that one of the men was covered in blue and white paint, it would be easy to find him, and handed over the bat and blade. The man ignored his information as well as the blade, a panga he called it, but studied the bat, turning it over in his hands.

"This. What is this?"

"A bat. An American baseball bat."

"What is it used for?"

"Well, it's supposed to be used to hit a little round ball."

"Like cricket?"

"You might say."

The policeman stood and swung the bat as if he were chipping with a nine iron.

"I think it is more difficult to strike with your bat. What do you call this part?"

"The barrel."

"The barrel?" He gazed quizzically at the Kiner. "Ours is called the blade."

"The blade? Like the panga?" Stephen nodding in the direction of the weapon.

"Where did you come by this… this bat?"

"I told you. One of those men tried to kill me with it."

The policeman glanced at Deos who only shrugged.

"Look here, it has a name on it."

"Yes, I know. Ralph Kiner."

"Exactly. That man who caused such a commotion the other night. It must be his."

"Nader? You think this is Ralph Nader's bat?"

"Yes. See here. It has his name on it."

"No, no. That's Ralph Kiner not Ralph Nader."

The policeman walked toward his desk, opened a drawer and withdrew a book. Unsafe At Any Speed. He held it up in the air. He pointed to Nader's name.

"You see. The same."

"No. No. Well, the Ralph is the same. But the last name is different. The bat is a Kiner. The book is a Nader."

"Well, of course, the man is not so stupid as to put his surname on the weapon. But it is close enough." He glanced again at Nader's name on the cover of the book.

"His mistake was making the surname so close to his own. All criminals are the same. There is no perfect crime. He did not think this through. You see, there are five letters in his surname and both end in er. Indeed, he is so foolish as to include an n here." He pointed to Kiner's last name.

"This man Nader was not thinking properly. I see from your injuries you did not make up this story. You have said this is an American bat. You and he are the only Americans in Buhaya. Perhaps you and he have had a disagreement. Something that began in America and was meant to be ended here. We shall arrest him."

"No. No. We've had no disagreement. Anyway, you can't arrest him. He's not here any longer. And that's not his bat. It's just a coincidence the names are so similar. Look, one of the guys is running around out there covered in paint. The longer we wait here the more time he has to wash it off."

The policeman looked at Stephens's shoes.

"Where did you come by such shoes? Are they American? I would like a pair of such shoes. My children would love them."

Stephen glanced at his shoes. What the hell? Dozens of minute six-pointed blue stars covered a field of white. How had that happened? What in god's name... Frustrated he said, "Forget it. Just forget it. I wasn't hurt. I won't press charges. I'm leaving soon. A trial would just tie me up. Just forget it."

Finally Deos spoke.

"What are you saying, Deos? So, you did see something. What did you say?"

"Deos speaks in Haya," the policeman told Stephen. "It is our native tongue. He says he noticed that bars on one of the windows had been sawed through. He says he thinks the two men were inside when you entered. He says he thinks you interrupted what they were doing, that you scared them." The policeman paused. "That may be so but it does not answer how they came by this man's," holding up Nader's book again, "bat."

XXXVI

THE DAY BEFORE HE LEFT FOR NAIROBI he sat with Jasmine beside the boulder overlooking the lake. Because of the rains he had seen her only sporadically. Once he had assisted her father in a side business he conducted during the rainy season. With an expression of great pride and confidence Mr. Patel had said, "You must come with me. I will show you American ingenuity. It is American capitalism here on Lake Victoria, isn't it?"

What he showed Stephen was a mammoth truck with its exhaust pipe running directly from the engine to the passenger side of the cabin where it bent almost ninety degrees extending at least two feet above the roof. The back of the truck was open, its sides slatted with wood, the chassis sitting high above the gigantic wheels. Stephen had never seen anything like it.

"It can carry two small vehicles or one large automobile and any number of travelers across the flooded road to Uganda. I take your American friend across in the automobile he rents from me."

"Nader you mean?"

"Yes."

"But how are you going to get the car he rented back?"

"He will leave it with my cousin in Kampala. My cousin will return it after the rains cease. This man Nader was delighted with my capitalism. He said even in America no one was as clever as me."

Patel drove him out the Uganda road to the flooded area where buses from Uganda left passengers on the far side, while travelers heading north milled about or huddled together on the Buhaya side, protecting themselves from the downpour with umbrellas, or banana leaves, or old newspapers, or nothing at all. Stephen decided that it was the Africans in their hollowed out tree trunks, paddling their two or three customers across the half mile or so of the washed out road, who were the true entrepreneurs. Not because they were competing with Patel but because of their aggressive and intelligent business acumen.

"I would have a monopoly, isn't it, Mr. Ledberg, if those Africans would leave my markers alone."

"What do you mean, Mr. Patel?"

It was early in the morning. Rain was hammering the cabin while Patel and Stephen, in ponchos and gumboots, sat inside. Joseph, an employee, sopping wet, was in the open truck. Joseph jumped from the truck with an armful of wooden stakes: Joseph close to seven feet tall, was meticulously treading the water, feeling for the road, implanting a stake; the water up to his chest, his arms held high grasping the stakes as if they were a weapon needing protection from the flood. Joseph completed his task, which was painstaking, taking over an hour of Patel's valuable time.

"You see, Mr. Ledberg, I would have a monopoly if the African would not pull my stakes from the ground every night."

"You mean Joseph plants the stakes so you know where the road is…"

"Yes. I cannot drive through the water except on the road. Anywhere else is too dangerous."

"So Joseph plants the stakes as he is doing now and at night those Africans in the dugouts pull them out?"

"Exactly. What am I to do? In America they would be arrested would they not? But here nothing is done. I complain to the police but they do nothing. You can see it costs me plenty of money. Time is money. Look at them carrying my passengers. My passengers. What to do?"

Stephen smiled inwardly, not answering Mr. Patel, as the truck, now filled with people and one automobile, lumbered through the water, the truck following the markers Joseph had implanted, the water lapping at the tires, the exhaust pipe belching and farting, while Patel muttered to himself, cursing his competition. Stephen was in no mood to contradict Jasmine's father, after all he was her father.

Now as he sat with Jasmine beside the boulder he said, "I'm going to Nairobi tomorrow."

"Why?" she asked.

"I have to find a friend of mine."

"In Nairobi? Is it a girlfriend?"

Recalling that Lewenberg had asked the same question, he responded, "It's a friend of mine from home. His name is Lefty. I saw his photograph in The Daily Nation. For some reason he was at a golf tournament in Nairobi. I need to find him. I can't explain why, I just feel I must."

"You won't come back. I know you won't."

"Well, you're wrong, Jasmine."

"Why would you come back? We come from such different worlds. Once you go to Nairobi you will forget all about me. I have lived here all my life and have never been to Nairobi. Yes, you will never return to Buhaya. Why should you?"

"To see you."

She stared at him. He felt a stirring in himself. He moved her head gently toward his own. As their faces drew closer her lips parted and quivered. Her whole body picked up that tremor as if her lips were a tuning fork that caused a series of vibrations deep within her.

A scuffle atop the boulder distracted him. He glanced up. Jesus Christ. Standing on the rock, blue eyes peering at him, was a silver-haired blue-balled monkey, his blood red penis erect, a lascivious grin on his face.

"Let's get out of here, Jasmine."

"You don't like me. I've done something wrong."

"Jasmine, for god's sake. You haven't done anything wrong, I just need to get out of here now."

He waved his arms in the air to frighten the monkey. He gave Jasmine his hand and helped her up. He wanted to embrace her at that moment but he could not. He wracked his brain for something to say. But he was speechless, as they walked side-by-side back to the hotel, their bodies brushing occasionally. He was scared. He thought she might be right. He might not see her again. He wanted to love her. He wanted to return to Buhaya. He wanted to teach her how to blow bubbles.

XXXVII

Nairobi caught him by surprise. Jasmine's uncle had said it was the Paris of Africa. But Stephen had never been to Paris. Nairobi caught him by surprise because the city made him feel vulnerable.

He wondered if that feeling were caused by the two ill-kempt taxicab drivers struggling over his luggage, one beaten off by an official wielding a knobkerrie, the victor telling Stephen, "It good, bwana, you not go with that one, him Mau Mau, steal your money, me Mbuyu, Mbuyu know all, you want woman, Mbuyu find woman, you want meet politicians, Mbuyu know all politicians."

Or was it the taxi itself, a familiar taxi, a black-and-white checkered taxi? Was Moses Short expecting him? He recoiled at the thought. Or was it just that Buhaya was a luxury, like an airplane flight, and now that his past was catching up with him in Nairobi, the Paris of Africa, thoughts of Ingy Reticent and Esther Maroon and Pete Codding to say nothing of Marcus Aurelius Brown and Catherine Reticent pestered his mind. He wondered if he should return to Buhaya.

Mbuyu pulled up to an old half-timbered building, the Gloucester Hotel, the reservation arranged by Lewenberg, the hotel owned
by a family friend, another Jewish family in the hotel business in
East Africa.

Stephen's anxiety increased as he paid Mbuyu, who glanced at
the money and said, "Thisi all you give?" Mbuyu kept the note but
hurled the coins into the street. Stephen felt embarrassed, thinking
perhaps he had not tipped enough. But he would not have given a
larger tip at home, would he?

His room, which he found to be claustrophobic, was in an annex
at the rear of the hotel. To reach it he followed a porter through the
lobby to a courtyard. At the top of the wall enclosing the courtyard,
broken glass protruded from a bed of cement, shards of razor-
sharp glass protecting the guests of the hotel. Those fragments,
he thought, a primitive line of defense, but as functional as barbed
wire. He stood on his tiptoes and delicately touched one of the
shards, a shiver coursing up his spine as he thought of anyone trying to climb over that barricade. He tipped the porter, holding his
breath, hoping it was enough, and walked back through the courtyard to the lobby.

Stephen thought the best place to begin to locate Lefty would
be the Muthaiga Golf Club where the tournament had been held.
Surely someone there would be able to assist him. But if it turned
out Lefty had gone home, he, Stephen, would return to Buhaya.
He would surprise Jasmine. He would prove her wrong. He would
show her how much he loved her. What would she think then?

As he was leaving the hotel he was surprised to see a familiar figure walking up the path. He realized it was Catherine Reticent. As
he held the door for her, thinking he would introduce himself, she
slammed her elbow into his solar plexus exclaiming, "I can open
my own door. I don't need anyone doing it for me." Stephen could
feel the shock and hurt clouding his face.

Jesus Christ. He stumbled outside, dazed. Across the street
Mbuyu grinned, as did the young boy tending a primitive cardboard

newsstand, the front page of The Daily Nation taped to it. Were they laughing at him? He felt ashamed, and a little crazy. He began walking. He had no idea where he was going or what he was searching for, if indeed he was searching for anything at all. He wanted to hide, to crawl into an invisible space. He wanted to be on an airplane or in an automobile or on a train, anywhere but Nairobi. Did Catherine Reticent know who he was? Had Brown told her about him? What was it Betty had said when she thought he was attracted to Catherine Reticent after he had seen her photograph in Ingy Reticent's office? Be warned. If you ever run into Catherine Reticent just keep on running.

Stephen wandered the streets of Nairobi. For hours he walked, until he looked up and saw far away in an almost vacant lot a smattering of men poised on their haunches and a man standing without a left arm, and a woman, not Betty, he could see that, embracing him. Was it Lefty? Not possible, Stephen thought, it must be his imagination. It must be another man without a left arm. But what he wished was to find Lefty and it seemed he had done so.

With an enormous grin on his clean-shaven face, Lefty said, "Ah knew you were out here somewhere. Ah just didn't know where. See, Mama, this here is the kid ah was tellin' you about. Kid, this is Mama. This is Mama Kitabu. Mama, this is Stephen."

Mama Kitabu? The woman in the photograph in the newspaper? The one who sang the national anthem at the golf course? That Mama Kitabu?

Mama Kitabu smiled, her face diffused with beauty, her voice quieting, a dove cooing, her handshake soft and delicate but firm. "It is so nice to meet you, Stephen. Lefty has told me much of you." He liked her immediately.

"Kid, you're just in time."

"I am? For what?"

Lefty placed his arm around Mama. "Mama and me we're gettin' married and you're gonna be mah best man."

Jesus Christ. Lefty and Mama were going to be married? The last time he had seen Lefty he was with Betty. What had happened to her? Did she know Lefty was marrying? He wanted to retreat to Buhaya, but Buhaya, he felt, was a millennium away.

"Come on, kid, ain't you gonna congratulate us?"

"Yes. Yes. Of course. Congratulations. That's wonderful. I…"

"Lefty, I have errands to run. Show Stephen around, dearest. Stephen, I hope I will see you later this evening. I will be singing at the River Road Club. Lefty will give you all the information." Lefty and Mama Kitabu embraced passionately.

"Okay, kid, before ah show you around why don't you get yourself a haircut. You're going to need one for the weddin'. This here's Mama's uncle. He gives the best haircuts in Nairobi."

Mama's uncle nodded at him, shook his hand, and directed him to the only chair in that vacant piece of land.

As Stephen was having his hair sheared in the center of the city, in the country of Kenya, he thought of a million questions to ask his friend. But the only one that mattered, he thought, would have to wait.

"How did you come to be here?" Stephen asked Lefty.

"Why one a the members at the Roarin' Brook Golf Club got into the tournament out here. Ah been caddyin' for him for years. He asked me to come out with him. Well, he was payin' all the expenses and ah knew you was out here somewhere, so ah did it. What did ah have to lose? Good thing too. Would never have met Mama. She's beautiful ain't she?"

"She is."

"Wait till you hear her sing. And ah would never been offered that job at their golf club."

"They offered you a job? What sort of job?"

"They want me to train their caddies."

"Wait, I'm confused, Lefty. You're training African caddies?"

"Yeah. Why?"

"Well, you didn't think much of the caddies at the New Falls Roaring Brook Golf Club."

"Them? Why these caddies out here have about as much in common with them as shit does with shinola. These caddies here want to learn. They're not in it just for the money. Why I'm training them to study their golfers, show 'em which clubs to use where, know their strengths and weaknesses. Why they even hang around after everyone closes up and they play a few holes. They're good. Why ah wouldn't be surprised to see one a 'em playing in a tournament one day. You ain't never gonna see any a those caddies at Roarin' Brook playin' in no tournament.

"Now we've talked enough. You got a good haircut. Let ol' Lefty show you around. When we get through there ain't gonna be nothin' you won't know about this town."

And there wasn't. Things he could not possibly have seen, or even wanted to, for himself. And when he got through he realized the only place they had not been was where the wazungu, the Europeans, lived.

Lefty took him to the Street of the Touts, a back street lined with betting parlors. Men milled about, studying racing sheets, radios blaring from open storefronts, blasting an Englishman's voice somewhere on the European continent thousands of miles away, that voice calling some faraway horse race. And in front of each storefront was a man standing on a ladder, chalk poised, white chalk on blackboard, waiting to scrawl the results of the race. The men on the street listened intently; those men dressed in tattered clothing, unkempt; the race over, chits of paper torn in two, confetti fluttering to the already cluttered street. Stephen heard no shouts of jubilation, no celebration.

"Has no one won, Lefty? Were they all losers? It looks like everyone has torn up their tickets."

"'Course someone won. Only none a 'em wants to admit they held a winnin' ticket. They tear up paper on 'em. They're afraid of gettin' robbed. They'll claim their money later."

"They will?"

"Sure. Ah don't know which part a Africa you been to but here everybody double locks their doors ands got askaris guardin' their house. Just ask Mama. The winners'll come back later when there ain't anyone else around."

Lefty even took him to the Street of the Beggars.

"A course that ain't its real name. It ain't got no real name. Mama calls it Dungudungu Street. Ah calls it the street a the Beggars. But see there ain't no street sign anywhere on this block."

A block nowhere near the heart of the city. A street over which a sweet sickly stench hovered. Men with one leg. Men with no legs. Men with one arm. Boys with clubfeet. Blind men. Blind boys. Even an albino child with translucent skin and white hair, white eyelashes, pink eyes, reminding Stephen of a rabbit. That boy's only deformity his albinism. Why were there no women on the Street of the Beggars? And just as no one could tell him where all the lake flies had gone the few times the sun pierced the clouds in Buhaya, Lefty was unable to tell him why there were no women on that street.

"Ah don't know," he shrugged. "Ah don't think anyone knows."

"But what is the point of having them all on this street so far from the center of town? No one can possibly see them here. No one can possibly give them a handout here."

Lefty said, "That's just the point. The government pays 'em to stay here. So the tourists can't see 'em. Mama says they use our money."

"They do?"

"Yup. Mama says it's an American project."

On the way back to the hotel Lefty said, "What's interestin' about them two streets, the streets a the beggars and the touts, is that there ain't no street signs on either a 'em. But everybody knows 'em by those names. Now you take some other places like the golf club, the New Falls Roarin' Brook Golf Club, now that's in New Falls that's for sure, but you ever see any roarin' brook anywhere near it?"

Come to think of it he had not.

"And the River Road Club where you an' me is gonna meet to-night, there ain't no river near there. And yet on a map, right there in black-and-white it'll show those places. Why even where Mama and me is gonna be married, Banana Hill, there ain't all that many bananas around there."

Stephen responded, "Well, at some point there must have been a roaring brook or a river or many more bananas."

And all Lefty said was, "Well, there ain't now."

That night Stephen took Mbuyu's taxicab to the River Road Club. It was the only cab around. Mbuyu parked next to the news-stand as if he had nothing better to do than wait for Stephen. Was there a reason for it? Something sinister? Why was Mbuyu so intent on Stephen as a fare? Had he been assigned to him? You stick to Stephen Ledberg. Whenever he needs a cab make certain you're the one who drives him.

Mbuyu had admonished him, "You not go there. Mbuyu not taki you there. It dangerous. River Roadi very dangerous. Mau Mau there. Mbuyu taki bwana to other club. It better. Lots of wazungu there." Mbuyu reminded Stephen of the cab driver in Houston who refused at first to take him to Moses Short's office.

But Stephen did not wish to visit another club. "The River Road Club, Mbuyu. If you won't take me there I'll find someone who will."

Mbuyu shrugged, ringlets dancing, as he pulled away from the curb exclaiming, "Okayi, bwana. You bossi. But you not blame Mbuyu if something happens."

If something happens? What could happen? Lefty would not place him in jeopardy would he?

The cab moved through the center of the city, neon signs flashing. The streets were crowded, the restaurants alive. They drove through the center, then past it, the streetlights sparser, the people fewer, the houses rundown, refuse strewn about, a street sign, River Road.

River Road was dark, illuminated only by the moon and an oc-casional fire in an oil drum, where men were warming themselves, here and there a neon sign in a bar window. Was Mbuyu going in the correct direction, he wondered? They were on River Road, but were they going toward the club? How come it was taking so long? He sat on the edge of the seat and told himself not to be stupid. Of course Mbuyu was going toward the club. Why would he do otherwise? Well, maybe he wants to make certain of his tip this time. Maybe that's why he was always waiting for you. Don't be ridiculous. He didn't want to come out here himself. River Road very dangerous, that's what he said. But suppose that was just a ruse. Suppose it was really Mbuyu, and not the other driver who was driven off by the knobkerrie, who was Mau Mau. Suppose Mbuyu, like Bre'r Rabbit, really wanted to be tossed into the briar patch, the briar patch being River Road.

He wanted to ask Mbuyu how much further. Instead, he sat on the edge of his seat, peering intently at each building and pedestrian until the taxi stopped in front of a cement block building, the door open, an old weather-beaten sign nailed above the entrance, River Road Club.

He tipped Mbuyu generously, and not only because he was relieved to be at his destination. He tipped him also because he did not wish an ugly scene in front of that club before all those people idling about the entrance.

He should have realized that it made no difference, that his stepping from the cab was attention enough. Heads turned, people wondering what he was doing there, wondering who the mzungu was.

And inside it was no different. It was as dark as the street, an extension of River Road. Heads swiveled, people on bar stools stared, he barely able to make out faces. The only illumination was from candles on the tables, a dim spot on the stage in the far right corner. Then he saw a figure waving at him.

He made his way around the tables until he reached Lefty.

"Sit down, boy, the show's about to start."

"Ladies and gentlemen, Mama Kitabu."

The club erupted with applause. Mama Kitabu walked on stage wearing a simple gray satin gown, her face radiant, a voice near the

bar shouting, Mama Kitabu Twisti. Mama's smile grew even wider.
Her trio played lightly in the background as she swayed slightly to
the music, the trio and Mama moving into Mama Kitabu's Twisti.

She was exquisite. Not because she was African or even because
she was a woman. Mama Kitabu was exquisite because she knew
exactly what she was doing, gliding about that stage as if she had
spent her whole life there. As if she belonged there and nowhere
else. As if she knew every crack, every splinter of that proscenium.
Her voice and body undulated in perfect rhythm. Mama was graceful, free, wild, at home where she belonged. A smile on her face,
the smile of a child who knew she was doing something well, something with which she was so familiar that she knew she was in absolute control, of herself and everyone around her. Mama ended to
loud applause, exited, returned for an encore, Mama Kitabu Twisti,
exiting again, the spots dimmed, Mama joining them.

Lefty and Mama embraced. Stephen looked away and felt a pair of
hands on his shoulders. Hands he knew instinctively even before he
heard her voice. Hands that had held him one sultry night in Houston,
making love on a floor covered in zebra skins. Jesus Christ. What the
hell was going on? Why was she here? Why were all these people in
Kenya? Was Jasmine Patel's uncle correct? You will meet everyone you
know in Kenya. Lefty and Catherine Reticent and now Stephanie. He
felt like fleeing to Buhaya. Just climb aboard an airplane and escape.

"I thought that was you. What the hell are you doing out here?"
A query Stephanie took right out of his mouth.

Stephanie wore a loose fitting white dress, her breasts pressing
against the material, her hair piled high, a gold necklace around
her neck. Her face seemed harder than he remembered, those light
brown eyes colder. Stephanie was about to embrace him when he
noticed a short thin man standing behind her, the man dressed in a
dark business suit, adjusting gold-rimmed glasses.

"Darling, come meet my friend. Stephen, this is my husband,
Kyangu. You remember the zebra skins in Mr. Short's office? Kyangu is the man who gave them to him. Aren't you, darling?"

Kyangu nodding, staring suspiciously, shaking hands.

Had Kyangu known what had transpired on those skins? Could he guess? Was it possible Kyangu knew that Stephen and Stephanie had been lovers on the gift he had presented to Moses Short? Was it possible, Stephen wondered, if Kyangu and Stephanie had themselves done the same?

Stephen said, "They're very unique. Did you give Mr. Short those beautiful birds as well?"

Kyangu looked puzzled.

"Yes, as a matter of fact he did. You know the birds he's talking about, darling. Why we were just talking about them the other day. The African birds you gave Short. You know, the ones that never make a peep."

"I was wondering about that. Why don't they make noises?"

"Oh please, Stephen. If you were shut up in that shithole would you make a peep? Kyangu didn't expect him to put them in that filth, did you, dear?"

"Why does he?" Stephen asked.

"Why does he? Why does Short do anything? He calls them his canaries, isn't that right, sweetie?"

Kyangu nodded.

"Canaries?"

"Yeah, he says the day they die will be the day he stops smoking. Why do we always end up talking about him? Why don't you introduce us to your friends?"

Which he did, Stephanie congratulating Mama on her singing and then adding, "I've heard the two of you are getting married. Congratulations. When is the wedding?"

To which Lefty replied, "Well, why don't you and your husband come on out to the wedding. It's gonna be on Banana Hill. Stephen here's gonna be mah best man. Everyone's gonna be there."

"Well, I might just do that," Stephanie answered. Turning to Kyangu, she added, "You won't be here, darling. What a pity." Taking Stephen's hand, pressing it warmly, more warmly, he felt, than she should have now that she was married. "Well, maybe I'll see you at the wedding." And they returned to their table.

Lefty said, "How do you know her, kid?"

"Remember when I went to Houston? She was the assistant for Moses Short, the lawyer for Marcus Aurelius Brown."

"That's the guy, this Brown, he was the guy who caddied at the club and wanted me fired, right? I told you about him, Mama, remember?"

"And he's out here somewhere. I ran into his girlfriend at the hotel. I suspect I will run into him, too," Stephen said.

Mama said, "Well, you should be careful, Stephen. Kyangu is not a nice man."

"Yeah, kid. Ah saw the way she squeezed your hand. You sure she was only Short's secretary? She looked pretty familiar with you if you ask me. And if ah saw it so did Kyangu."

Stephen felt himself blush. He hoped the dimness of the club protected him.

"Yeah, kid, those things you told me about. Those guys in the warehouse, you fool around with that woman out here, it'll be hyenas you'll have to worry about, not baseball bats or pangas. Ain't that right, Mama?"

"I'm afraid so, dearest. And I wish you had asked me before you invited them."

"Oh, ah'm sorry, Mama. I apologize. Sometimes ah just get carried away by mah excitement. Ah'm sorry."

"That's all right, Lefty. Stephen, why don't you and Lefty drive out to my farm one day before the wedding? You will love it, won't he, darling?"

"Yup. Mama's got this pig farm outside a Nairobi. We'll drive out together. You up for that?"

"I guess so."

"You guess so? You got to be more enthusiastic than that, kid."

"Sorry, Lefty. I can't wait to see it."

XXXVIII

THE DAY BEFORE THE WEDDING Lefty drove him to Mama's farm. He did not imagine it would be possible for Lefty to drive. But he did. He drove a Land Rover with the steering column on the left, just like in America. "The only model the dealer had," Lefty said. "Someone had driven it from French Africa. So, see, this way ah can use mah hand to shift gears." Lefty showed him how well he accomplished what would have been an impossible task had the steering column been where all the others were in former British East Africa. Lefty balancing the steering wheel with his stump as he performed the necessary acceleration. Lefty adding, "The only thing is you have to holler when ah should pass. Okay?"

"Okay."

The road led north outside the city. The road was in early morning shadow, the sun filtering through the trees on the right. Women and children walked shoeless on the brown red earth at the side of the road. Their feet and shins were covered in brown red dust, that dust settling into the cracks of their skin, that skin dried by the sun into hard tough rawhide. The women were dressed in dirty loose garments, their backs bent by loads of wood, wood strapped to their backs by leather strips, leather which wound around the wood, over their shoulders, and across their foreheads, leather not far removed from the skin covering shoeless feet.

"How come there are no men carrying wood?"

Lefty shrugged, shifted his toothpick, spit some tobacco juice out the window, the wind stream catching it, blowing it past the vehicle. "Don't know. That's just the way it is. Them women is in Mama's tribe. They Kikuyu."

The Land Rover passed Banana Hill. People waved. Lefty waved back and said, "See, over there. You see that hill. That's where me and Mama's gonna be married."

Stephen glanced at his friend's face. Lefty's face was relaxed, contented, untroubled. Perhaps he really was in love with Mama Kitabu. Perhaps it wasn't just the farm. Else it would show, wouldn't it?

Ever since Mama Kitabu had mentioned her farm, Stephen was devilled with the thought that that was the reason Lefty was marrying. Hadn't he always said he wanted to retire to a farm, just put his feet up and relax? How else to explain the wedding after all his racist remarks in America? It did not make sense. Yet here they were, the day before the wedding, driving to the farm and as far as Stephen could make out Lefty was as content as he had ever been. Surely if Lefty had nefarious motives he would not be able to conceal them, would he?

Mostly they drove in silence, Stephen mulling over everything that had happened since he arrived in Nairobi. He wondered again what had become of Betty, but hesitated to ask Lefty since he was marrying Mama Kitabu. Shouldn't he just let sleeping dogs lie? But, he wondered, had Lefty told Betty he was getting married? If he had, how did that affect her? Stephen would have been hurt, he thought. Suppose Jasmine told him she had fallen in love with another person. He thought he would be devastated. He felt close to Betty. She had encouraged him to come to Africa. Despite her drinking and chain smoking he admired her courage. She spoke her mind. And, it seemed her instinct was correct about Catherine Reticent. Perhaps the child in her class, Adam, the half-caste boy whom Esther Maroon had adopted was Catherine and Marcus Aurelius Brown's child. Stephen even wondered if Betty had been correct in intuiting a connection between himself and the Reticents. Betty would have had the courage to ask.

"Does Betty know you're getting married?"

Lefty inhaled deeply, stared straight ahead, Stephen thinking he should not have asked, thinking he had embarrassed his friend, when Lefty said, "Sorry, kid. Ah shoulda told you before. Betty's dead. She died. Betty died."

"What? Betty died? She's dead? How? When? I…"

"Cancer. She'd a had cancer many years before. Seems they didn't get all a it the first time. But you shouldn't feel bad. Ah talked to her about comin' out here. She said, go. Africa, she said, what an adventure. Go and find our little friend, she said. But aren't you scared a dyin' I said to her. Scared, she said. What's to be scared of? I'm lookin' forward to it. What an adventure. You'll be in Africa. I'll be god knows where. But it'll be exciting."

Stephen was swept by a wave of despair, an emptiness vaguely familiar, a hollowness he did not want to give in to. An image of himself lying on his bed, a summer day, a special day, come in here, son, before we give you your presents, his thirteenth birthday. Betty dead? And he had not known it? Betty dead and his life going on and not even knowing? How could someone he knew die and he not know? No sign. No intimation. No hint. Betty dead.

"When?"

"Just before we came out here."

"Was there no warning? No indication?"

"Nope. Only one day she just felt rotten. Couldn't breathe, she said. She went to the hospital that night. The doctors said there was nothin' they could do. It had spread all over her body."

The Land Rover moved down the asphalt road, a stillness and sadness everywhere. Stephen was stunned by the enormity of the news, not comprehending what it meant, not understanding that Betty was dead, gone, poof, he would no longer hear her voice or buy her a drink or watch her teach children. And what of the children? What would the children she taught think of their teacher's death? Did Adam slam an umbrella even harder against a desk? Did Esther Maroon reprimand him even more loudly for doing so? And what did Esther Maroon feel about her old friend dying? His mind spun as Lefty made a sharp right off the road onto a deeply rutted path.

The path wound up a hill, twisting left and then right, branches scraping and banging against the cabin. Then they were in a clearing in front of a large expanse of freshly mowed lawn. A log house stood on the other side, around it a border of neatly turned earth, cultivated, cared for, flowers, oranges and rusts and mauves and violets, flourishing. A thin plume of blue-white smoke rose from the chimney.

In the middle of that lawn was a mysterious tree, with the broadest trunk he had ever seen. It was gray-barked, with gigantic limbs, dark green leaves, the branches and trunk entangled by vines, a tree which seemed to hover over most of the lawn. Elms, maples, oaks were majestic and graceful, but none were as foreboding as that tree: a tree that was alive but sinister as if it had malevolent human characteristics, as if, if he approached more closely those branches would slowly envelope him until his very being would vanish and no one would know and no one would care. A shiver coursed his spine.

"What kind of tree is that?"

"That? That's a fig tree."

"A fig tree?"

"Yup. It's one a the reasons Mama bought the farm. That fig tree is worshipped by the Kikuyu."

"It is?"

"Yup. Their god – Ngai they call him – lives in that fig tree. Mama says the whole world began here."

" Mama says that?"

"Yup. Mama says everyone in the world's a relative of the Kikuyu."

"They are? How does Mama explain you and me?"

"She doesn't. She just says this is where we all started. At this here fig tree."

"Did you know that Jesus Christ killed a fig tree?"

"He did? Why'd he do that?"

"Well, it's a long story. The man who owned the hotel in Buhaya told me the story. It's in the Bible. Jesus woke up one morning and wanted a fig but it wasn't the season so he got frustrated and just killed the fig tree."

"Really. Well, maybe it wasn't them Jews who killed Jesus. Maybe it was Ngai.

"Maybe he was just pissed off enough at Jesus to do him in. Maybe Ngai wanted to show Jesus who was boss. You can't go around killin' mah fig tree. Ah was here way before you was."

Ngai was responsible for Jesus' death? What was Lefty talking about? He was just showing off, wasn't he? But wait. Suppose Jesus knew about Ngai. East Africa, after all, wasn't that far from the Holy Land. And he was the son of that God – did Ngai have a son? – and that God was a jealous god. So perhaps it was not about hunger or petulance as Lewenberg and I. F. Stone imagined, but about vengeance. Yes, maybe that was it, Stephen thought. Kill the infidel, show them who is boss. Scare the bejesus out of them. Destroy their fig tree. Murder Ngai. See what you can do if you have faith. My god is better than your god, even if your god came first. His brain spun madly as he thought of the deaths of Betty and George Morris, his best friend who stole his girl, but George had given him a warning, Betty had given him none. He followed Lefty down a dirt path and into the pigpen.

He expected to see the pigs wallowing in a sea of mud. Instead, he found dozens of oinking, sniffling, fat, pink, bristle-haired animals all pushing into one another, wobbling about on a field of cement. The floor of that barn was one long wide avenue of concrete. And on it, milling about, were awkward and ugly pigs. Wooden partitions separated them into groups, according to their progress to the market, the littlest ones at the farthest end.

"Ya see, kid, most people think pigs is dirty. But they ain't. What you got to worry about most is sickness. Worms. That kinda thing. Wadudu they calls 'em out here. But there ain't no way they're gonna get sick on this cement. Fact is there's more worms in people 'round here than in mah pigs. Yup, that's a fact. There's more a them wadudu in 'em, particularly the kids, than in mah pigs. All those kids you see walkin' barefooted at the side of the road? Watoto they calls 'em. Well, them watoto have more wadudu in 'em than mah pigs. Why we wash this here floor down three times a day. Think a that. Ain't no way these pigs is gonna get sick. And the pig factory's just down the road, so's we don't have far to take 'em. Mama says there ain't nothin' wasted on pigs. Tail, snouts, innards, bristle, everythin' is used. Why Mama says the Queen a England brushes her hair with pig bristles. Think a that. The Queen a England could be brushin' her hair right now with bristles from some a mah pigs."

Stephen was upset, thinking something was not right, and not just because Lefty was using the possessive adjective even before the wedding had taken place. No, what disturbed him was the fact that more effort seemed to go into caring for those pigs than for the women and children walking barefoot beside the road.

"Lefty, why should Mama's pigs be looked after better than those children we passed on the road?"

"Why? 'Cause it's a business, that's why. Ah bet the pig farms in America are the same. Ah bet the cows and sheep and pigs in America got more lookin' after than some a the children."

"That doesn't make it right. I don't get it. All the animals are going to be killed anyway, aren't they?"

"Yeah. So what?"

"Well, it doesn't make sense to me."

"It would if you owned a farm. Now let's go get somethin' to eat. Ah just heard a car come in. Mama must a arrived. Let's go greet her."

Mama climbed out of her car, and she and Lefty embraced. Lefty said, pointing to Mama's dress, "See here, boy. This is another a Mama's businesses. You see the dress she's wearin'? I bet you never saw anythin' like that before? You'll never see anythin' like it in America."

Stephen had noticed the cheerfulness of the canary yellow dress. But not until he was closer did he notice that there were colored images of book covers on the dress, reds, mauves, sepias, greens, the titles of the books and their authors legible: Mine Boy Peter Abraham, Things Fall Apart Chinua Achebe, The Palm-Wine Drinkard Amos Tutuola, People of the City Cyprian Ekwensi, Foriwa Efua Sutherland.

Stephen said, "I'm embarrassed to say I've heard of none of those books. Where did you find the dress, Mama?"

"I did not find it, Stephen. It was designed for me. All over the country I have groups of women who sew for me. They sit together while a reader reads from one of the books. Lefty thinks this is a business and one day it might be. But for now the women sit and sew and stitch and when they are finished they send the dress to me and my own tailor alters it to fit my figure. Two things are accomplished. The women hear a story written by an African. I get a dress and people see me in it and like you wonder what the books are about and perhaps they will be inspired to go to a library and take one out. All the work on the clothing is done by women. Kenyan women drive the country, Stephen. If Kenya succeeds it will be because of its women."

"You're not talking about the women Lefty and I passed in the car coming up here, are you?"

"Which women were they?"

"They were carrying bundles of wood…"

"Particularly them. Now let's go in and have lunch."

Lunch was slices of cold pork and potato salad and cold string beans in a vinaigrette, with Tusker beer. And lunch was Lefty pointing toward the window in the direction of the fig tree.

"Ya can't see it today, kid, 'cause a them clouds, but if it was clear over there you could see Mount Kenya. Ain't that right, Mama?"

"Yes, it is dearest."

"Ah'm hopin' tomorrow we can see it from Banana Hill, ain't that right, Mama?"

"Yes, Lefty, it is. And Kilimanjaro, too."

"You can see both mountains from here?"

"Yup, kid. If it's clear we can see both a 'em. Fact is them two mountains remind me a Mama an' mahself."

"How is that?"

Lefty with a broad smile said, "This here Mount Kenya reminds me a mahself and Kilimanjaro is Mama. Kenya's got a summit, the other a crater. You got it? When you see both a 'em at the same time it's like they was courtin'. Only they got all this space in between, in all these years they never got together. But Mama and me did, ain't that right, Mama?"

Mama blushing, "Yes, Lefty, it is."

Lunch ended with tinned plums and fresh yogurt, both products of Kenya. It was a dessert Stephen found succulent, the sweetness and tartness of the plums contrasting with the acidity of the yogurt, he helping himself to extra servings.

"Kenya is a paradise, Stephen. There is nothing we do not have. You should consider staying. Lefty would love that, wouldn't you, dearest? Now give Stephen and myself some time to ourselves. I want to show him the house."

Proudly she escorted him to the library. Hanging on the wall opposite the door were two large black and white photographs, of a man and a woman. Beneath the photographs on a small round table, a color photograph of another woman, a ceramic vase overflowing with flowers resting behind it. Stretching the length of the room, were bookcases crammed with books.

"Who are they?" Stephen pointed to the two black and white photographs.

"My mother and father."

"They must be very excited about tomorrow."

An expression of great sorrow passed over her face. She shook her head. "They are no longer here. They passed away."

"Oh, I am so sorry. If I had known…"

"It has been almost fifteen years now. They were killed during the emergency."

"The emergency?"

"Yes. The Mau Mau uprising. Are you familiar with it? A reprehensible part of our history."

"I heard the expression the day I arrived."

"Oh? How was that?"

"Two taxicab drivers fought over me. The one who won told me the other was Mau Mau and if I had gone with him he would have robbed me. Then the other night when I heard you sing he said the same. He didn't want me to go to River Road. He said Mau Mau were there. He wanted to take me to another club."

"Oh, dear. Yes, they do that. They think it intimidates the tourists. They think they will be given larger tips and probably they will be paid by the owner of whatever club they take you to. We have tried to stop them but it is nearly impossible."

"Well, I have to admit he did intimidate me."

"Not so much that you didn't arrive safely."

"True."

"But the driver was correct in one sense."

"What was that?"

"Most people assume the English killed my parents. But they did not."

"The Mau Mau did?"

She nodded. "It happened while I was away at university in England. They came in the middle of the night. They wanted my parents to swear fealty to Mau Mau. My parents were Christian. They refused. So they killed them. It happened to so many. The Mau Mau killed their own people or maimed them senselessly. Why?"

Mama walked toward the round table. She picked up the photograph. "This is Nicola Woodson. She was my mentor. She took me under her wing when I was a child. My parents worked for her. She gave me my first book to read, Winnie the Pooh. The cover was a gorgeous green with gold lettering. Lefty thinks I acquired my stage name because of my singing. He imagines it is because I hide nothing when I perform. He says when I sing I am like an open book. I have tried to explain to him that Miss Woodson gave me that name, kitabu, it means book in Swahili, as I devoured book after book she provided me. But he will have none of it. The Mau Mau murdered Miss Woodson too."

She paused, and said, "You don't approve of the marriage, do you?"

The question stunned him, not because he did not expect it, somehow he sensed its coming, but because he had no response

"Your silence betrays you."

"It isn't that I don't approve."

"You mustn't hurt Lefty. He is so happy you are here. And, if truth be told, my own family questions what I am doing."

"They do? Why is that?"

"They imagine I am marrying beneath myself. But they do not understand. They think they want the best for me. They see Lefty and all they see is someone who has no profession nor speaks proper English to say nothing of his missing arm. But they have not seen him work with and teach caddies. They have not seen his face as I have as he watches me sing. They do not see me as he does. They do not hear me as he does. They think I should marry a politician or a civil servant or a businessman. God knows I had enough opportunity to do that. They don't understand. Those people tell me how much they love my singing and they buy me gifts but they do not hear me or see me. For them I am just another step in what they imagine is their success. Lefty is different, I sensed it right away. That is why we are being married tomorrow and you are his best man. So, please be kind to him. Now come, I will show you the rest of the house."

That night he lay on the bed in his hotel room reading The Daily Nation, thinking on what Mama had said but not able to rid his mind of Lefty being so emphatic about his farm and his pigs. He was thinking perhaps what brought them together was the uniqueness of having lost their parents when they were young, congratulating himself for that insight, when his eye caught a small item datelined Buhaya, Tanzania. He sucked in his breath in anticipation of reading something that was about to disturb him.

Owner Expelled. Hotel Expropriated.

Mr. Peter Lewenberg, owner of the hotel that bears his name, was ordered to leave the country within the fortnight. The hotel is to be renamed the Hotel Uhuru and is to be managed by the People's Food Cooperative under the supervision of Mr. Abraham Jacobson.

Mr. Lewenberg, responding to a question, said, "My mother is even now in Israel. I will go there. But Tanzania will always be our home. The only item I will take is the Torah. We will have it repaired in Jerusalem. Everything else will remain."

Jesus Christ. He felt like throwing up. He felt remorse. He knew instinctively he had played a role. No, not played a role but bore sole responsibility. Why had he mentioned Lewenberg to Jacobson? Why had he questioned the writing on his arm? Why had he been provocative? There was no need. He cursed himself and began to pace the room. There must be something he could do. There must be some way to help Lewenberg. Call the minister. Call Nyarimbere. Call Dar es Salaam. But it was the middle of the night. Tomorrow, do it tomorrow, but tomorrow, he thought, would be too late, besides tomorrow was Lefty's wedding day. He paced up and down cursing himself, wishing it were morning, wishing Lewenberg knew he was thinking of him, but he murmured to himself, if Betty could die without his knowledge, how would Lewenberg ever learn of his feelings?

Feeling claustrophobic, he left the room. He walked toward the courtyard and as he did he smelled a familiar aroma, a certain familiar pipe tobacco permeating the cool night air. He knew it was not Lewenberg's, although he wished it were. An image formed in his mind as he stood sniffing the rich, sweet, mysterious, and expensive scent, a scent that contained more than just a hint of latakia.

He turned and down the corridor he could see the door to one of the other rooms partially opened, a sliver of light slicing across the floor. He knew what he would find. It was the last thing he needed. Don't go there. How many more blows do you want in one day? But just as he could not stop himself from going through Nader's suitcase neither could he prevent himself from approaching that seductively open door.

Holding his breath to listen more clearly he heard the voice that belonged to that tobacco, the voice of Ingy Reticent, saying, "For god's sake, man, put your glasses back on. You know I can't bear looking at your eyes. You know they cause mine to tear up."

Who the hell was Reticent talking to? Whose eyes were affecting Reticent much as the publisher's had affected his own?

"There, that's better. If we're going to talk let's at least be civilized about it. So you think Short is your friend, eh? Well, let me tell you something, you're only here because Moses Short made a mistake. You were never supposed to be bailed out."

"You honkies are all the same. You think I believe that? You're trying to split Moses and me. The only person I trust is Moses Short. Nothing you can say will change that."

Stephen imagined a smile curling across Ingy Reticent's face. A smile bred from years of power and access to information and wealth. That smile as much a part of Ingy Reticent as his pipe, its tobacco, and the flamethrower that lit it.

"Think what you want. It's the truth."

And then he heard still another voice, not as familiar as the first two, but a voice that was certainly more familiar to Ingy Reticent than to either himself or Marcus Aurelius Brown. It was a voice that had startled him a few days ago and it startled him now.

"I thought that's what was going on. He's not lying, M.A. For once he's telling the truth. You were paying off Short to keep M.A. in jail, right? That's why he was never bailed out. Well, let me tell you something, he's out now and he's going to stay out. And there's nothing you can do about it."

"I think there is, Catherine."

"You think so? Then let me tell you this. Adam's going to have a brother or sister and that's my truth. And it's M.A.'s child again and that's his truth. And no matter what you try we're going to stay in Africa. So stuff that in your pipe."

" I rue the day I took you out to the golf course, Catherine. You never would have met Marcus Aurelius. What a mistake I made. There hasn't been a day I haven't blamed myself. If I could do that day over I would. I haven't been to the course since. I've thrown away all my golf clubs. You know you can't have this child, Catherine. We were lucky with Adam but we can't take another chance. The odds are just hugely against us."

Stephen, mouth open, amazed that Catherine Reticent had met Marcus Aurelius Brown at the Roaring Brook Golf Club, wondered what the hell Ingy Reticent was talking about. He felt sad that Betty was not alive to hear her insight confirmed. Adam, the half-caste child in her class, was Catherine Reticent's child, but why was Catherine lucky with Adam and why did her father think she should not have another child? Because Marcus Aurelius was black?

"You're a liar. We've asked for proof. You have none. Why should we believe you?"

"You have to believe me, Catherine. You have to trust me. I'm not lying. I'm your father."

"You're not my father. I hate you. I wish you were dead."

Stephen stumbled away from the door, wishing he had not heard. He placed his hands over his ears, not understanding what was going on between father and daughter. Proof? What was Catherine Reticent talking about? And what had it to do with him? Why had Ingy Reticent sent him to the golf course to interview Lefty if Ingy himself had not been there for years? His head spinning, he found himself in the shadowy courtyard, which was illuminated by a half moon, the top of the wall visible, those shards of glass sparkling in the moonlight. A self-destructive impulse momentarily hurtled through his mind, a shiver shuddered through his body. He returned to his room, agitated, scribbling a letter to Nyarimbere, the minister of cooperatives in Dar es Salaam, begging him to help Mr. Lewenberg. Why hadn't he returned to Dar es Salaam as Lewenberg wished? He could have interceded for Lewenberg instead of writing the letter, which he now held in his hand, and which he was certain would arrive too late. Why had he come to Nairobi?

He left the room, dropping the letter in the hotel's mailbox, returning, feeling like retching. Restless, he picked up the telephone book, looking for Ledbergs but knowing that even if he found someone with that name it would mean nothing. Disgusted, he hurled the book to the floor, turning on himself, knowing that no telephone book, no book whatsoever was going to tell him what he wanted to know.

XXXIX

HE HAD NOT SLEPT AT ALL AS NIGHT BECAME DAY. Mbuyu was in his taxicab outside; the newspaper boy was hawking his wares. Everything was in its place except his own head. As if nothing had been amiss the night before. As if the world spinning on its axis had not missed a beat. And perhaps it had not.

Lefty was dressed in a white shirt, dark brown tie, and brown trousers. He was freshly shaved, his hair neat and combed, his shoes highly polished. It was Lefty and Mama's day. The Land Rover headed north past that cinnabar earth, those shoeless women bent over, backs supporting wood, watoto tagging along.

"How do you know you're really in love with her?"

"In love with her?"

"With Mama I mean."

"How do ah know ah'm in love with her? What kind a question is that?"

"I don't know. I just wondered, that's all."

Lefty glanced suspiciously at him, then back to the road. "Why the minute ah heard her sing ah knew. The minute ah heard her sing that national anthem ah knew. Ah never heard nobody sing any national anthem like that before. That's why they got Mama doin' it. Ah wish you'd a been there. You'd a heard somethin'. Ah been tryin' to get her to start her singin' at the club with that but she won't. She says it shouldn't be wasted like that. She says it's only for special occasions. Maybe that's what's wrong with our national anthem. We sing it at every damn occasion. That and the fact that ah ain't never heard no one sing it like Mama does hers. Fact is ah don't believe ours was meant to be sung at all. Fact is the best ah ever heard ours was played by a symphony orchestra." Lefty emphasized the last five letters in the word "symphony".

"Yeah, that was the best ah ever heard it. There oughta be a law it can only be played by a symphony orchestra and then only on special occasions. That way people will come to respect it like they do here. Why you could hear a pin drop it was so quiet the day Mama sung it. Sent a shiver right up mah spine and ah didn't even know the words. Hell, we start teachin' ours the moment a kid steps inside a school. But you bring in a symphony orchestra and you play that thing on special occasions, maybe once or twice a year, well, shit, those kids are sure as hell gonna respect that, they're gonna feel a tinglin' from their toes to the top a their head. Yup, they oughta make that national anthem a mystery. Don't play it so much and when they do no words and only on special occasions."

"You fell in love with her over the national anthem?"

"That and other things." He smiled.

Stephen did not smile back. Instead he said what he knew he should not. A restraint tearing away, a layer flaking. A dog really kicked.

"So it wasn't just the farm?"

Lefty braked the car, spewing up dust as he rolled to a stop at the side of the road.

"Get out. Just get out. Ah don't need you doin' nothin' for me."

"I'm sorry, Lefty. I apologize. I don't know what's the matter."

"The farm? What the hell are you talkin' about? The farm? Is that what you think? What's the matter with you today? You got a stick up your ass? You're supposed to be happy about me gettin' married and all you're doin' is askin' a bunch a half-assed questions. You know what ah think your problem is? It's that Jasmine woman."

"It's not Jasmine. It's not her. You know what it is. You never thought much of the caddies at the club and how could I ignore that?"

"Shit, boy, those caddies have about as much in common with Mama as a Chinaman and a Eskimo. But ah'll admit it ain't just the caddies. Ah ain't gonna bullshit ya. Ours is different than the African."

"Come on, Lefty, you don't know what you're talking about."

"Ah don't? Ah sure as hell do. You been out here. These people have pride and tradition. If ours had stayed here maybe they'd be different. But they didn't and no matter how much they'd like people to think they're related to the African why they just ain't. Why ah bet most a ours got white blood in 'em by now. Look at that fella you been chasin' out here, that Marcus Aurelius. Didn't you tell me he's got blue eyes? Blue eyes. Well, whoever heard a a blue eyed nigger? Not out here. Out here that fella'd be on Dungudungu Street. You won't find any blue eyes in Mama's tribe. No sir."

Stephen did not bother to correct him. He did not bother to tell him that Marcus Aurelius Brown's eyes were gray. The most translucent gray, evidently, that Ingy Reticent had ever seen as well. Nor did he feel like telling him what had transpired last night. Perhaps that was it. Perhaps if he had not read the newspaper article about Peter Lewenberg, or overheard the disconcerting exchange between Ingy Reticent and his daughter and Brown, or even had had half an hour of sleep he might have been more civil. But he had read the article and he had overheard the conversation and he had had no sleep and he felt he had ruined Lefty's day. He felt disgusted with himself.

Nearing Banana Hill they passed parked cars, cars that had not been there yesterday. Cars – Mercedes, Peugeots, Renaults, Fords –

that clearly were not driven by the elderly couple climbing the hill, the man in an ancient tuxedo jacket, the jacket at least two sizes too large for him. His wife wore a khaki shirt, a heavy green tweed skirt, nothing on her feet save for cracks and dust.

Lefty parked the Land Rover in the shade on the west side of the hill. Then turning in his seat, he picked up a brown jacket, draped it over his stump, reached into a pocket and withdrew a small blue box which he handed to Stephen.

"See that you don't lose it."

"I'm not going to lose it."

"Ah wasn't sure."

Stephen placed the box in his pocket, patted the pocket twice, conscious that he had upset the mood of this, his friend's day.

They walked to the crest of the hill, the east side drenched by sunlight. Sunlight and people and the smell of burning wood. People were everywhere, men, women, and children, some families dressed like the ones they had passed on the hill. Others – he thought from the city –dressed as if they were going to a wedding for royalty.

He followed Lefty down the hill toward a table standing where the hill plateaued. People greeted them, smiled, and nodded, Lefty making his way to the table where a man in a khaki suit awaited him. The Reverend Ng'anga. They shook hands, Lefty introducing him as the crowd gathered around, then parted, oooohing and aaahing, forming a path for Mama Kitabu. Mama who was dressed in a white satin gown, wore a glorious, excited smile on her face. Stephen had no doubt why she was marrying his friend.

The cleric went on for almost half an hour, his intonation interrupted only three times. Once by the crowd quite spontaneously, with gasps, heads turning, fingers pointing toward the northeast where Mount Kenya had popped through the clouds. Jagged snow-covered peaks. Stephen thought the mountain handsome and more mysterious than Kilimanjaro. The second interruption was with Mama saying I do. Do you Agostino

Njoroge take Gabriel Abrams as... I do. Gabriel Abrams? The third time by the minister turning toward him and requesting the ringi. The ringi? Oh yes, as he reached into the wrong pocket, panicking for a moment, then locating the box, handing the ring to his friend, Gabriel Abrams placing it on Agostino Njoroge's finger. Gold on brown, each color enhancing the other, the richness astounding Stephen, the gold and brown complementary, the beauty subtle and refined as if gold were meant to adorn only the skin of brown hued people. Gabriel's I do, the ceremony over, a band striking up Mama Kitabu Twisti.

"You never told me your real name was Gabriel Abrams."

"You never asked."

"That's not true. I did, I'm sure of it. For the article in the paper. And you said the only name you went by was Lefty."

"Ah don't remember. Anyway what difference does it make?"

"Yes, but you said..."

"What? Ah said nothin'."

"Yes you did. You said your father was given last rites. I remember that. I thought last rites were for Catholics."

"He was. What did you think?"

"Nothing."

Stephen rushed down the slope toward a group of men sitting around a fire, thinking, Gabriel Abrams? Wasn't Abrams a Jewish name? But what's in a name? A rose arose to arouse Romeo, perhaps that was it, it had nothing to do with names, only Romeo arising as he was aroused by Juliet. That was what the Capulets feared. Maybe that was what Ingy Reticent was upset about as well. Maybe that's what all fathers were upset about when it came to their daughters, he thought, as they walked briskly down the hill.

"See those men down there?" Lefty interrupted his reverie, pointing. "Yes."

"Well, ah don't think they will but in case they give you a hard time 'bout bein' with me you..."

"A hard time? Why would they do that?"

"'Cause you ain't a part a their age group like me. That's why. But you can be if you listen to what Mama told me. See, she says you should pretend ah'm your uncle. That's if they say anythin'."

"My uncle?"

"Yup. See, Mama says out here that a first son is named after his father's father. The second after his mother's father. Well, ah couldn't be either a 'em. But the third son is named after his father's brother and ah could be that. So ah'm gonna be your uncle. It's a little white lie. Just in case. Okay?"

"Okay."

"Oh, one other thin'. They're gonna give you muratina to drink. Ever hear a it?"

"No."

"Some a it's just homemade beer. But if you see it bubblin' that means they put a special fruit from a special tree in it. If it's bubblin' and there's no fire under it, you be careful. You watch out for it."

They headed down the hill toward those men, lineal relationships to say nothing of family names, spinning in his head; toward those men sitting in a circle, a mound of raw meat stacked next to the fire, flies flicking about, and beside that meat, resting on the ground a gigantic smoke-blackened kettle, the brew bubbling but not because of any man-made heat. Those men greeted Lefty, greeted Stephen, not caring who he was, sitting there passing around a cow's horn. A cow's horn? A cow's horn filled with muratina. The horn was passed to Stephen – just be careful of it Lefty had said – an amber colored liquid, mottled, with specks of dirt floating on the surface. He hesitated, wondered how the uncleanliness might affect him, sipped, swallowed and passed the horn on.

Just watch out for it. Watch out for it? Once that amber liquid was inside there was no way he could watch out for it. He felt no sensation as it went down. No raw, fiery feeling. He sat waiting for something to happen. Maybe he did not drink enough the first time, taking a larger gulp as it passed his way a second time, Lefty admonishing him again, you be careful.

And now, he began to feel something. Now he felt a slight numbness beginning in the soles of his feet and the tips of his toes, that numbness spreading throughout his body. Unlike anything he had ever experienced before. As if someone had injected him with a drug. Everywhere a lightness. Everywhere good cheer, everywhere a glow. Even his face was affected, as if it did not exist. It was as if his body was simply plasma, flowing freely, lacking boundaries, floating, spreading light, warmth, and joy.

He became hungry. Ravenous. He eyed the mound of raw meat. Beef and liver. Spurts of saliva saturated the inside of his mouth. Gastric juices jumped. Raw. Bloody. Grab. Tear. Lick. Lust. Blood. Sun. Muratina. Giggling. Floating.

For hours they sat eating meat and passing the horn. The only interruption was from an old woman wearing a dress of burlap, material which once had held rice or maize or beans and now covered her bent-over body so loosely that he could see her breasts, wrinkled, flat, caked with dust, nipples like tiny dried up berries. What did she want? Cackling at him, pointing, a harridan, the men trying to move her on. But she would not go, only drawing closer, circling, pulled toward him as if he were a star and she some object loosed in space.

She was eyeing a coconut, gathering a panga, raising it with both arms above her head, and with every ounce of strength slicing the coconut, the meat of the coconut startling him, its whiteness shimmering unsullied unlike any other white he had ever seen, ensconced in a dark brown membrane, the hag lifting the coconut to her toothless mouth, draining the liquid, swirling it around as if it were a mouthwash, all the while staring at him, spitting it, ptooie, down the front of her body, washing her bare dusty deflated breasts with coconut milk, rivulets of wrinkled brown skin where dust had been. Jesus Christ, he thought, no such thing as black or white, no one's skin as white as the meat of the coconut or as black as the print of a newspaper. So why call brown-skin people black? Where did that come from? Everyone was a subtle shade of tan, weren't they? Why did journalists describe people as black or white rather than hued? Because it was easier. How many shades of brown were there? What caused light or dark skin? Forget it, not important, you had a deadline to meet. But wait, perhaps it was more complicated. Perhaps black was a code word. A code word? For physical characteristics, yeah, maybe that was what black really meant. Texture and shape of hair, shape of forehead, size and shape of lips, of nose, of penis, but wait, wasn't that what the Nazis did? We're not talking coconuts here, as he recalled Lewenberg's description of his father rummaging in the kitchen for coconuts, shouting nazi, nazi, nazi. But it was not the season. What are we talking? Twinkle twinkle yellow star how I wonder what you are, does yellow mean I will die unlike the stars in the sky. But the stars in the sky did die, their light traveling billions of miles and billions of years to reach his eyes and by the time it did the source of the light might have expired. How long, he wondered, would it take the light from the yellow stars to penetrate the earth's surface as well, unaware that the men were standing whooping and hollering, smacking him on the back, she want you. The hag was beckoning him and even through the numbness of the muratina he was swept with embarrassment. The men recognizing this raised their arms threatening the woman, chasing her away, the woman limping back up the hill from whence she had come.

They sat there for hours, on the ground or on a dead log or on their haunches. They sat drinking and eating and telling tales. Only when the sun dropped behind the hill, when they became chilled, did anyone leave, and that person was Lefty. Lefty leaving? What was that feeling that suddenly cut through all the numbness? Was it abandonment? Lefty shaking hands, thanking everyone, heading up the hill.

Mama was already in the Land Rover, her family gathered around. Lefty stopped, embraced Stephen, told him to look after himself, "take care a yourself, kid, you come visit whenever you want", then opened the car door and climbed in. He started the engine, waved, everyone smiling, everyone happy. Everyone but him. Why? He was standing on that hill, among all those other people, alone. He watched the Land Rover move down the hill, noticing for the first time the metal tag attached to the rear fender, a large red L on a field of white. The L could have stood for Lefty or Ledberg but all it really meant was that the driver was a Learner.

He felt a pair of hands on his shoulders, like the other night, and a night before that. "I did not see you at the wedding," he said.

"I got lost," she said. "I arrived late. Do you know how many Banana Hills there are in this part of the country? I'll give you a lift back to town." It never occurred to him how he might return to Nairobi. He wished it were not with Stephanie.

He followed her down the hill. Her car was a chocolate-colored Mercedes with tan leather seats. He climbed in, the seat embracing him, comforting him, the aroma of leather everywhere.

Stephanie settled into her seat, her stomach bulging slightly against the material of her dress. That wasn't weight she had put on. Was it possible? Was Stephanie pregnant? A faint fear grasped his intestines as he stared at her stomach.

"Yeah, I got a bun in the oven. What do you think about that?"

"Well, congratulations."

"Yeah, sure." Stephanie started the engine.

The car headed back to Nairobi, speeding silently down the tarred road, the blood- red sun bathing the brown-red soil, making it appear a darker red than it really was.

The silence was interrupted by Stephanie. "So your friend got married. What are you going to do now?"

He wanted to say he'd go back to Buhaya. He wanted to say he'd see Jasmine. But even thinking on her could not erase the emptiness he felt.

He said, "I'm going home," knowing it was the truth the moment he said it.

"You are?"

"Yes."

"Take me with you. Get me out of this shit-hole, Stephen. It's nothing but a zoo. Take me with you. I want to go back to America. Things are about to explode out here, Kyangu, Moses Short, they're all going to be in trouble."

"Trouble? What kind of trouble?"

"They own everything. They bribe everyone. All sorts of politicians and the police. There's going to be a story in the papers any day. Please. I hate this place, Stephen. I hate Kyangu. I only married him because I thought it would get me out of Houston. I made a mistake. Take me with you.

"You want to know who was sending those checks to Short, don't you? I know now. Only take me with you."

He said nothing. He knew already who sent the checks. He no longer needed that information. And more, he no longer cared. He had not slept, he felt, for days. He felt alone, abandoned by Lefty, exhausted. He turned toward her and, nodding in the direction of her stomach, said, "What about that? What about your baby?"

She glanced at him in an odd way, a smirk crossing her face. A glance and smirk he did not want to believe. Not possible. More, not true. He began counting months even before she answered. July. August. September. October. November. He had no idea how large the stomach of a woman who was five months pregnant would be. Was it possible she was really carrying his child?

"Yeah, I got a bun in the oven, Stephen, and you provided the water and flour. It's your child. It's not Kyangu's although he thinks it is. It's yours so take me with you."

Jesus Christ. His child. It couldn't be true. Stephanie was lying. Stephanie would do anything to get him to take her with him.

"You're lying."

"Am I? You better not fuck around this time. You take me with you or I tell Kyangu."

"You wouldn't dare."

"Wouldn't I?"

The car hurtled down the tar road, the wheels suddenly making a rhythmic sound. Your child. Your child. Your child.

"And don't think you can pull anything. I have friends at your hotel. They'll call me the moment you check out."

The Mercedes, its wheels keeping up that rhythm, headed smoothly, effortlessly back to town, he exhausted, not believing but believing, wondering, wanting only to leave Africa and escape to home.

XL

IN THE DAYS SINCE HIS ENCOUNTER WITH STEPHANIE it had occurred to Stephen that perhaps it was Mbuyu, the taxi driver, who was her source of information, if in fact she had a source at all. Else why did Mbuyu seem to be there each day waiting for him? He had never seen him pick up any other hotel guest. Granted the days between the wedding and today he had rarely ventured from his room. He had no interest in running into Ingy Reticent or his daughter or Brown, to say nothing of Stephanie. He slept a lot. He watched television. He ate little.

Now, as he stepped outside the hotel the first thing that caught his eye, other than Mbuyu sitting in his cab, was the seventy point banner on the front page of The Daily Nation pinned to the newspaper boy's stand.

ISRAEL SACKED

What? Israel sacked? He had seen nothing on television, heard nothing on the radio. There had been no buzz in the hotel. He glanced around. It was a gorgeous sunny day. There was a man riding a bicycle, a woman with her children, a street sweeper with his broom. Students dressed in school uniforms walked by the hotel.

He crossed the street, bought a copy of the newspaper and opened it to page three where the headlined story continued. There he saw a photograph of Abraham Jacobson. The front page contained a typo. It had accidentally dropped one important letter, perhaps the most important letter in the English language. The dateline: Dar es Salaam, Tanzania.

The Israeli, Abraham Jacobson, who managed the People's Food Cooperative in Buhaya was sacked two days ago for selling South African wine at the Hotel Uhuru. The Honorable Minister of Cooperatives, Robert Nyarimbere, lauded Mr. Jacobson for the effort he had given to the cooperative but said, "The incident is unfortunate. We cannot turn a blind eye. He knows there is an embargo on all South African produce."

Mr. Jacobson, before boarding an El Al flight to Israel said, "I don't know from where the wine came. It was there before we took over. But it makes no difference. We are going home. We have a son in the army."

Then Mr. Jacobson in a sardonic tone and with a smile added, "If your British had their way I would not need to be at the airport. I could have walked across the border."

A reporter asking what he meant received the response, "You have no idea from what I talk? You did not know the English they wanted Uganda to be our home? It was a joke. Yah, it was a good English joke."

Had not Joyanti Patel said the same thing about Uganda? Could both be correct? Or were both mad?

He chucked the newspaper into a trash bin. He placed his bag in the trunk of Mbuyu's taxi. "Take me to the airport, Mbuyu."

Mbuyu smiled, looked at him in the rearview mirror and said, "Yes, bwana. You going back to America?"

Stephen did not answer. He thought now as the taxi passed all signposts to the airport that if Mbuyu was Stephanie's plant, he would have to call her after he dropped him off. As it turned out Mbuyu was no one's fool but his own, and a brilliant fool at that.

As the taxi parked in front of the terminal, Mbuyu, as if he knew exactly what to expect, calmly watched Stephen empty his pockets and wallet of all the local currency. Stephen would have no further need of it. He felt as if the act put, even more than an exit stamp, finality to his odyssey.

Mbuyu with an enormous grin, a tip of his cap, an "I'll find bwana a porter", thanked him, wishing him a good trip, "Americans are good, Americans are the besti, when Mbuyu come to America he call you, yes? Heri, you give Mbuyu bwana's telephone number and if bwana return Mbuyu waiting for him. Mbuyu showi you everything. Mbuyu drivi you all over the country. You telli your friends about Mbuyu, yes?"

"Yes."

Mbuyu pocketed all that loose change and paper currency, tossing none of it away; driving off, that grin on his face, a wave of his hand, ringlets dancing, Mbuyu not in the least interested in contacting Stephanie or anyone else. Mbuyu interested only in that airport loot and an American telephone number, a fictitious one at that.

Stephen checked his bag, anxiously glancing about the lounge, not entirely certain Stephanie would not miraculously appear. He did not see her. Stephanie was nowhere to be seen. But Moses Short was. Shit.

Short was pacing up and down, glancing at his watch, then at the clock on the wall, and back to his watch. Pacing, pacing. He reminded Stephen of an animal in a cage.

And then the flight was announced. Stephen breathed a sigh of relief. Short was exhaling as well, moving to the boarding line. Stephen settled in his seat, on the aisle and toward the front, recalling that Short always sat in the rear, relieved as Short settled somewhere far behind him. The plane moved slowly to the runway, stopped, and waited. Sitting. Waiting. A green light, the engines whining loudly, the plane poised for takeoff.

Stephen sat back, eyes shut, relaxed, thinking how foolish he had been to imagine Stephanie might show up. She was bluffing and not just about knowing someone at the hotel. The child was not his. Relaxed, eyes shut, he anticipated the acceleration.

They sat that way for two or three minutes, the engines whining, everyone expecting take off. They sat that way and then the engines were throttled.

What the hell was going on? It wasn't as if traffic was backed up. Ten, fifteen minutes passed. There was no announcement.

As he craned his neck to look out the window he saw a gray government Land Rover making its way toward the plane. Had he exhaled too soon? What in god's name was this about?

He heard a commotion in the first class section. He watched the curtains separating first class from tourist, part. An African in a khaki uniform, epaulet on his shoulders, a swagger stick beneath his armpit, led a Sikh in a white uniform who himself preceded a European in policeman's gray.

They moved slowly down the aisle studying each passenger. Stephen exhaled as they passed him by. A moment later he heard Short shouting, "You can't do thish to me. I'm an American shitishen. I'm your brother. We're brothersh. Here, theshe are American dollarsh." Stephen turned in time to see the swagger stick strike Short's hand, scattering greenbacks: George Washington, Abraham Lincoln, Alexander Hamilton, Andrew Jackson, Ulysses Grant, Ben Franklin, Tom Jefferson, swirling through the air, fluttering to the floor.

Short screamed as they led him down the aisle, passing Stephen, grabbing his arm, "Tell them who I am, Mishter Ledberg, tell them, you know me, we're friendsh, help me, Mishter Ledberg, tell them," Stephen aware that all the passengers were looking at him. He was tempted to shuck Short's grasp, imagining what the other passengers thought, Short a crazy person, just get him off the plane, but instead he said, "I am sorry. There's nothing I can do."

An astonished expression saturated Short's face as if he expected less, much less, as if he did not expect Stephen to acknowledge him at all, to deny him, as the officers led him from the plane. Stephen watched from the window as they escorted Short to the Land Rover, the vehicle turning, moving toward the terminal, moving out of sight.

The engines roared again, whining, the plane moving, faster and faster, suddenly airborne, free of the earth but not its gravitation. Heading home. Down that river. Down the Nile that was twisting and bending, pouring over rocks, forming rills, the plane heading back, back from whence he came.

Home

XLI

WHAT WOULD HE FIND WHEN HE ARRIVED HOME? Would he be willing to pepper his mom and dad with questions about his real parents? What would they say? Would they get angry? Would they turn on him? Would they disown him? Would he have no one? It frightened him to think of the worst possibilities. Why take a chance, why not just let sleeping dogs lie? But you pushed Lefty, he told himself. Lefty was angry, but he did not abandon you. He wanted to kick you out of the car but he did not.

As the plane crossed a continent and an ocean, flying over New England, America, Stephen caught glimpses of frozen terrain and dustings of snow between high-flying clouds. They approached New York, the city exquisite, sharp, crisp cold in an early December light, the plane setting down perfectly on the wet black runway. America.

He called home between flights. His mom was surprised but said she would meet him at the Wichita airport. "I wish you had given us more notice, Stephen. We would have prepared a real welcome."

"That's all right, mom. It's just going to be nice to be home." Wondering what he would do when he arrived there. Wondering if he had the courage.

His mom met him, his college parka under her arm. She wore her frayed blue cloth coat, an off white scarf draped about her neck, galoshes on her feet. She appeared older and smaller than he remembered. Her body was bent slightly like the bodies of those African women carrying wood at the side of the road. He thought perhaps it was the winter coat and galoshes that gave that impression. An impression that he was quite certain would give way soon enough to the one he always carried in his mind's eye.

They embraced. "Thanks for bringing the parka, mom. How did you know I had no winter clothes? I forgot to mention that on the phone."

"I thought you would have no coat. After all, you left in the middle of the summer, didn't you?"

He marveled at her memory and attention to detail, surprised in a way she had not brought galoshes for him as well. Wichita a dry, crystal cold, their shoes crunching on the snow, as they walked to the car.

After placing his bag in the trunk he walked instinctively to the driver's side. His mom handed him the keys saying, "Do you want to drive?"

"No, mom. Out there the driver's seat is on the other side. I thought this was the passenger's side." He unlocked the door for her, opening it, leaning across the seat to pull up the lock for himself, handing her the keys, then walking around to the other side and climbing in.

The inside of the car was freezing. Their breath fogged and then froze on the windshield. His mom started the engine, cold air blowing on his legs, his mom rubbing her white-mittened hand over the glass, clearing it, the car moving, the chains on the tires clacking on the roadway.

He closed his eyes, exhausted, resting his head on the back of the seat while the car moved almost by habit down that slick black snow-framed highway.

She woke him when they reached home. He followed her up the shoveled walk, dazed, fatigued, wanting only to throw himself upon his bed. The house was warm, comforting, the couch, chairs, piano, rug, Lincoln and Washington all where they belonged. Nothing had changed. As if he could have gone away to other planets and other constellations and returned and still found everything the same.

"Dad will be home shortly, son. Why don't you go upstairs and finish your nap. You must be exhausted."

"I'm really glad to be home, mom."

"And we're so happy to have you home."

XLII

It was dawn when he heard movement across the hall, his mom waking up on an early December morn. The radiator pipes knocking and hissing, the house waking to his mom's rhythms. Like always. Nothing changed. Always the same, and this morning comforting. Why? Why did he find his mom moving about the house so comforting? His dad in the bathroom, the sound of the shower running, Stephen able to sense the humidity and the shaving cream without being there.

When the aroma of brewing coffee reached his room, he threw off the covers and walked to the window. He pulled the shade all the way to the top: the morning was crisp, crystal clear cold. The rising sun struck parts of the playground, reflecting off the crusty snow. Jeweled reflections. Prisms of color. Other parts still in shadow. Purples and mauves. The playground under that snow in that light was like a desert. Sands of snow, he thought.

He went into the bathroom. The smells so familiar, camphor and eucalyptus and others even more intimate; the mirror dripping with humidity. He showered and shaved, dressed and went downstairs.

His dad rose to greet him, that shock of silver hair over his forehead, his body thinner than Stephen remembered, his face craggier, more lined, his posture slouched slightly, also something he had not recalled from the past, something he was certain would revert back to the familiar as had already happened with his mom. His dad shook his hand. Certain characteristics never altered. His own hand was smarting. Washington and Lincoln watched with approval while his dad said, "Sit down, son. Sit down. Mother's made a wonderful breakfast for you. I bet you didn't have waffles and sausages over there."

"Not mom's at least, dad."

"Now why don't you sit and have your breakfast and tell us everything."

"Everything, dad?"

"Well, what were the most interesting things that happened to you out there?"

"A lot of things happened, some of it you probably won't even believe."

"Try us."

"Well, I'd have to say that the most exciting thing for me was that this caddy I wrote a story about for the New Falls Sun Times married a famous African singer and I was his best man."

"Really. You never told us that. What was the story about?"

"It was only a human interest story but I got to know the caddy, his name is Lefty, well, that's the name he goes by, I got to know him really well while I lived in New Falls. He had been caddying out at the club longer than anyone else."

"How did he come to be in Africa?"

"One of the members of the golf club in New Falls was in a tournament out there. I happened to see a photo in one of the African newspapers and Lefty was in it. So, I decided to leave the little town I was in and go to find Lefty in Nairobi. And I did."

His mother broke in. "I see. And just how did this Lefty meet the African singer?"

"He met her at the opening ceremony of the tournament. She sang the Kenya national anthem and they just fell in love."

His parents glanced at one another.

"This Lefty, is he a black American?"

"No, mom, he's not. Why would you ask that?"

"No reason, Stephen. It just sounds like such an improbable story."

"Well, to tell you the truth I felt the same way. But they love one another and if you ever decide to visit Kenya you'll definitely have a place to stay. Mama Kitabu, that's Lefty's wife, owns a pig farm outside of the city."

"A pig farm, eh? Why grandpa was interested in raising pigs at one time. Did you know that nothing is wasted on a pig?"

"I did know that, dad." Stephen paused. "And since we're here in the kitchen, there was a man from Israel who was working in Tanzania who actually thought Abraham Lincoln was a Jew." Stephen nodded in the direction of the portrait on the wall.

"Abraham Lincoln a Jew? Where on earth did he get that idea?"

"My thoughts exactly, mom. He said no other American president had a Jewish name. He said it wasn't just the Abraham, but the name Lincoln was Jewish as well."

"Well, that's not true, son. There is one other American president with an Old Testament first name at least, Benjamin Harrison. And come to think of it, there were rumors about Harry Truman. Some people claimed he was a Jew. They claimed the letter S for his middle name really stood for Solomon. They claimed that early in his life he owned a haberdashery with a Jew and the only reason he recognized the independence of the state of Israel was because of all that. They claimed his family had changed its name. But it's all nonsense. Harry Truman comes from a farming family, just like us. No, it was his political enemies who spread all that."

"Really, dad? I wish I had known those stories when I was in Buhaya."

"That's where you met this man who thought Lincoln was a Jew?"

"Right. Abraham Jacobson was his name. He was running retail cooperative stores for the Tanzanian government up there."

" What were you doing there?"

"There were some problems with the retail stores and the minister of cooperatives had asked me to go up and help him, see if what he had heard was correct."

"Was it?"

"I didn't think so. But while I was there I stayed in a beautiful hotel owned by another Jew actually, a man named Lewenberg. But he had lived his whole life in Tanzania."

"It's strange. I wonder why there were so many Jews in Africa. What were they doing there? Seems an odd place for a Jew, Africa."

"Well, there were only those two that I met, dad. But they were both interesting characters. They actually didn't like each other very much. Mr. Lewenberg thought the reason the rest of the world treated Jews with such scorn is because the Jewish people had chosen the wrong person as their third patriarch. Lewenberg said it should have been Esau and not his brother Jacob. In fact, Mr. Lewenberg suggested that Esau was a better man than Jesus Christ."

"Whoa, now, Stephen, no one is a better man than Jesus Christ. You had better think before you repeat something like that. Lewenberg is a Jew. Of course he would say such a thing."

"No, dad. Do either of you know the story of Jesus and the fig tree?"

His mother said, "No, I don't think we do. What is it about?"

"Jesus Christ killed a fig tree."

"Oh, please, Stephen," his father said. "Jesus Christ never killed anything. I don't know what this Lewenberg was up to, but Jesus never killed anything or anyone. Wait right here, I'll be back."

"You had better know what you're talking about, Stephen. He's gone for his Bible you know."

"I know, mom."

"Okay, son, now where do I find this story?"

"I'm not certain, dad."

"You're not certain. Stephen, you know you can't just make some scurrilous remark about Christ and not back it up. Now where in the Bible is it?"

"Well, I remember Mr. Lewenberg saying it had something to do with the parable about moving mountains."

"You mean if you have faith you can move mountains?"

"Exactly. That one."

"Let's see. I don't recollect any fig tree having anything to do with that. Hmmmm. Well, I'll be darned. Here it is. Here it is, mother. What do you know about that? Stephen goes halfway around the world and a Jew tells him about this. Matthew 21:19. Listen to this, mother. We'll have to ask Reverend Finley about this.

" 'And seeing a fig tree by the wayside he went to it, and found nothing on it but leaves only. And he said to it. "May no fruit ever come from you again." And the fig tree withered at once.' "

There was silence in the kitchen. It seemed to Stephen as if Washington and Lincoln were also silent with disbelief.

"But I've saved the most disconcerting story for last," Stephen said. "I met Ralph Nader out there."

"Why that's wonderful, Stephen. Why should that be disconcerting? What was he like?"

"He even offered me a job."

"He did? Why that's wonderful. What's wrong with that?"

"But then, mom, he backtracked."

"What do you mean?"

"He told me how helpful I had been. He showed up in Buhaya. He was setting up an international consumer project. He asked me all sorts of questions and I told him everything I knew. It impressed him. He offered me a job in his organization. He told me to contact him when I returned. But then he said he had one further question to ask me."

"I'm sure you answered it correctly, Stephen."

"I don't think so, mom. He said if I had an important assignment and I had to be in the office to complete it but one of my parents was in the hospital what would I do?"

"What did he mean, what would you do?"

"Would I visit either of you or go to work?"

"What a strange thing to ask. Why you would visit whichever of us was ill and then go straight to the office where you would spend as much time as you needed. Of course."

"That's exactly what I said, mom. But I had the distinct impression that was not the answer he wanted. I think what he wanted me to say was, why go straight to the office, Mr. Nader."

"No, Stephen, I'm sure your impressions are wrong. You write him now that you have met him. You write him and tell him you always wanted to work for him. I'm sure you misread the situation."

"I'm not so sure, mother," his father interjected. "I'm not so sure Stephen did not get it right. Listen to this. I thought the story Stephen was telling sounded familiar. I believe Reverend Finley preached this just a few weeks ago."

As they were going along the road a man said to him, I will follow you wherever you go. Jesus answered, Foxes have their holes and birds their roosts; but the Son of Man has nowhere to lay his head. To another he said, Follow me, but the man replied, Let me first go and bury my father. Jesus said, Leave the dead to bury the dead; you must go and announce the Kingdom of God. Yet another said, I will follow you sir; but let me first say goodbye to my people at home. To him Jesus said, No one who sets his hand at the plough and looks back is fit for the Kingdom of God.

His father closed the book, looked first to Stephen, then to his wife. "Luke 9:57 to 62."

"You think Nader thinks he is…"

"I don't know what he thinks, son. But that's what your story brings to mind."

Again there was silence in the kitchen. Five people stunned by his father's insight, ruminating, pondering, wondering. Stephen noticed through the kitchen window an icicle melting dripdrip-dripdrip. He turned and said, "You know mom, dad, one of the things I don't understand. A lot of people think Ledberg is a Jewish name."

"Who thinks that, Stephen?"

"Well, those two men in Africa."

"Yes, but they were Jews themselves."

"Right. But even when I was younger some kids thought Ledberg was Jewish."

"When you were younger? You never told us that. Why didn't you mention it to us?"

"I was frightened."

"Frightened? What were you frightened of?"

"I don't know."

"Stephen, we are Svenska. We are Swedish. Now I have to admit there are lots of Swedish names that sound Jewish. I don't know why that is. Ledberg is not Jewish. Ledberg is Swedish."

"But how do I know I'm not Jewish?"

"What are you talking about, Stephen?"

"You know exactly what I'm talking about, mom. I don't want to hurt either of you. I love you. But don't you think it's time now to tell me all you know."

"All we know about what, Stephen?"

His father slammed shut the Bible and said, "For god's sake, mother, tell him. You've kept it a secret long enough. It's only right he know now. We should have told him long ago. Do you want him gallivanting all over the place for the rest of his life? Go upstairs and get it right now."

Go upstairs and get what? What was his dad talking about? His mom looked forlorn, rubbing her right hand over the left, a tragic expression on her face.

"Well, if you won't I will." His dad left the kitchen, climbing the stairs, entering their bedroom.

"Mom, it's all right. You know I needed to know." He stood, walked to her, placed his hand on her shoulder, sensed the flesh beneath his touch, his mom's body tense in anticipation of what?

He could tell by the way his dad descended the stairs that he had not found what he was seeking. His dad entered the kitchen, fists clenched, face livid, shouting, "What did you do with it? I can't find it anywhere. It's nowhere up there. Where is it?"

He walked directly toward Stephen's mom, his fists still clenched, a child's expression on his mom's face, as if she were about to cry not because she might be struck but because she knew she was guilty.

"What did you do with it?"

She whispered, "It's gone."

"Gone? Gone?"

"I… I destroyed it."

"What? You destroyed it?"

For a moment Stephen imagined his father might strike his mom. His hands, those scarred hands white at the knuckles.

Stephen broke the tension. "What are you talking about? What was destroyed?"

His dad relaxed, unclenching his fists, telling him, between angry glances at his wife, how they had found him not, through a woman who wanted them to adopt him, that was a story made up, Washington and Lincoln not believing their ears it seemed, but at grandpa and grandma's farm.

It was Stephen's turn now to be shocked. He felt a flush rise to his cheeks, a numbness spreading over him even though he had known, even though he had sensed all these years.

Hearing his dad as if through a haze, "… a newspaper. There was a newspaper stuffed in the bottom of the basket. Mother had kept it, but now they are gone. It was that newspaper fellow, that Reticent, the one who wrote you. We knew when you received that letter offering you a job that he had kept track of you all those years. We should have told you then. I wanted to tell you then. We should have."

Glaring again at his wife. Walking over to the coffee pot, picking it up, walking back toward his wife, what was he going to do with that? He wasn't going to get even after all these years, was he? Standing in front of her, holding the pot, scowling, then walking to the table and pouring himself another cup.

Five stunned people in that sunny kitchen, a bright cold December morning, the rest of the world going about its business, the two gentlemen hanging against the wall looking on as if in disbelief, the butter and syrup lying cold and coagulated on the plates.

Stephen was unable to respond in any way. Feeling not elated but strangely sapped. So was Ingy Reticent his real father? Esther Maroon his mother? Catherine Reticent his sister? Thinking back to the day he had accepted the job, understanding why his parents had not wanted him to take it – and with good reason – can't you find a newspaper closer to home? He remembered how relaxed his mom's face had become when he told her he had been fired, and now look at her. He did not understand why he felt as he did when he had just unraveled what had taken years to weave. The evidence evaporated. Pouf. Did it matter? He recalled suddenly that Betty had been correct again. But how had she known, what would she say, emptying her glass, snuffing a cigarette, jiggling her leg, if only she were alive? Thoughts cascaded, knocked about. Silence in that kitchen. Silence in the kitchen but not in his brain.

Silence until his dad jerked his head and said, "Wait. Wait a second." He stared at his wife. "You think you've outwitted me, don't you? You think you're smarter than me, don't you. You think you've put one over on me."

He placed the coffee cup on the table and went into the living room. He returned with a photo album. He looked again at his wife, "You haven't outsmarted me this time."

Then turning to Stephen he explained, "You remember we always photographed you on your birthday. It wasn't really your birthday of course. Only the day we found you. But we took a photograph of you on that day as well."

His dad opened the album, studying each photograph glued to the black page, Stephen beside him looking on. While his mom sat transfixed, as if someone had freeze-framed her, that pathetic expression on her face. His dad turned the pages until they found a page where two photographs had been removed, crusty mucilage the only indications anything had once been there. His dad exploding anew, his fingers grasping the edges of the book so hard that his knuckles again turned white.

"Damn you. Damn you."

"It's not important, dad. It's not."

"Not important? Of course it's important. She thinks she's put one over on me."

His dad thumbed through the book once more, turning pages swiftly, until he reached the last one, noticing on the inside cover a pouch which contained a multitude of jumbled negatives. He removed a number of them, holding each to the light. As he did he muttered, "Now we'll see how smart she really is." His mom was rubbing her right hand over her left as if she were comforting herself. As if she did not, now that her husband had turned on her, no one would.

Stephen walked over and placed his arm around her shoulder, patting it lightly, consoling her, "It's all right, mom. You know I had to find out some time. It's all right."

His dad tossed negative after negative onto the kitchen table. Until he said triumphantly, "Aha. Aha. Come here and look at this."

Stephen patted his mom's shoulder once more and returned to the table.

The negative was of an infant, a rather grotesque infant at that, Stephen thought, all darks where lights belonged and light where dark was meant, in a picnic hamper. Except for his dad's words he had no way of knowing it was himself.

"Now go and get my magnifying glass. It's in the drawer beside my chair."

Stephen returned with the glass and his dad examined another negative, studying it as if it were a secret document, handing glass and negative to Stephen.

"Now look at this one."

This one was of the hamper alone, the child gone; the child gone but not the newspaper cradled on the bottom, translucent lettering, New Falls Sun Times… Window on the World June 13, 1945.

Stephen's eyes, those of a good journalist, flicked over a minor headline, Gov. Martin Presses… Conservation Measures… Delaware to be cleaned up. Unaware until that moment that that problem was as old as himself.

And then, "The date is not the same as the day you found me."

"No. It's not. Probably he picked up anything he could find. But there's your proof."

Proof of a sort. "You never tried to contact him?"

"Contact him?"

"Reticent I mean. You never contacted him at all?"

"No. Why should we have? We had no idea who left you at the time. As far as we were concerned the newspaper was incidental."

"Why did you keep it then?"

"Keep it?"

"The paper I mean. What made you keep it at all?"

"Because we just thought we ought to. Suppose somebody had come looking for you? We needed some sort of proof. That was all we had. Then when you received that letter offering the job, well, we knew."

"Why didn't you tell me the truth when I was writing the articles about adoption for the college newspaper? Why didn't you tell me the truth then?"

"We should have told you then, son. We should have. That was the moment to have done it, when you were writing that story."

"Why didn't you?"

"We were scared. Plain and simple we were scared."

"Scared? Scared of what?"

"Of what?" His dad blushed, a tinge of crimson rising to his cheeks. "You see, your mom and I always wanted a child. We thought perhaps this was the way it was meant to be. We thought if it was not meant to be someone would turn up. Someone would find out. But no one did." And again looking at his wife he said, "Now, now, mother, it's all right. It's better this way. It's better it's all out."

His mom was standing now, silent, rubbing her hand, consoling herself, an expression on her face as if everything that had once been in place, apastron and periastron, had broken loose; out of control, hurtling through space, seeking other orbits, other bodies.

Stephen was touched by his dad's explanation. Tempered by it. Not even considering that they might have wished children of their own. Not wanting to know why they did not.

"Just because there was a copy of the newspaper doesn't mean it was Reticent. Anyone …"

"True. That's true. Anyone could have but they didn't. It's too much of a coincidence that they offered you a job right out of the clear blue sky."

"But if that's the way it happened how did you get me a legal birth certificate? How was that possible?"

"Grandpa took care of that. We never asked him how he was going to do it. But he took care of it. Then, of course, we are teachers. Everyone knew us. No one questioned us. As the years passed, well, people forget. Yes, over the years people just accept and forget certain things.

"Now, son, you go back to New Falls. You get this cleared up. Your mother and I love you. We will be here when you return. If there is anything you need us to do just call. We've been paying the rent and electric and telephone bill on your apartment. You should get that squared away as well."

"I will, dad."

And then, in that kitchen, in front of the portraits of those two men, Stephen embraced and kissed his father and mother. He was not at all certain what he would find when he returned to New Falls. Wishing Betty was still alive. Puzzled by Ingy Reticent's firing him after all the trouble he went to to hire him.

XLIII

Except for the date on the calendar, Ingy Reticent's office was exactly the same.

"You think I'm your father? Are you crazy?"

"Here, look at these."

Reticent held the negatives to the light. "I can't make head nor tail of all this. You never were very good with photographs. You should have brought me a print. Leave these here, I'll have the boys in photography print them up. All that film you shot out at the golf course. Garbage. It was all useless. It was all overexposed. Couldn't see a thing."

"One is a negative of a picnic hamper which is lined with a copy of the New Falls Sun Times. The other is of me as a baby in that hamper."

"I don't do picnics. I wouldn't know a picnic hamper from a laundry basket. Besides, you have brown eyes and mine are blue, aren't they? I don't produce brown eyed children."

For a moment Stephen hesitated, then brought his gaze to Reticent's eyes, amazed that his own failed to tear. Why was that? What was going on? What had changed? He had no idea.

"Why did you tell Catherine she couldn't have her baby? Why did you tell her it was too dangerous to do that?"

"What? What the hell are you talking about? Are you nuts?"

"No. I overheard what you said at the Gloucester Hotel in Nairobi. You said she was lucky with Adam. Why? Why was she lucky?"

Reticent pushed a button on his desk.

"Security. Get security in here right away. I want this numb-skull out of my office right now."

Ingy Reticent was not his real father? Ingy Reticent was deny-ing him? Stephen did not believe him. Stephen thought he was lying, as he was led from the publisher's office to the street.

When Stephen had arrived in New Falls, before he visited Ingy Reticent, he went straight to his apartment. It was small-er than he remembered. Smaller and seedier and chillier. The barred window was open a notch just as he had left it. The fan on the floor, the bed unmade, books scattered about, Ralph Nader's photograph pinned to the wall. Except for the tempera-ture and the thin covering of snow that had sifted in through the window, everything was the same, everything but his own impressions.

He walked to the Nader photograph and ripped it from the wall, crumpled it and tossed it into the trash basket. A sweet sad-ness swept through him, as if something, he did not know what, had changed within.

He tossed the mail onto the bed and walked to the window. He ran his hand along the sill collecting the snow, compressing it into a ball and tossing it out between the bars. Then he shut the window and turned on the radiator, the steam hissing violently as if for months it had been bursting to escape.

He walked back to the refrigerator, opened it, and nearly became ill at its odor. Only two cans of beer appeared respectable and he dared not touch them. He slammed the door shut.

He found the instant coffee, picked up the kettle, and turned on the faucet. It farted and spat, kicking out a brown liquid. He let it run but it remained rusty. Disgusted, he shut it off and put the kettle down.

He looked around for the telephone book, could not find it immediately, and then saw that it supported the television set. And this time, knowing exactly what he was searching for, he turned to the B's. Dialing the Bridle Street School, asking for Esther Maroon, he waited, wondering if she knew he knew about Catherine Reticent's affair with Marcus Aurelius Brown, wondering if she knew he knew that Adam was their child, wondering if Esther Maroon knew he knew Catherine Reticent was pregnant again, wondering if she knew what the hell her former husband, his former boss, was talking about when he told Catherine she had to abort her second child. He wished that Betty were still alive and teaching at the Bridle Street School so he could talk with her. When the secretary asked who was calling he wanted to answer "Mrs. Maroon's son," but gave his name instead. He shuffled through the mail as he waited, discarding the trash, coming upon a blue air form postmarked Vancouver B. C., a return address, Joyanti Patel, was about to open the letter when Esther Maroon came on the line.

She greeted him as if he had been out for no more than a ramble in the countryside these past months. As if he had not been to Africa and back, to say nothing of to his past and back. But only out for a midsummer's stroll on a lazy afternoon and was presently calling her.

"Mr. Ledberg. What a pleasant surprise. How was your trip? A success I hope."

What do you say to that, when you had not spoken, knowingly that is, to your mother, your real mother, in twenty-two years? You say sort of. Or words to that effect.

"When did you return?"

"A couple of days ago."

" Does Pete Codding know you're back?"

"No. No he doesn't."

"I see. What can I do for you?"

"I was wondering if I could come over and see you."

"Of course. When had you in mind?"

"As soon as you can do it. Whenever you are free."

"Is it that urgent?"

"Yes."

"Well, hold on then and let me see."

As he waited, shivering from the coldness of the apartment, he opened Patel's letter.

My Dear Ledberg,

My family and I send our greetings from Vancouver, British Columbia. It is a stroke of luck, is it not, that we go from British Africa to British Columbia.

It is a fortunate sign. Laksmi smiles on us even so far from home. My friend, already I am working for a big insurance company and business is splendid.

My wife and I speak often of Steven Ledberg. We hope soon to renew our acquaintance. Herewith I enclose address and telephone number.

I am yours,

Joyanti Patel

He was disappointed there was no news of Jasmine as he glanced at the address on the envelope to see if his first name had been misspelled there as well – it had not- and tossed the letter onto the bed as he heard Esther Maroon say, "How about four thirty today?"

"Today?"

"Yes."

"Fine."

"You don't want to give me an idea what's so urgent before you come over?"

"No, I'd rather wait."

Having time on his hands he had strolled over to the New Falls Sun Times building, found Ingy Reticent to be in, confronted him, wondered why the publisher had lied, had been escorted from the building and now here he was, cold and uncomfortable, standing outside the Bridle Street School. The sky was turning to dusk; the air was damp, an indication he thought that foretold the onset of snow.

He was cold, but he was hesitant to enter the school building, not because he feared what Esther Maroon might say, would she lie as well, he wondered, like her former husband, but because he had never been in an environment where someone he knew had died. What would it be like in the school without Betty? He stood with his hands in his pockets, his feet cold, his breath vaporizing, sucking in air, as he forced himself to enter the building.

He pulled open the door to the stairwell, smelling that cleansing agent, walking past those finger paintings, different now, other names, past collages, also changed, up those stairs, past some bubble gum, was it the same? Did it matter?

As he opened the door to the second floor he heard a plaintive melody, music he had heard before, but where? Images of splashing paint, blue and white paint, triangles locking, hurling cans, he the king of the mountain. He asked Esther Maroon's secretary, "That music. That music I hear, what is it?"

She was answering, "I don't know," as Esther Maroon opened the door to her inner office, wearing a grand smile, a sea green turtleneck sweater, and gray skirt. "So good to see you again, Mr. Ledberg. That?" Esther Maroon added. "That's the Israeli national anthem. Hatikvah. Do you know it?"

"I've heard it once before."

"They're rehearsing for assembly. We are proud of our creativity here. We play the national anthems of nations in conflict. Then we ask the children and the faculty which anthems they like best. We ask them why. That leads us into the histories of the countries and how they came to confront one another. As far as I know no other school in the world is that inventive. You would be amazed at some of the things that come up."

"And that tune?" Hatikvah had ended and another piece was being played.

Esther Maroon cocked her head as if to free her ear to hear more clearly.

"That? Hmmm. I'm not sure what that is. But it must be the national anthem of Egypt or Iraq or Syria or Lebanon. It must be one of them. But this isn't why you were in such a rush to see me, is it?"

"No. No, it's not."

"Well, come in then. Come in and tell me what is so urgent."

Esther Maroon's office, like that of her former husband, appeared exactly the same. Stephen felt as if he had not been away for months, but had only stepped out for a moment to go down the hall.

"I suppose you've come to tell me you've met Catherine. Pete Codding called a number of weeks ago to tell me."

"No. That's not why I've come. And I haven't really met Catherine. We sort of brushed by one another in passing. But why didn't you tell me she was living with Marcus Aurelius Brown? Why was that such a big secret?"

"I'm sorry. I apologize. I should have told you. But I was hoping they no longer were."

"Well, they are. I suppose you know Catherine is pregnant again."

Esther Maroon lit a cigarette and sat down. "Again? What do you mean again?"

"Oh, come on, Mrs. Maroon. Adam, that child who was in Betty's class, he's not adopted. He's Catherine and Marcus Aurelius Brown's child. And now they are going to have another baby."

Esther Maroon appeared very pale. "You have uncovered a great deal. Do you want to explain how you uncovered all this?"

"Not really."

"Not really? Then why have you come to see me on such an urgent basis?"

"This." He withdrew the envelope from his pocket.

"An envelope?"

"What's in it." He handed her the envelope.

"What is in it?"

"Negatives."

"Negatives?"

"Yes."

"What do they have to do with me?"

"Why don't you look at them and see."

She stared at him suspiciously, withdrew the negatives and held them to the light.

"What are they?"

"A baby in a picnic hamper and the picnic hamper by itself."

"I don't understand."

"That infant is me."

"You?"

"Yes."

"Well, that's very nice, Mr. Ledberg, but I don't quite see what all of this has to do with me."

"If you look closely at the negative of the empty basket you'll see it is lined with a copy of the New Falls Sun Times."

Esther Maroon adjusted her glasses, lifted the negative to the light again, this time for a longer period of time.

"I still don't see…"

"I am your son."

The moment he said it a hush fell over the room. A stillness in which he imagined those books and papers and pencils and erasers and paper clips and chairs and desk ceased what they were doing, pricking up their ears, holding their breath. Stopping in their tracks, as if they had been waiting years to hear what had just been spoken. I am your son. The room snapped to attention. An incandescent sign blinked on and off. I am your son. I am your son. The world, for a moment, Stephen imagined, in its place.

"Don't be a fool, Mr. Ledberg. You don't know what you're talking about. My son is dead."

"Betty said you would say that."

"Betty? Betty was a drunk."

"She may have been, but she told the truth. She guessed that Adam was Catherine's child. I don't know how she did it but she had clarity of insight. She thought I might be your third child. She told me you would say the child died. But she didn't believe that."

Esther Maroon stared at him. She lit another cigarette. He wondered if those were traces of tears at the corners of her eyes. Was Esther Maroon about to cry?

"Yes. Yes. I apologize. I should not have said that about Betty. How terrible of me. She passed away, you know."

He nodded.

"She always said the one part of our life we have no choice over is our parents. She said the one moment in our lives when we were freest, unshaped, ourselves, well, as much as we could be, was in the years of our early childhood. Her goal, she always said, was to permit the children in her classroom to express what it was they loved. 'Finger painting, dreaming, playing, dressing up. I always want them to remember what it is they loved as children in the hope that when the going gets rough, and it will,' she said, ' they might fight their way back to what they loved when they were children. That will save them,' she said."

Stephen did not care about Betty's philosophy. He barely heard what Esther Maroon was saying.

"Why did you and Mr. Reticent abandon me? Just because I had brown eyes? That's crazy. Whoever heard of such a thing. Why did you let him do that?"

"It was so long ago. How old did you say you were?"

"Twenty-two."

"Twenty-two. Twenty-two years. So many years."

"Why did you let Ingy Reticent take me?"

"I was so young. He had all the power. He had all the money. I didn't know what to do. I didn't know where to turn. I was terrified. It happened so long ago. I don't know what to say to you. But you've turned out well. Whoever that bastard left you with, did well. Probably much better than I could have done."

"But I don't understand. Just because I was born with brown eyes he couldn't deal with that? He dropped me off halfway across the country because my eyes were brown and not blue? What kind of madness is that? And then why hire me at the newspaper and then fire me? What does it all mean?"

She nodded. "He's crazy. No one understands why he does anything. Perhaps he hired you to get back at me in some warped way. But here's the thing, since it's come to this. Here's the thing." She paused, inhaled deeply and said, "You're lucky. You're very lucky."

"Why is that?"

"Because you do not have any of that bastard's seed in you."

What? What the hell was she talking about? He felt sick to his stomach.

"He's not your father. Reticent's not your father. Actually, I don't know who your father is. I don't know his name, that is."

Stephen felt his legs quiver, as if they might give way. He clutched the back of a chair, feeling faint, wondering if he should have let sleeping dogs lie, not wanting to go any further, but you've come this far…

"It's quite a long story really. I haven't thought about it for years. You see we had a maid once. When we were married, that bastard and I, we had a maid." She snuffed out her cigarette. "That's another thing, that bastard never let me smoke cigarettes in the house. Oh, he could smoke his stinking pipe. He could do whatever he wanted…"

"You had a maid once." He had no idea he had said that. Where had it come from? Something deep inside his being.

"Yes, yes. We had a maid. She was very beautiful. She was a black woman. Her name was Claire. Claire Brown. I don't know how long that bastard had been carrying on with her but he had. I gave up a long time ago trying to figure out the whens and whys and hows. The long and short of it was that he got her pregnant. I might never have discovered anything if not for that. He got her pregnant. She left of course. He refused to do anything for her. Oh, I think he gave her a little money, nothing that could be traced, but that was all.

"She died in childbirth. You might have guessed, the child was Marcus Aurelius Brown."

Jesus Christ. He stood anchored to the chair, paralyzed, as she lit another cigarette.

Then he spoke. "Do Marcus Aurelius and Catherine know they are brother and sister?"

"Half brother and sister. Yes, of course they know. But they don't believe us. They think we are just trying to break them up."

"So that's why Mr. Reticent tried to persuade Catherine not to have another child."

"He did? How do you know that?"

"I overheard them at the hotel I was staying at in Nairobi. But Catherine said there was no proof of what you have just told me."

"She was correct. That asshole destroyed anything that had to do with his relationship with Marcus Aurelius' mother. We have no proof that Marcus Aurelius is my former husband's child. I was so young. So young.

"He hurt me. I don't think a man could hurt me now like he did. But he hurt me then. I wanted to get back at him in the worst way. I swore to myself that I would hurt him as much as he had me. I thought of all the ways I might do that. I knew there was only one that would equal what he had done to me. My problem was with whom."

Stephen felt he did not need to hear any more but he understood he was under some sort of spell, drawn to the ending no matter what it held, unable to escape the paralyzing pull of Esther Maroon's voice, the voice of his true mother.

"I thought at first of seducing one of his best friends or even someone he respected and trusted on the newspaper. After all, what a story that would make for the boys in the newsroom. But he had everyone frightened. Everyone was terrified of him. No one dared lay a hand on me. I thought they were a pretty pathetic bunch.

"Then I remembered some of the girls at the golf club telling me stories about things that went on on one of the greens. I wasn't much on golf but I checked the stories out and found they were true. You'd be amazed at what the girls around here know that their husbands don't. You look pale. Are you all right? Shall I get you some water?"

"No. No. Go on." Sensing what he was about to hear, unable to bolt.

"Well, I went out to play a little golf one day. It was early enough so that there were not many people around. I didn't care which caddy I drew. I never knew his name. No, I never knew his name but I can tell you this…"

Her teeth pressed gently against her lower lip. Her eyes, those celadon green eyes, gazed into the distance, a distance that came hurtling at him, he unable to prevent it, unable to deflect it, knowing what he was about to hear even before he heard it. He wanted to place his hands over his ears. He wanted to turn and run. But so mesmerized was he that he just stood unblinking, holding his breath as Esther Maroon's words tumbled out.

"One thing I'll never forget was his arm. One of his arms was missing. Left or right I don't remember now. But the people out at the club can tell you. He had no arm. Just a stump…"

He bolted from the room. He turned and ran, through the outer office, past a bewildered secretary, hearing the national anthem playing somewhere down a hallway, oh say can you see, down the stairs, hurtling three at a time, past the bubble gum, collages, finger paintings, disinfectant.

Outside, he breathed heavy vaporous breaths, stunned, embarrassed really, better always to let sleeping dogs lie, what did it matter, had Ingy Reticent hired him for this moment? Lefty his father, Esther Maroon his mother, a light snow cascading, recalling that someone had said – a teacher? his parents? an article in a newspaper? – that each flake was unique, like a fingerprint. But he wondered now how that could be proved? How could anyone examine all the flakes in the world before they melted? His head thrown back, agape, as snowflakes fell from a pitch-black sky, gentling upon his upturned face.

The End